CW00602358

Jeremy Mills

Jeremy Mills lives in Suffolk where he is currently working on his second novel.

Married with two children, Jeremy has spent many years working for businesses in the book industry and is now enjoying life on the other side of the fence as an author.

OUTSIDERS

Jeremy Mills

OUTSIDERS

Vanguard Press

VANGUARD PAPERBACK

© Copyright 2010
Jeremy Mills

A CIP catalogue record for this title is
available from the British Library.

ISBN 978 1 84386 577 3

*Vanguard Press is an imprint of
Pegasus Elliot MacKenzie Publishers Ltd.*
www.pegasuspublishers.com

First Published in 2010

**Vanguard Press
Sheraton House Castle Park
Cambridge England**

Printed & Bound in Great Britain

For Wilma, Daniel and Lauren

CHAPTER 1

It was so very quiet in the city. As it had been for a long time. The buildings still stood tall and the old streets were still there, but now there were no people.

There was a time when he used to seek out the peace and quiet but now he missed the noise. That was why he had set off through the quiet streets that morning. The problem these days,though, with finding any noise was that it could mean also finding trouble. That morning he found both.

Hugh Hanson was seventy-two. He could still clearly remember the buzz of walking to work through the crowded city streets. That was over fifty years ago. All the noisy traffic and the people who always seemed to be in a hurry. All the shop windows and the interesting side streets – he used to soak it all in, watching the different people who had come to his city from all over the world. When he walked with Louisa in the evenings, they would often stop to look at the restaurant menus and think about going out with their friends. They took great delight in springing surprises by finding a new restaurant that none of them had been to before.

Now there was no Louisa and no friends.

He had always loved the history of the city. He knew that he would never need to walk far before seeing a monument or a building which could tell so many stories from centuries before. St Paul's was his favourite, and it was towards the great old dome that he set off that morning. He never made it.

Over two-hundred-thousand miles away Carder stretched slowly and stood up. At six-foot-three, he towered over the man with white hair who he followed to join the others in the darkened room, and as he took his seat he knew that his life was about to change forever.

The white-haired man stood at the front of the room and started to speak in the familiar steady and neutral tone.

'Now we are all here I can give you the itinerary.'

The wall in front of Carder was flooded with light and a map of the planet stretched from left-side to right-side. The amount of blue on the map never failed to surprise him.

Carder looked round and saw three others in the room plus the white-haired man who he knew as Maldini, a man with an impressive track record. He had been there and back six times over the years, the first time being when no-one knew the level of the risks.

'There will be two operation sites,' Maldini continued, 'London and Seville, which are both areas with unusual activity.' As he spoke the map was populated by two red dots. 'You will operate in pairs. Carder and Scott, you will land in London. Silves and Mercer, you will be going to Seville.'

Carder grimaced. London, that was a good location he thought. At least the people there would speak the same language. But Scott? No, that was not so good. He had something of a history with Scott. A few years ago they had both been on a training exercise and Scott had panicked, nearly killing them both. When they returned to the base, Scott tried to lay the blame at Carder's door. Maldini had seen through Scott but the incident still rankled with Carder.

Maldini then sprang a surprise.

'There have been several previous operations as you know, but this time we will be doing things a bit differently. For this reason, you'll be staying for longer than the normal twenty-four hours. This time it will be a week and you will be expected to mix in with the communities. We need to learn who the leaders are and what their agenda is.'

Carder led the interruption.

'You're asking a lot there Maldini. Just surviving for a week hasn't been done before and you're asking us to do that, and go looking for trouble.'

Maldini turned to face Carder, his eyes were hard but Carder had known Maldini for many years and he trusted him.

'You know the stakes, Carder. We've been away over fifty years now and we have maybe two years left before we must return. We have to make the place safe for that return, it has to be safe for us and for the next generation. You have all been picked out because we think you have the mental and physical strength to do the job.'

Silves stood up slowly.

'You are asking us to die, Maldini. A week is long enough to get virus exposure. We have heard it still lingers in Europe and Africa. You're giving me a one-way ticket to Seville.'

Maldini clicked the mouse and a bar chart showed on the wall.

'Virus depreciation over the last twenty years has accelerated to the point that we are here,' pointing to the chart on the right. 'Air concentration levels are now negligible across the planet. Yes, there may still be pockets but you will have monitors and can assess that risk rapidly on the ground.'

Scott laughed. 'It's okay, Carder, if I see you turning green I'll tip you in the River Thames.'

Maldini moved onto the next slide. It just showed one number. Five million. The talking in the room drained away and everyone was silent before Maldini spoke.

'That, gentlemen, is the new number. Five years ago it was seven million. You know what that number is? The estimated total population of our planet. Our home.' There was just the sound of breathing in the room. 'As you can see, we are running out of time... and options.'

CHAPTER 2

Hanson knew that he was taking a risk. His daughter had pleaded with him to move out of the city. To join her at the Village. His daughter... Hanson paused on Waterloo Bridge to think about Sarah, the one and only other survivor in his family. She was thirty now, headstrong but beautiful. And she was safe and at peace. She had found happiness at the Village, a tiny community sprawling around Stonehenge, which Hanson thought was a good choice of location for a new beginning. If that's what it was. Hanson wasn't so sure... but he wasn't sure of anything anymore, except that he needed the comfort of familiar surroundings. He didn't want to lose the memories.

He continued walking north across the bridge, a solitary figure in the bright glare of the May morning. To his left, he could see the old Houses of Parliament still standing proudly although the famous clock tower no longer called out to the city. The sun was beginning to strengthen and Hanson knew that it would be another scorching day. Thirty-two centigrade in May was not unusual in London nowadays.

There was something different though about this morning. He would normally have seen someone by now. Heard a dog barking. Maybe even had to take a detour to avoid the occasional group of scavenging dogs which ran loose on the streets. Today he heard nothing and saw nothing moving, except for the relentless ripples of the Thames.

Looking over again towards Westminster, he saw no boats and no activity on the river. It was as if the City was waiting, perhaps waiting until it was safe to show itself.

At last he saw some movement. Two men walking towards the north end of the bridge. Talking to each other and then turning. Coming his way. They looked young, maybe in their early twenties.

He met them on the north bank. Three men meeting at a road junction that was once alive with the noise of cars, buses and people.

'Good morning.' Hanson offered his hand. The two men stopped and looked at Hanson.

'Morning, old timer, are you not going to watch the show?' One of the men replied. Hanson could see that he was thin and hungry looking. The man had an arrogant look in his eyes and he began to feel uncomfortable.

'What show?' He asked.

'Over there, here they come,' and the second man pointed behind Hanson, back over the bridge.

Hanson turned and he could see plenty of people now. Covering the width of the bridge walking north. At the front of the crowd he could make out three figures, tied together with hoods covering their heads, being pushed slowly along by the men behind them. Men with dogs. It wasn't quiet any longer. The mixture of the dogs barking and the jeering from the crowd had taken over the peace of the morning. They stopped in the middle of the bridge.

The three figures were pushed forward but after that Hanson lost sight of them as the crowd was blocking his view. He could hear a voice though and although not making out every word, he knew that he was listening to some kind of a kangaroo court and it sounded like it was at the last stages of the proceedings. The voice was getting louder, talking about punishment, talking about crime against the authorities, talking about an example needing to be set.

'What did these people do?' Hanson asked his two companions.

'They stole food,' came the reply from the thin one, 'They were not prepared to work for their own food and they were caught raiding some storehouse down near Bishopsgate.'

'All this for stolen food?' Hanson asked, incredulous.

'You got a problem with that, old timer? People have to play by the rules or they get disciplined. This is all about showing everyone what will happen to them if they break our rules.'

'Our rules? Who are you then and what will happen to them?'

Hanson's companions didn't need to answer. Three shots rang through the air. The shots echoed around for what seemed like an eternity and then it fell silent again. London had just witnessed its first public execution for many years. The small crowd of watchers cheered wildly and then, to Hanson's growing bewilderment and rage, he saw a group of them rush forward and tip the bodies over the bridge and into the Thames.

Shock had taken over Hanson and he found that he could not move. He couldn't believe what he had just seen and he suddenly felt very old and very alone.

CHAPTER 3

Eighty-five miles to the west of the city, a group of children were outside in a meadow playing and chattering. The air was alive with their excited laughter and the birds were loud with their singing. There was a breeze rustling through the leaves which just took the edge off the heat of the sun. It was a timeless scene and Sarah Hanson was standing watching and drinking it all in.

She had been worried recently; preoccupied with the life her father was living in London. She knew the city was his life and that he would always struggle to break away from it, but she had heard an increasing number of worrying stories from the travellers, stories about the new authority developing in the city. An authority that was corrupt and increasingly powerful. A group of self-elected bullies who were diverting all the scarce resources to themselves.

She allowed her mind to drift back to when she had been in London as a child. She didn't know her mother who had perished when she was very young, but she had fond memories of times with her father. It must have been a terrible struggle for him, protecting her in that huge lawless city, but somehow he did it and the two of them managed to have fun from time-to-time. She used to love the boat rides they took down the Thames. They would go for miles without seeing a soul but the time passed in a flash as her father talked non-stop about all the places on each riverbank. They would stop for a picnic and just lie on the grass by the river. The world had changed forever but her father had tried his best to make sure that she had a happy childhood.

She wished that her father would join her now so that she could care for him, and let him see the new community that was beginning to take shape. It would be safer for him here. If only she could persuade him to leave his beloved City.

Sarah lifted her gaze above the children and onto the ancient stones that watched over them. Every time she looked at the strange circle she got some sort of comfort. She didn't understand why, but she knew those stones had seen so many things and had watched people come and go. Good people and evil people. Not for the first time, she thought that the stones were standing guard over the small community that had grown below them, a community that was fragile and just clinging to an existence, but was gathering a little strength each day.

The Village was her home and she was glad of it.

She rang the bell for the start of lessons.

CHAPTER 4

'Yes, a week is what he said.' Carder replied to the girl's incredulous question. The girl was called Carla and she was getting out of Carder's bed, ready to face the new day. This day she was upset. Very upset.

'You're not going to come back, David, it's too long a time to stay safe,' she protested as she walked to the shower.

Carder watched her but didn't reply. He was lost in his own thoughts. The shower burst into life and Carder lay back on his pillow, and tried to pull together what he knew about the blue planet. He had looked at it often enough from the observation platform. A shining blue and white marble two-hundred and forty-thousand miles away, hanging miraculously in the vast dark blanket that filled the sky.

He had never walked on the Earth but he had read a lot about it. He had listened to Maldini and picked his brain to find out what he had seen on his visits. He had seen the news recordings of the years running up to the clandestine evacuation. Sometimes, he would dwell on the suffering of the people and on other occasions, he would not be able to shift the feeling of guilt which try as he might would never quite go away. The secrecy of the evacuees. The guilt of the evacuees. The generation before his. Carder didn't evacuate. He was born at the base but he still felt the guilt.

That morning, though, his thoughts turned to the film records he'd seen and for some reason he couldn't shake the image from his mind of all the of people across Earth, enjoying themselves in huge festivals at the end of the second millennium. Fantastic fireworks, parties, music and most of all, a vast outpouring of happiness and hope from the billions across the globe. Looking back now, the year nineteen-ninety-nine seemed like a watershed year for humanity. At the end of that year somehow the world changed, something intangible happened but Carder kept thinking how much he wished he had been there at that time. Hope and energy and compassion and love were all compressed into that one night's celebrations and he thought that maybe the people then did know, somewhere deep down, that they were on the edge of something. No-one could know exactly what or why, but everyone seemed to sense that they should enjoy the day and then cope with what tomorrow brings.

Carder thought some more about this and still puzzled over why, when it really mattered, they had not coped. Why, with all the medical resources, they had still been defeated by a virus.

No-one seems to have known how the virus started or even where it started. Carder still struggled to understand how something could have crept up so silently and had such a devastating effect and yet its origins had remained a mystery.

Maldini called Carder in that afternoon. Alone.

Carder thought the old man looked troubled. He was certainly deep in thought as Carder knocked and walked into his office.

Behind his desk was a large window and outside, the barren lunar landscape stretched into the distance. On the far horizon, the thin crescent of the Earth hovered just above the horizon.

'I'm not sure what you will find, Carder.' Maldini said. 'Our latest reports suggest that the virus is all but gone but we cannot be sure of that. I didn't say it in the briefing, but there has been no sign of human activity in the southern hemisphere now for the last six months. There are people here who think that the virus is likely to still be strong.'

'Well, we have to find out and soon by the sounds of it,' Carder replied. 'We can't stay here forever.'

'No, exactly… and that's what I wanted to talk to you about.' Maldini paused before continuing. 'When you return, if you report the all clear then we may bring forward the day when we leave here. I think it is in everyone's best interests to leave here and make a new home on Earth as soon as possible.'

Carder sensed an unease about Maldini.

'Problem, sir?' He asked.

Maldini looked at the young man sitting in front of his desk. He liked Carder. He was pleased that Carla had found someone so solid. And strong-minded.

Maldini had watched Carder grow up and had always been there for him to offer advice and guidance. Soon he knew, though, that he would have to tell Carder about where he came from. And that would not be easy.

'Not a problem yet Carder,' he replied, 'but we need to be sure that when we do all make the journey, then we all have the same goals. For the sake of everyone's future…'

Carder frowned, not yet understanding where Maldini was coming from, but he let him carry on.

'Timing is everything. We have a number of strong-minded individuals here. It is important that the right views prevail when we set foot on Earth.'

Maldini was silent for a moment before turning to look straight at Carder.

'There are some here. Some who may see the settlement of Earth as a time for individual opportunity. That will be disastrous. We need to have a set of common goals and these must always be for the good of the community, not for any one individual. That is how we have survived here and it is how we will survive on Earth.'

'Who are these people?' Carder asked.

'Look around you, Carder. Look at the social groups developing here. Look at who meets up with who. I suppose it is inevitable… the longer we stay here the more likely it is that… factions will develop.'

'But you lead us,' Carder replied, 'you and the committee. All that we do is for the common purpose. You have always ensured that.'

'Yes… yes, but I see the first small cracks appearing. I see it in their eyes. I hear it in the words they say and the words they don't say.'

Carder was quiet as Maldini continued.

'Carder, you will be my eyes and ears on Earth. You will have to make decisions and I trust you to make the right ones. You will have some hard choices to make but you will choose correctly. I want you to rely on your instincts and what you feel inside when you have to make a choice.'

Carder nodded. 'I will do my best.'

Not for the first time he realised that this old man, his mentor over the years, had the extraordinary gift of looking ahead and visualising how the future might pan out. He could somehow see all the scenarios and see the risks.

'Another thing, Carder. I'm pulling the Seville trip. Silves and Mercer will stay here for now.'

'Why?' Carder asked.

'I need to see how you get on in London first. Seville could be tricky,' Maldini replied.

Carder was puzzled but he had enough to think about with his own trip. He didn't dwell on Maldini's reply. The significance of it would only hit him later. Much later.

'When you return,' Maldini continued, 'I would like you to lead the settlement project. Carla will also be involved and we will build a momentum here so that everyone pulls together.'

Maldini smiled. 'So your report back will be the key, Carder. If it is a safe haven that awaits us then we will start to make our plans.'

Carder stood up and shook Maldini's hand. 'Thank you, sir,' and turned to leave the room.

Maldini turned back to look out of his office window. He gazed at the thin blue crescent hanging there in the black void.

'Good luck, David Carder,' he muttered to himself, 'and come back with the right answer.'

CHAPTER 5

Carder leaned forward towards the craft's window and looked out at the Earth.

The land shapes were clearly visible now but still the overwhelming colour was blue. Carder marvelled at the huge Pacific Ocean and even more so at the tiny islands that were dotted around in it. They looked so isolated and so vulnerable, just like the planet itself - a fragile globe just hanging there in the vast blackness of space.

He had heard so much about Earth and read so many things, but nothing had prepared him for the sheer beauty of it. He felt a weird sense of protectiveness towards the land and water passing below him. He glanced across at his fellow passengers and Silves was like him, looking out in awe as the craft moved into Earth's orbit.

Scott was sleeping. Sleeping, calm as you like. Carder could not understand how anyone could imagine missing this moment. However, he knew that Scott was different. Ambitious, arrogant and cold. Scott was after personal glory on this trip. He coveted promotion and power, and Carder knew that he would be very driven in his pursuit of both. Not the ideal partner.

They would be in orbit for four more hours, so Carder settled back and watched the planet below. His thoughts turned to the few vague stories he had been told about his father who grew up and lived down on this planet. Maldini had told him very little, other than his name and the area he had come from. But Carder had read about the lives people on Earth had led, and he had built up his own picture in his mind about his father's life.

He imagined him as a child, playing and running across fields, climbing hills, swimming in the sea. He had tried to imagine his father's friends and then, of course, how he met his mother. Maldini had no information on his mother and had been strangely reticent on the subject. Just like most of the others on the moonbase, Carder had precious little to go on. He had no memories of his early childhood and the pictures he had in his mind were all his own creation.

He had seen videos and read so much about the lives of the people who had lived here. He had listened to music. Great music. Songs that told stories in themselves. Always though, Maldini had brought him and everyone back to the harsh reality. That one world had died and that there would need to be plenty of hard work done if another was to take its place. The life he had led on the moonbase, up until now, was totally alien to what he was about to experience.

Alien... Carder dwelt on the word. In many ways he was an alien to this world he was looking at. He had never walked on it or breathed the air. Sure, he knew he looked the same as the inhabitants, but he also knew that from their point of view he did not belong.

'Hey, take a look at our place Carder.' Silves interrupted his thoughts and was pointing outside his window. Carder stretched over and craned his neck so that he could follow the pointing finger. He saw the moon from a distance for the first time. In its own way it was beautiful, hanging there in space, but it could not compare to the Earth. There were no colours and there was no vibrancy about the distant orb. However, Carder felt the pull of home. All of his thirty two years had been spent there. His girl was there, his friends were there. He belonged back there in that strange, protected, sterile atmosphere.

Carder went back to his own thoughts, forcing his mind away from the moon and the only life he had known, to the task ahead. He did not have long to wait before a slight change in engine noise signalled the start of the preparations for descent.

CHAPTER 6

As Silves brought the ship through the Earth's atmosphere and downwards, Carder's adrenalin kicked in. This was it. The culmination of a lifetime's training. And a lifetime's dreams.

The Earth below was dark. Where once the pattern of lights would have marked out the cities and the roads, there was now nothing but darkness. As the ground became closer, Carder could dimly make out some variations in the darkness. There was water that reflected back. Then a lake and some hills. They were travelling over some undulating landscape. Occasionally there was a building that reflected back, but everywhere looked lifeless. There were too few people left now to leave tell-tale signs for anyone flying above.

The ship was hovering now. 'Three hundred feet,' Silves voice came over the earphones.

And then, slowly, very slowly, the ship made the final descent.

For long seconds Carder waited for it. The soft bump that would tell him that they had landed on Earth. The seconds dragged out. Carder glanced out of the window. He could see something in the distance. Trees. There were trees. For the first time in his life he was looking at trees. It was very dark and difficult to make anything out clearly, but definitely they were trees.

And then it happened. A bump and then another one. The ship had landed. Carder had arrived.

'All clear out there. Doors opening.' Silves's voice came over again. 'You have five minutes to disembark.'

Carder and Scott unstrapped themselves from their seats. They dragged their backpacks out and made their way to the doors.

They both stood there for a moment at the top of the steps, twenty feet above the ground.

This was a moment Carder would never forget. Although he could see very little in the dark, he could sense a million things. There were noises. A noise came from the air moving. The trees made small noises. He could smell the grass…

'Good luck.' Silves's voice shouted from behind them and they started to walk down the steps, Carder first, followed by Scott.

Carder paused on the last step and then he planted his foot on the ground. There was a bit of give in the turf. There was a softness that took Carder by surprise. It was instantly different to the solid floors and rock that was all he had known before.

He walked a few steps and turned back to see that Scott had joined him. He too was looking down at his feet. No amount of training could have prepared them for what they were both feeling at that moment.

The bigger surprise though was the wind. Air movement was alien to him and he stood with his face into the wind, relishing the feeling. It felt fresh and it made him feel very alive. Something in Carder's mind triggered thoughts of his parents again. They had known this. They had known the wind. Now it was his turn at last.

On some impulse Carder looked up and saw a glimpse of the half moon slipping out from behind the clouds. He caught his breath.

'Take a look at home now, Scott,' he pointed, 'it seems near somehow… it seems very close.'

For a moment Carder felt the strong pull of the only home he had known. Long before humans had ever walked on Earth, the moon had looked down on the planet. It was always there. It was a permanent light in the sky when all sorts of mayhem was raging down on the ground.

For once, Scott seemed caught up in the mood. He stood for several moments looking at the half moon before eventually turning back to Carder.

'We should get moving, we can't stand around all night gawping. It will be light in three hours and we need to look like we live here.'

The night was mild as the two men made their way from their landing field. As they neared the edge, they heard some rustling beneath their feet and they could feel that the ground had taken on a slightly different texture. Carder hesitated and crouched down. He ran his hand over the ground and felt the leaves which had fallen there. He scooped up a handful and looked at them. Even in the dim moonlight they looked beautiful. But they were also fragile. Once they had been growing vibrantly on the trees but now they had died, and Carder opened his hand slowly and watched them flutter away in the breeze. As the two men walked through the leaves, both men were dumbstruck by the assault on their senses. They had lived in a sterile, protected environment all their lives and now they were experiencing a living, moving world. It was thrilling and disconcerting at the same time.

They headed south and made their way along the edge of fields at first, before finding more established paths and then finally a road.

Two hours later, the two men were making their way through deserted suburban streets and onwards towards the centre of a once great city.

CHAPTER 7

Maldini had explained to his committee that he had pulled the Seville landing because he wanted to assess the reports back from London first before risking a double landing.

His committee were not happy. Apart from Maldini, there were four others on the committee and they were all there, sat around the metallic table in Maldini's office.

Commander Pirrin was head of the operational forces and the most powerful person in the moonbase, apart from Maldini.

Pirrin was the longest serving person on the moonbase, apart from Maldini himself.

They had both arrived as boys. They had always had a rivalry and Maldini sensed that Pirrin was never totally comfortable that Maldini had the overall command.

He was very agitated about the aborted mission.

'We are just wasting time, Maldini,' he complained. 'If there are still problems on Earth then we have the firepower and resources to deal with it.'

Pirrin had served Maldini well, particularly when tough decisions had to be implemented. He had coordinated resources with an authority that no-one else in the team had. But Maldini knew that there were troubled times ahead. At sixty-two, Pirrin was only three years younger than Maldini and saw himself as the natural successor to the overall leadership.

Maldini knew that Pirrin harboured this ambition but he also knew that he would not be right for the job. His style would be harsh and cold and that was not what would be required when the time for change arrived.

He looked at Pirrin now and saw his pent-up fury and frustration. He was a short man with cropped dark hair framing a square, hard face. He kept his beard neatly trimmed and was always immaculately dressed. Pirrin thought that he was born to lead and that worried Maldini. It worried him a lot.

Peter Straker was also there. He was the blond, blue-eyed boy in many peoples' eyes. He was charm personified and had used this to rise to a high position in the moonbase, but although Maldini valued his extraordinary intelligence and diplomacy, there was something about Straker that he couldn't quite work out. Something that Straker seemed to be always holding back.

Samuel N'Gomo was the brilliant Chief Technical Officer and very popular with everyone. He combined a sharp brain with great humour and a big personality and without him, Maldini knew that the moonbase community would have perished a long time ago.

The remaining committee member was the quiet and diminutive Mai. She was Maldini's sounding board. There was always a sense of calm around Mai. Calm reasoning with no panic. Maldini loved the little Chinese woman, although he had never told her so. It was Mai who was the first person that Maldini would turn to or confide in, although even she did not know the real reason behind Maldini's decision to pull the Seville landing.

Maldini had told her that Seville could be hostile but Mai suspected that there was more to it. She trusted his judgement though and decided that she would not push him on the subject.

Straker chipped in. 'You said it yourself Sir, time is running out for us here. Would it not be better to press ahead with both landings?'

'Not right now, Peter,' Maldini replied. 'A few weeks won't make any difference. Silves has gone with Scott and Carder and he will hold the ship in Earth's orbit whilst they are down on the ground. It will be a good experience for him and will complete his training.'

'A mistake.' Pirrin said abruptly. 'I think we are hesitating when we should be decisive.' And with that he stood up and excused himself from the meeting.

Maldini sighed. The cracks were widening all the time.

CHAPTER 8

'What was that?' Scott asked, stopping abruptly.

Carder had heard it too. A low guttural sound coming from somewhere to their left.

Both men stood still in the middle of the road. The dark buildings on either side of them showed no signs of life. There was a long abandoned car on its side to their left, and further along there was a burnt-out and decaying vehicle which Carder guessed was a public bus. He had read about these at sometime in the past and from what he could see, the vehicle had rows of seats on two levels. The roof had gone though and the whole shell was blackened.

'Don't know. It seemed to come from that old car over there. Maybe the wind blew it a little.' Carder replied, unconvinced with his own explanation.

They stared at the car but could see nothing and heard no other sounds. They walked slowly on down the deserted road.

'They liked their food here,' Scott laughed, 'all types of eating houses.'

Carder nodded. He had seen the signs above some of the buildings. Some of them were losing their letters or had fallen off completely, but there seemed to have been all types and nationalities of food available in the buildings on each side of the road.

Behind them they did not notice the movement from behind the old abandoned car.

They came across a church on the left hand side.

'There's plenty of these too.' Carder said. 'Thousands of churches all over the country. And not just for one religion. Even on a tiny island like this they must have had lots of different religions and beliefs.'

'Ah, yes, religion,' Scott replied. 'Maldini's forbidden subject. He doesn't want any factions or different beliefs.'

Carder thought about this. Scott was right. Maldini had gone to great lengths to preserve the unity of the moonbase as he saw it. But at what cost? Carder thought. It was artificial. People did have different viewpoints. They had a right to...

The thoughts vanished from his mind as he heard the sound again. So did Scott and it was louder this time. The two men froze, before slowly turning round in the direction of the noise.

Behind them, less than twenty yards away, was a dog. A large dog with bared teeth. The low growl came again and sent a chill through both men.

'Don't move,' Carder said. 'Just stare it out.'

But Scott was impatient. He moved his right arm towards his gun. The dog saw the movement and in that instant launched itself across the twenty yards straight at Scott.

Scott froze, his eyes wide with terror as the beast closed in on him and jumped up towards his face.

Scott fell backwards onto the road under the weight of the dog and screamed as its foul smell invaded his senses. He waited for the tearing pain as the teeth sank into him but it did not happen. Instead, the lifeless dog rolled off him onto the road and Scott stared up at Carder who had fired his gun at the last moment.

'Hell!' Scott cursed, badly shaken. 'Welcome to Earth!'

'You were lucky, Scott. No bites, no scratches. I dread to think what diseases that dog was carrying.'

Carder put his gun back and pulled Scott up to his feet.

As the two men walked on, the buildings on either side became taller and the streets wider. Over to the east of the City the sun just appeared over the horizon. Scott and Carder were about to experience their first day on Earth.

CHAPTER 9

Scott saw her first.

An old woman was walking slowly along the pavement ahead of them. She was hunched up and carrying a bag which looked as though it must be heavy.

'First contact,' Scott said. 'Now let's see if the people are more welcoming than the dogs here.'

They caught the old woman up and approached her from the side to try and minimize the alarm it may cause her to see two total strangers coming towards her. It didn't work. The moment she saw the two men she dropped the bag and put her hands up.

'Please... please just take it.' She cried out to them.

The bag had fallen open and some apples and potatoes had fallen out.

Carder stooped down to pick them up. He examined the fruit. It didn't look inviting. The potatoes looked mouldy. He put them back in the bag.

'Don't worry please,' he said softly. 'We mean you no harm. You can keep your bag.'

'I have nothing else,' she said. 'Please don't harm me. I have nothing else to give you.'

Carder was horrified at the distress they had caused the old woman. She was obviously wary of being attacked here. It did not bode well.

'Do people attack you for this?' Scott asked her, pointing at the bag.

She nodded.

'Why do they do that?' Scott asked, but the old woman did not reply. She grabbed her bag and scuttled away, looking anxiously over her shoulder as she went.

'Nice place this.' Scott remarked sarcastically.

'It's broken.' Carder said simply. 'The place is broken. Once it worked and maybe worked really well. But not now. Too many years have gone by.'

They continued to head southwards, gazing up in awe at massive buildings, some of them seemingly made of just glass. A lot of the glass had been smashed or cracked and many of the buildings had been burnt long ago, but Carder could still feel something about the place. He could still feel something of the massive energy and bustling life that must have once been there.

They came upon a massive square with a tall monument rising from the centre of it. There were a few people in the square setting up some tables. Carder and Scott walked up to one table and watched a man putting some bottles on it. They looked like bottles of water but the man spoke a strange language and seemed very wary of the two strangers, constantly looking around him nervously.

After a few minutes, a man came up to the table and exchanged a jar of some amber-coloured liquid for two bottles of water.

'This is primitive,' Scott said. 'It's a market place. A market place for survival rations.'

As Scott and Carder turned into a nearby road, Carder read the sign nailed to the wall. The Strand was a long, wide road with large buildings on both sides. As he looked down it, he could see a couple of dogs lying in doorways and a man lying in another one. There was no-one else around except in the distance where Carder could just make out a small group. He peered closer at the group and then realised there were just three figures. It looked like there were two men who were assaulting an older man. The old man was taking blows to his body and was not offering any resistance.

Carder started towards them but Scott put a restraining arm out.

'Don't go there, Carder. You know the rules. We don't want to get noticed by interfering in a local squabble. Keep focused on the mission.'

Carder pushed Scott's arm away angrily. 'Local squabble! That guy's getting the crap beaten out of him. He's not able to take much more. Lets go and even up the odds for him.'

Carder ran down the road and yelled at the assailants. They let go of the old man who fell to the ground. They turned to face Carder and something about them made Carder feel uneasy. These men were not run of the mill thugs just looking for easy pickings. They had a deeper menace. They were both large and thickset and they were both alert. His eyes flicked to the old man who had not got up and then looked back at the two men who had moved a little closer.

'You like easy odds do you? Couldn't find anyone else to play with?'

No reply.

Carder sensed this was not going to be straightforward. The two men were weighing him up and then Carder saw one of them move his right arm fractionally towards his coat pocket. He knew then that he had a gun.

It all happened in a second or two, at most – no thinking time, just instinctive reaction and decision-making.

The man went for his gun but Carder was a fraction of a second ahead. Locking eyes with him and confirming his intentions, Carder reached his decision. He knew what he had to do. He pulled out his gun and fired at the man's shoulder and then flung himself sideways, rolling over twice before coming up and aiming at the other man.

His gun was also on the way out but Carder fired – another shoulder shot before swinging round to the first man and putting another bullet in his knee. A reverse swing and Carder was now back on the other man who dropped his gun to the ground.

'You idiot, Carder!' Scott yelled from twenty yards away.' 'Those bullets will give us away. We will have to return. You've screwed it all up.'

'Shut up, Scott, help me with the old man.' Carder walked slowly forward to help the man up from the ground. He started to help him up but was stopped in his tracks when he heard a voice from behind calling.

'Stay where you are, don't move.'

Carder turned round to see a group of five armed men walking slowly towards him. He looked round for Scott but he had vanished.

'Drop your gun.' One of the men shouted.

Carder had no choice. Five against one was not good odds. He dropped his gun.

Within seconds he had been tied up and blindfolded and then bundled into the back of a vehicle, together with the old man who he could hear grunting with pain as his injuries took fresh knocks.

Where had Scott gone? Carder thought. He must have dashed down a side street and got away. He was in deep trouble and could only hope that Scott could somehow dig him out of it.

The journey in the van was short. A corner was turned sharply and Carder hit his head on the side of the van, but then it stopped abruptly and Carder could hear some raised voices from outside. After a few minutes, the doors were flung open and Carder and the old man were pushed out of the van and shepherded into a building.

They heard some voices and someone asked for the blindfolds to be taken off.

Carder felt the hands roughly untying his blindfold and he squinted as it fell off. His hands were still tied so he couldn't rub his eyes. He looked across at the old man who looked very uncomfortable and in some pain.

He stared ahead of him at the short bald man looking directly at him. Carder had not seen such evil eyes before. The man's eyes were fixed and they were black and cold, and seemed to delve deep into Carder's soul.

The man said nothing. He looked curiously at Carder's clothes and then looked at one of the men behind Carder.

'Lock them up Stein, and bring them to me later when I call you,' was all he said as he took one last look at Carder, and then turned and walked away.

The blindfolds went back on immediately and then Carder felt a shove in the back, and on his shoulder, as he was pushed along down a corridor.

The blindfolds came off again, only after they had descended a flight of stairs and been pushed into a room. They were untied and then the door shut behind them, and they were alone.

CHAPTER 10

'Anything broken?' Carder asked the old man. 'My name is David Carder and I'm beginning to regret trying to rescue you.'

'Thank you for trying. I'm Hugh Hanson. I'm okay, nothing broken, just an old man's pride.'

'Why were they attacking you?'

'Because I don't belong to their crowd. They are corrupt and they know I'm not with them.'

'So why did they have all the guns, why all this, Hugh? Why not give me a good beating and then move on?'

Hanson sighed. 'I don't know where you've been living but it's obviously not London. This place has been taken over and the old rules just don't apply anymore.'

Carder paused. 'If I told you where I was from, you wouldn't believe me. But you're right, I'm not from London.'

Both men were sitting on the floor facing each other. Their eyes were becoming accustomed to the dark. Hanson looked at the stranger opposite him and grimaced.

'My daughter, Sarah, told me I was mad to stay here. She left for a more peaceful life out in the sticks. I hope she's okay, but I haven't seen her for five years. I should have gone with her. Now, I don't suppose that I will ever get to see her.'

'You'll see her... ' Carder started.

'No, you don't understand. They won't let us go. They'll question us, then torture us and then get rid of us.' Hanson paused for a moment before continuing. 'A few days ago I saw an execution on Waterloo Bridge. A man was just killed and sent over into the water. I'm sorry, David, but this is not a good place for you to walk into trouble.'

Carder sat there looking at the old man, thinking about what he would report back to Maldini if he ever got himself out of here. It seemed as though anarchy had taken over in London. It was not a safe place.

'I don't understand, Hugh? Why would they torture us? What do we know that could be of use to them?'

Hanson was breathing deeply, and he rubbed his chest where he had been hit. He lifted his head and looked at Carder.

'These people want power. They started to control all the essentials, like food and water supplies, a few years ago and now they control almost everything. They're in it for themselves and they won't let anyone stand in their way. They'll want to find out where we each live so that they can go and ransack our homes and take anything valuable.'

'Who are these people?' Carder asked.

'The Council of London run everything. There are twelve in the Council, led by a man called Gorman. That was the bald man you just saw. I've met him only once before and that was enough. He is evil and he is also very powerful. Today, we were captured by one of their street patrols that run around flushing out people like me.' Hanson paused before continuing. 'Three years ago, we would have been fined and probably beaten. Now, the penalty is more final.'

'Why didn't you leave with your daughter?' Carder asked.

Hanson flashed angry eyes back at him.

'Because it is my city. It is where I grew up. It is where I met Louisa. Where Sarah was born. Why should I leave now? I knew this place as a great City and I am not going to be driven out by thugs.'

Carder nodded. Hanson was stubborn. Brave, but stubborn.

The old man was in a lot of pain and Carder moved over to help him, but Hanson waved him away and then continued. 'Thank God Sarah got out of here, but I pray they don't catch up with her at the Village.'

'The Village?' Carder asked.

Hanson looked at him, sizing him up. There was something about this stranger that made him trust him. An inner instinct told him that Carder could be an important ally. He did not know the man at all but he always trusted his inner instincts.

'They live out at Stonehenge. There are a few people out there trying to re-build a decent life. They are trying to be self-sufficient. Sarah teaches the children.'

Carder had not heard of Stonehenge, but had no time to ask further questions because they both heard footsteps approaching.

Hanson smiled thinly. 'It was good to meet you David Carder but you should have ignored me and not got involved.'

The door swung open and two men stepped in.

CHAPTER 11

'We've got a problem.' Maldini said, looking at the four committee members. 'Scott has messaged up to Silves to say that Carder has been captured. They ran into some trouble in central London.'

'What sort of trouble?' Pirrin asked.

'Some sort of a fight. We don't have any more details.' Maldini replied.

'If Carder talks…' Pirrin started.

'He won't,' Maldini interrupted. 'Carder will not say anything.'

Pirrin shrugged. 'It doesn't really matter I suppose. We should just get down there ourselves now and sort it all out. All of us. We should do this properly.'

'Not yet,' Mai said. 'We need to get a full report back from Scott. This may be just an isolated incident and Carder got unlucky. It may not be a widespread problem. Let's wait for Scott's report.'

'Does Scott know where Carder has been taken?' Straker asked.

'I don't know. I hope he's trying to find out right now.' Maldini said grimly.

'One day!' Pirrin exclaimed. 'Carder hasn't even been there one day and he's been captured.' He turned to face Maldini who was disconcerted by the look in his eye.

'The time is fast approaching when we need to be bold and take the decision to return to Earth. I have said this to you before and I am not alone in thinking this. There are many here on the moonbase who are growing restless.'

'Commander Pirrin,' Maldini spoke evenly. 'Mai is right. We will wait for Scott's report. Then, and only then, will we decide on the next course of action.'

The meeting ended and Maldini was left alone in the room. He sighed and called for Carla. She needed to know that Carder had been taken.

Maldini was proud of his daughter. She had proven her abilities time and time again in training exercises and although Pirrin had resisted her climb through the ranks, even he eventually had to accept that the girl had fighting qualities.

He had never talked to Carla about her mother though. That was because he couldn't. Not yet. As with all things the timing had to be right for that. Initially, Maldini's silence on the subject had hurt Carla but she trusted her father, and she knew that many others on the moonbase were in the same position as herself. She steeled herself and adopted the pragmatic attitude that Maldini had fostered upon his community. She got on with her life and just like all the others; she focused on the one goal which had been drummed into everyone for years now. The goal was a return to Earth as one united community.

'What are his chances?' Carla asked her father after hearing the news.

'He's a survivor, Carla. If anyone can make it, he can.'

Carla looked at her father. 'He is important to me.' She said simply.

'I know,' Maldini replied, 'as soon as I hear more I will let you know.'

Carla left the room and Maldini smiled to himself. Restraint. Emotions held in check. His daughter was a good example to others on the moonbase. Maldini held the view that to fall too deeply in love or to have too strong feelings, good or bad, for anyone on the moonbase would be a dangerous thing for such a small, closed community.

Yes, he was proud of his daughter.

CHAPTER 12

Carder had to think quickly. This was as good as the odds were going to get. He had to seize the chance.

'Can you help the old man up, he can hardly walk,' he said to his captors. He shot a quick glance at Hugh and gave him the slightest of nods. The message was clear and Hanson had understood it.

Tony Stein was the older of the two men at the door. He had been working for the Council for over a year and had dealt with the prisoners for the last three months. He had lost count of how many there had been – more than fifty. Not one of them lived now. Some had talked, some had not, but they had all suffered the same fate.

'Pete, you grab the old man. I'll watch the weirdo.' He said to his sidekick, Pete Myers, who was a vicious looking youth of about twenty.

Carder pretended not to be interested but in his mind he was calculating. He had to trust what Hugh had said – these men were killers. He looked at the distances and weighed up the chances of success and reached his conclusion.

Hanson, at first, resisted being pulled to his feet. He complained that he hurt too much.

Myers tried to hoist him up and Hanson pulled back and then, just when the balance of weight was shifting, Hanson made the switch and summoning all his dwindling energy, he leapt up and jabbed Myers in the eyes and grabbed his right arm before it could reach for the gun.

Carder reacted instantly and flew at Tony Stein, landing a blow in the solar plexus and then bringing a knee up to crack his nose. Carder grabbed Stein's gun and cracked him on the head with the butt before swinging round on Myers.

'Move a muscle and you are dead,' he said quietly, before reaching over and taking his gun.

'Hugh, walk away to the door and stand behind me.'

Stein and Myers had been taken completely by surprise and were mad with rage.

'You fools,' Stein said. 'You'll suffer twice as much for this.'

Carder motioned Hugh to back out of the door.

'Okay you two,' he said, 'you have a choice. You can die now or you can play by my rules. Rule number one, lie face down on the floor. Go on, now.' He kept his voice quiet and steady. Stein hesitated, but moved when Carder stared at him. When the two men were on the floor, Carder said 'Rule number two is you stay there and stay silent because I'm going to be at the door, and any sound or any movement means I will have to silence you.' He glanced at Hugh.

'Okay, Hugh, you get out of here whilst I take care of these two and find out what's going on here.'

Hugh made to protest but Carder urgently signalled to him to say nothing. The old man then limped his painful way down the corridor before coming to a left hand turn where he could see the corridor led into a large hall. He looked back at Carder who motioned him to go on. As Hugh turned the corner and got out of sight, Carder gave him ten seconds before he made his move. He grabbed the door, slamming it shut and locking it before running down the corridor to catch Hugh.

He caught up with him as Hugh was surveying the large hall. There was no-one in it and it looked like the door at the far side led to outside. The two men started to cross the hall.

Behind him, Carder could hear the banging on the door he'd just locked and shouts from Stein and Myers. He then picked up another noise, closer to him.

It was a padding sound and at the same time as Carder turned round he heard a low growl. Two Dobermans were coming towards them and they looked like they meant business. Carder glanced at Hugh and knew that the old man could not fend off dogs like this.

Carder could handle one of them but not both. He drew his gun but was too slow as both dogs sprang at Hanson and pulled him to the floor. They chose the weaker man from instinct and they were going for the kill. Hanson shrieked as the fangs tore into his flesh. Carder had no choice. Two bullets later and both dogs lay dead on the floor, but Hugh was in a terrible way with blood pouring from neck and shoulder wounds.

Carder picked the old man up, ran to the door and pushed it open as shouts came from the house behind them. It was thankfully very dark and the moon was Carder's friend as it hid behind clouds, and he ran as fast as he could. A shot rang out behind him but he was away, round one corner, down an alley and then across a further larger road before taking another turn and down some steps. He was near the Thames and could hear the old river washing up against the concrete embankment. There were no other sounds, just the relentless wash of the river.

He could go no further carrying Hanson and laid him down on the ground. The old man was shivering and looked dreadful. Carder knew that they had to move again before morning but he doubted whether Hanson had the strength.

CHAPTER 13

Tony Stein was not often afraid, but he was now. Up until this point he had an unblemished record in working for the Council, but he knew he had been complacent and underestimated the strength and will of the weird man he had pulled off the streets. He stood next to Pete Myers and struggled to look into the face of his boss, Elliot Gorman, who sat behind the table in front of them. He knew Gorman did not tolerate failure and he knew he had failed badly. He had seen what happens to people who fail to deliver for Gorman.

Gorman was about fifty, bald and stockily-built with the sort of cruel, dark eyes that could see right through people. Those eyes were fixed on Stein and Myers as he asked, 'Which one of you should die for this?'

There was no answer.

'Okay, if you can't choose, you can both go. You are both responsible for allowing the prisoners to escape.'

'Give me a day to catch them' Stein said. 'I'll bring them to you by the end of tomorrow.'

Myers chipped in, 'Yes, we can catch them back for you boss. Then we'll make them suffer.'

Gorman paused, and then looked across the room to one of the street patrollers who had been watching and waiting for his signal. Gorman just gave this simply by looking at him. The young man silently moved across the floor and stood directly behind Stein and Myers.

'I like your attitude, Myers, we need more like you.' Gorman said. Myers smiled with relief and opened his mouth to speak. His mouth stayed open but no words came out though as the bullet lodged in his brain. Slowly he toppled forward and crashed to the floor.

'Clear up the mess, Stein.' Gorman said. 'And bring those two back to me by this time tomorrow.'

As the room cleared, Gorman was thoughtful as he looked again at the objects on the table. They had been taken from Carder's pockets when he had been captured. The communicator and the gun were not the usual sort seen on the streets of London. Gorman held both of the objects in the palm of each hand. He then smiled and reached for his communicator.

CHAPTER 14

Carder decided he could afford to rest with Hugh under the bridge for about thirty minutes before moving on. They would come to track them down, but for now there was no sound in the dark night apart from the gentle splashes of the Thames.

He looked down at his new friend. 'We'll stay here for a bit, Hugh, and then see if we can get further away. Just take it easy and rest up. Let me take a look at your wounds though.'

Hugh was very weak and in a great deal of pain. He looked up at Carder. 'You go on now, my friend. I'm only going to slow you down and on your own, you just might have a chance of getting away.'

Carder looked at the bites and cuts on Hugh's face and neck. Two of them were very deep and had bled a lot. Carder knew that Hugh needed a level of medical treatment that he just couldn't give him.

'I'm going to try and get you to a safe shelter before it gets light, and then I'll get you some help for those wounds. Where is the best place for us to head for, Hugh? – as you already know, I'm not from round these parts.'

Hugh didn't answer him at first. He was deep in thought as though he was weighing up something very carefully in his mind. 'Where *are* you from David? Your clothes are a bit strange and you just seem... you just seem very different.'

Carder thought about his answer but Hugh had drifted into unconsciousness. He did his best to clean Hugh's wounds but he knew that he was running out of time.

'Hugh, stay with me. Keep awake.' Carder spoke urgently now. 'We have to move soon and then I'll get help.' There was no response from Hugh and Carder let him drift further into the deep sleep. Still, there was no sound at all – his pursuers must have called off the chase.

'I'm not from here, Hugh.' Carder began, as he leant back against the concrete wall and looked across the river. 'My father was from here,' he began. 'Well, not from London but further north... a place called Derbyshire, I think. Jack Carder was his name. His family were there and he grew up there. I've been told he would have been twenty-one when the virus hit. He lost all his family in the space of two months.'

Carder looked down at Hugh who was breathing very heavily, and still not showing any signs of regaining strength.

'I'm told the same thing was happening all over the country.' Carder carried on, unsure if the old man could hear him. 'I can't imagine how he felt knowing that he was one of the very few survivors.'

Hugh stirred and his mouth moved a little as if he was trying to speak, but his eyes stayed closed and no words came. Carder felt he could hear though and carried on.

'I don't know much about what happened to my father after that. I know he ended up in a place called Sheffield, but after that I have no idea what happened to him. He

55

didn't travel with my mother and...' Carder paused, '...and I was told that my mother died giving birth to me. My father died before I knew him. I can't actually remember him. And there are no photographs. Nothing. How they both got to the moonbase I just don't know.'

Carder had said the word... moonbase. Because it had seemed the right thing to do, he had confided in an old man he barely knew.

Hugh's eyes were open now. 'Moonbase, David? Did you say moonbase... good grief, is that where you are from...' His breathing was laboured and every word was a huge effort. 'It really is true then. What I heard.' He paused for a moment before summoning up another effort.

'The moonbase. People talked about it but I wasn't sure whether to believe it. I heard that there was some kind of international cooperation. Some joint project to set it up years ago. Back in the forties I think. But it was all highly secret. I... I'd forgotten all about it.'

The old man's eyes closed for a moment and Carder thought that he may have lost him, but then he coughed and grimaced in pain before continuing.

'Your father... he must have lived through a terrible time... people dying... everywhere... the burials were dreadful... All the corpses...' Hugh's voice was fading. 'They left us to it... left us to do all the cleaning up. Left us to look after ourselves and then I heard... the moonbase...'

Hugh trailed off.

'What Hugh, what about the moonbase? What did you hear?'

'I'd forgotten about this as well. It was all very serious but I heard that they took sperm samples from some of the survivors and then... they just left us...'

'What? What did you say Hugh?' Carder was puzzled. 'Sperm samples, what do you mean?'

Hugh coughed violently and some blood dribbled out of the corner of his mouth. Carder leant near to him so he could hear his whispered words.

'David... find Sarah. Find her and protect her... please...' Hugh was drifting away and Carder held him close.

'Hugh, stay with me,' he implored the old man. 'We'll find her together. I promise... Stay with me.'

It was too late though. Hugh had gone. His suffering was over.

Carder had hardly known the man. Just for a few hours, that was all. He had tried to save him but instead had brought him death.

He felt a terrible guilt and he also felt a great sense of loss... Carder didn't know which was worse. He lay there holding the old man close to him, trying to make sense of it all as the relentless old river ebbed back and forth.

After a while he could see the first signs of the new day pushing back the dark blanket of the night. A grey smudge in the east meant Carder had to move, but he was still lying there thinking about what the dying man had said when the decision was made for him.

He heard the faintest of noises first. A pebble rolling across the concrete. Carder was alert. Then silence. Maybe he had imagined it. He stayed very still and very quiet. Then there was another very slight noise. An unmistakeable scraping against some more pebbles. Something was moving in the dark and it was getting very close to Carder.

Without a sound he stood up. And pressed his back against the wall of the bridge so he was kept in the darkness. A couple of minutes went by before he heard another sound. Breathing... he could hear someone breathing and then he could dimly make out a shape.

Carder waited until the shape passed by him less than three feet away. The shape stumbled... it had walked into Hugh's body lying on the ground. Carder leapt out and pinned the shape's arms back whilst closing his hand over its mouth. 'One sound from you and it's the last one you'll make.' He hissed. Then he realised with shock that the shape was Scott.

Somehow Scott had found him and for once Carder was relieved to see his fellow traveller. He let him go but regretted it immediately. Scott hit him... hard in the face.

'You idiot, Carder. You've messed up big time here.' Scott had real venom in his voice. 'I wanted to leave you, but I was ordered back to find you and get you back to the ship... before you do any more damage.'

Carder gingerly felt his bloodied nose. 'It's good to see you too, Scott.'

CHAPTER 15

After they had weighted Hugh's body with stones and slid it into the Thames, Scott and Carder had started the long walk back to the ship but were barely exchanging words. They had attracted some curious looks from the occasional passers-by but in the main, the streets were deserted.

The two men were re-tracing their steps from the day before and recognised the same old abandoned buildings and streets. They even saw the same old woman with the bag of fruit, but she hurried off in the opposite direction as soon as she saw them.

'Feels like we're being watched.' Carder broke the silence.

'Maybe,' Scott replied, 'it is weird that we haven't met anyone.'

'How did you find me?' Carder asked.

'I asked a couple of people. No-one seemed willing to talk so I applied a bit of pressure.'

'What do you mean?'

'I had to rough up a young guy. He had seen the incident with you and the others and he knew where they were taking you, but he wouldn't say. He was too afraid.'

Carder was silent for a moment before replying. 'Everyone is afraid. Everyone in this city is afraid of these people. They're called the Council and they are ruling by terror.'

Eventually they reached the edge of the city. A pack of wild dogs passed by on the other side of the road but left them alone.

Both men were exhausted. They had only eaten and drunk small rations and neither of them had slept. They had been told that through living on the moonbase, their levels of stamina and endurance had developed to far higher levels than they would have done on Earth but nevertheless, they were both reaching their limits and needed some rest.

The ship was not there. Scott had arranged the rendezvous time and he knew that they were on time. 'Let's get into those woods over there and I'll call in the ship,' he said. 'This is not a good time to land a ship undetected. We'll have to be quick when it lands and make sure we're away again within a minute or two.'

Safely under the cover of the trees, Scott made the call. He waited a few moments but there was no response. 'Maybe they've had to delay for some reason.' Carder said, but he was puzzled that the ship was not responding to their call. He was tired and aching from his ordeal in the city, and he was also beginning to think something was wrong.

Then, both men heard them at the same time. A long way away but there was no doubt what the sound was. Dogs. Hunting dogs being driven on by men.

'Let's move, Carder,' Scott said urgently. 'They will find us here. I'll give the ship new landing coordinates once we get clear. The men started to run through the woods but at that moment, Scott's communicator beeped loudly. With relief he flipped it open.

'Come in now, right now, and we'll be ready. We have hostiles approaching and probably have about two minutes to embark. Not the original landing site. We're running through woods due north – lock onto us and go for the first landing space north of the woods.'

In the ship above them, Silves could see the two men's thermal images showing clearly on the tracker screen, and about half a mile south of them several two and four legged images heading towards them.

It was difficult running through the woods. At times the path narrowed to a single track and branches and brambles had to be avoided or pushed away. The going underfoot was sometimes hard and sometimes soggy and for two men used to a far more sterile and pristine environment, it was very testing. They could hear the ship now overhead but could not see it as the trees canopy was too dense.

'Four hundred yards, Carder,' Scott yelled. 'The ship has got us tracked and is coming down in a field ahead of us.'

Carder was aching all over but his adrenalin was pumping and keeping him running. Thorny branches were ripping across his face and the ground underneath was getting worse, but he knew he had to keep going. He could tell from the increased volume behind him that the dogs had their scent.

The noise of the ship grew louder and they caught a first glimpse of it through the trees. It was very low and just ahead of them.

'Through there.' Scott pointed and set off down a track that led to the edge of the woods. Carder turned too sharply and went flying into the bushes. His foot had caught something and he ended up rolling down a hidden slope, hurtling against fallen branches until eventually he came to a stop at the bottom of the slope. Bruised and battered and cut all over but as far he could tell nothing broken.

He could hear Scott yelling for him from up above somewhere. 'Go, Scott, get on the ship and come back for me.' He yelled back. He heard no more from Scott and started to clamber up the far side of the slope. From behind him he could hear the dogs approaching and men yelling wildly.

At the top of the slope, Carder staggered towards the light coming from the edge of the woods and then flung himself to the ground. A desperate scene was unfolding before him.

Scott was running across the field towards the waiting ship which had its embarking steps down and the doors open. Dogs and men were closing in on Scott and Carder knew at that moment that Scott would not make it.

Scott was running for his life and thought he might just make it, but then he froze in horror as he saw the embarking steps retracted and the ship's doors close.

'No!' he yelled. 'You can't leave me here.'

A few seconds later the ship was airborne, hovering over the figure of Scott surrounded by howling dogs and at least twenty men pointing guns at him.

The ship hovered about fifty feet up and turned slowly round so that the front of the ship with its vaporising guns faced the men and animals in the field. Carder could not believe what he was seeing. 'No,' he gasped. 'This is wrong, so wrong…'

The guns opened up and a second of blinding light followed.

After Carder had removed his hands from shielding his eyes, all he saw was an empty field. And there was silence. Every man and animal had gone. Including Scott.

The ship continued to hover and it took Carder several seconds to realise that it was waiting for him.

Carder did not move though. It was very tempting to just walk out into the field and attract the ship's attention, and his mind was telling him to run to the ship and return to the safety of his home. Something was holding him back though. Some inner instinct was telling him to keep out of sight of the ship. The ship began to move along the edge of the woods towards Carder.

Carder withdrew carefully a few yards into the trees. He suspected that the ship could not pick up his thermal image because of the distortion caused by the vaporising guns. He could not be seen.

A part of Carder's mind was telling him to walk out of the woods and catch a lift home.

He could not understand though why Silves had fired the vaporiser. The ship was not under threat... why? Then Carder realised with a jolt that Silves alone did not have authorisation to fire the gun. He had received instructions from someone.

He stood there in the trees trying to make sense of it all but try as he might, he could not figure it out. Maybe Silves had panicked. He just did not know.

He thought of Carla and all the friends he had back home. It was the only life he knew, but he also knew that he had just witnessed a terrible massacre and that meant something must have changed. Something was happening that he didn't understand.

He remembered that Maldini had told him that he would need to trust his decisions and in that moment, he had just made one. He was staying.

The noise from the ship increased and then it moved swiftly away and upwards. Carder watched it go until it was just a silver speck against the blue sky. And then it was gone and Carder was totally alone.

CHAPTER 16

Maldini paced across his office floor. The ship's report had arrived and reported both men killed in action. One hundred per cent positive confirmation of Scott's death, minimal chance of Carder surviving the vaporisation.

He sat down heavily in the leather chair behind his desk and rested his head in his hands. It had been a disaster and he had to blame Carder for that. Carder had acted with his heart and not his head. He had taken a risk and lost and now he and Scott were dead. And now he had to tell Carla.

He looked out of the window at the blue marble shining in the black void and he felt despair. He knew from Scott's report that there was anarchy on the City streets. What was happening in London was probably the same everywhere. It was human nature...

His thoughts were interrupted by a knock on the door and Carla walked in. Beautiful Carla, his daughter and his pride and joy. When she had got involved with Carder, Maldini had been wary because he knew Carder to be a restless soul. He knew at some time that his daughter would get hurt. That time had arrived.

'Carla, the ship had to take action. Pirrin said that it was under attack. He had to order Silves to do it. We could

65

not risk them being captured.' He began. Carla looked at her father impassively as he continued 'I'm sorry that David perished... there was no trace of anyone after the vaporising gun stopped.'

'It was murder', Carla interrupted, 'cold-blooded murder... we...'

'No.' Maldini spoke quietly. 'Can you imagine the harm it would do if the people on Earth knew about us now. We have to position this right with them. When the time comes. We have to...'

'Spin it?' Carla asked. 'Come on, Dad... you know what's happened here. We've preserved our shiny reputations for a future day by... by killing our own people and also killing people who have had to survive horrors on Earth. If this is humanity evolving I think we're going backwards!'

'Carla,' Maldini kept his voice even although he knew his daughter was mad at him. 'David would have been tortured and killed. Those people surrounding him were from the London Council. We know about them. We know what they can do.'

The door opened and Peter Straker walked in. Straker looked grim-faced as he stood looking at the father and daughter. At just thirty-two, he was the youngest committee member and Maldini knew that for all his smooth charm, he was deeply ambitious.

He had watched Straker grow up and always seen in him something different to all the others. He had a confidence in himself but he seemed to want to hide it. He always gave the impression that he was holding back on something. Always wanting to give the impression that he was like all the others. He didn't want to stand out in the crowd.

His looks made him stand out. Tall and muscular with startling blond hair and blue eyes.

But his eyes were hard. Maldini had seen the edge in them even though Straker could camouflage them when he turned on the charm. Maldini knew that he would need to watch Peter Straker very carefully.

What Maldini did not know was that Straker wanted Carla for himself.

'Sorry to interrupt boss… Carla,' he began, 'but I have some more bad news.'

'More bad news? What now, Straker? What could be worse than losing two of our best people?' Maldini replied.

'We've lost three, Sir.' Straker paused before continuing. 'We've lost Silves as well. Something malfunctioned in the ship just as he left Earth orbit. The ship… just blew up.'

'Blew up!' Maldini replied in a calm steady voice. 'Our ships don't just blow up. What did N'Gomo say about it?'

'He's trying to find out the reason, Sir. But he's not got much to go on. One moment Silves was there, saying that he was heading back here, and then… nothing… just silence.'

'Damn! How can that happen? How can we lose Silves too? He was a good guy. Damn! Now we will never know what exactly happened in those last seconds. Why did he feel so threatened that he had to use the vaporiser? He would have known that was a last resort.' Maldini looked distressed.

'They must have been shooting at the ship, Sir. Straker said evenly.

'We don't know that for sure though,' Carla said, 'and now we will never know.'

'One other thing, sir'. Straker added before pausing.

He looked at Carla and then back to Maldini. 'It's Carder, boss. Silves reported that there was no tracking of Carder's location despite doing two Earth orbits. Enough time would have passed after the vaporisation for Silves to pick up Carder's location if he was still alive. If not on the first orbit, then definitely by the time he flew over the spot again.

'What are you saying, Peter?' Carla asked.

'I'm saying...' another long pause as Straker looked at the two faces studying him. 'I'm saying that we didn't just lose Scott and Silves. We have to accept that Carder is dead as well.'

Maldini sighed. 'I... I had come to the same conclusion. I think it's highly unlikely that Carder would have survived.' He turned to face Carla. His daughter's eyes were shining with moisture but she was keeping her emotions in check. She was doing what all the others on the moonbase would do. She controlled her emotions. Just like she had been trained to do.

'I'm sorry, Carla,' Maldini said softly, 'but Carder's gone.'

Carla nodded and for a long moment said nothing. Then she looked straight at her father and stuck out her chin a little in a determined fashion before saying, 'Carder would want us to carry on. He would expect us to carry on planning and training and then getting it right for the next time.'

She turned and left the room.

Straker turned to Maldini. 'Perhaps now, sir, we need to re-think our plans a little. It looks like Pirrin may have been right. It is hostile over there and the time has come for us to show up in numbers.'

Maldini said nothing. He just turned to look out of his window and out across the void to the blue planet.

Straker left him to his thoughts and closed the door quietly behind him as he left.

CHAPTER 17

Eight months later.

Carder thanked the elderly couple and bade them farewell. He was truly thankful to Tom and Trish Langford for they had been his lifeline. As he had struggled out of the woods and into the fields to the north of London, he had arrived on their doorstep tired and starving and very confused.

In return for Carder doing work around their farm, the couple had fed him and provided a roof over his head. They had asked no searching questions about him and in turn, had been grateful for the work he had done during the cold days of that winter. They had even included him in their own homespun religious ritual at Christmas.

Carder had been fascinated by this. He had heard of the Christmas festivals that happened on Earth but it still took him by surprise.

He had not expected to feel such a deep sense of history. Such a connection to the past. He could feel the belief that the couple had, and feel their need to remember the past lives of their loved ones. He felt very new emotions wash over him as he listened to the gentle couple saying their prayers and singing their hymns.

He wondered if Jack Carder had enjoyed his Christmases in Derbyshire. When Maldini had told him his father's name and where he came from, Carder had not given too much thought to it. There was no point in him investing time and emotion on the subject. Jack Carder would be long gone now.

All of Carder's training and development on the moonbase, just like all the others, had been about looking forward, not back. But somehow, these strange rituals that Tom and Trish had introduced to him were faintly stirring something deep in a corner of his mind.

When he called it a very human festival, the old couple looked at him strangely. When he spent ages looking at the makeshift decorations they had put up around their house, and then made some of his own, they smiled at him and perhaps felt sorry for him for he clearly had no family to spend the special time with.

It was his turn though to feel compassion when Tom showed him old photographs of the extended family they once had. The pictures showed happy faces of the extended family.

Children and grandchildren, lots of lights, a Christmas tree and many beautifully wrapped presents had all been captured on film. The old man's eyes glazed over with moisture as he told Carder the name behind each face.

Tom and Trish had each other, but they were both living off the memories of much happier times.

As the dreary month of January fell away though, Carder knew he must move on and he knew where he had to go. The voice of an old dying man came to him time and again, often waking him in the middle of the dark nights. That voice pleaded with him to 'find Sarah' and it reminded Carder of the promise he had made to Hugh Hanson, the debt that had to be repaid if Carder was ever to shake himself free of the feeling of guilt that burdened him.

So he knew that now it was time to head west towards a place called the Village. The old couple at the farm had not heard of the Village, but they did know of Stonehenge and they had given Carder two priceless gifts. Rough directions to find his way there and also an old bicycle. Carder loved the bike and although he had not found it easy to balance on it immediately, he now felt at home on it and he also felt a strange sense of independence for the first time since he had arrived on Earth.

He had about a hundred miles to cover and he had three days food and water in his rucksack. It was not enough, but to carry any more would have slowed him down.

It was an eerie journey to begin with. Carder cycled along deserted motorways, passing signs that meant nothing to him other than following the town names given to him by Tom and Trish. He tried to imagine that the six lanes of the motorway were once full of traffic speeding along, although Tom had told him that often the vehicles would be almost stationary. He had been told that the M25, as it was known, just became too congested as more and more people crowded onto this small island.

For early February, the weather was kind to Carder. He had experienced rainfall many times but each time he had marvelled at how soft and refreshing it felt when he was out in the wet. On a bike however, he would soon get wet through if it rained and he was grateful for the crisp blue skies above him. It was cold at night, but finding shelter was not difficult with so many deserted buildings to choose from.

For the first two days of travelling he saw no-one and made good progress. On the third day however, he awoke to a different world. For the first time in thirty years, snow had fallen in southern England.

Carder was amazed at the transformation. White pristine snow all around him. His boots were sinking in and leaving a clear imprint. He scooped up a handful and let the white powder blow away in the air. Then he picked up another handful and studied it. The white flakes which were still gently falling were so pure and clean. He compacted the flakes into a ball and threw it.

He had seen pictures of this and he knew that snow sat at the tops of the high peaks around the world, but to be standing right in the middle of it was an experience that humbled him. It was wonderful but it was also painfully sad. He was alone. He thought of Carla and longed to be able to share this moment with her. He also felt sad because this beautiful world was nearly empty now and it deserved to have people enjoying all of its wonderful surprises.

He lit a small fire to keep warm and sat nearby looking out on the deserted countryside, trying once again to imagine what it had once been like. This precious place had been home to millions of people, and it struck him there and then how much those people must have loved their home and how terrible the end must have been for them.

As the snow kept falling his mind drifted back to some of the old films he had seen back at the moonbase. He had seen films of the many wars between different countries on this planet. Maldini had been keen to show everyone these films. To show them how the conflicts arose and how human beings had the capacity to wipe each other out. Maldini had always said that the wars were senseless, but it was only now that Carder could really feel that for himself, sitting alone in the white countryside.

By mid-afternoon, the snow had stopped and melted sufficiently for Carder to set off again to try and get two more hours travel in before the sun set. As he was preparing to look for shelter that night, cycling down into a broad valley, he realised that he had company.

The woman and child had come out of an old farm building and were walking slowly towards him. The boy cannot have been more than about ten and had a shock of unkempt black hair which matched the woman's. Carder's friendly smile slipped away as he saw the woman point a gun at him.

'Hold on, I mean you no harm lady.' He said. 'I am travelling west and need to stop somewhere for the night. Do you know of anywhere nearby where I can rest?'

The woman replied. 'Throw down your gun and walk away from it.'

'I have no gun.' Carder said. 'I have only food and water in this sack and not much at that.'

The woman hesitated. 'Throw down the sack then'

Carder threw the sack onto the ground. The woman motioned with the gun and spoke quietly. 'Back away from it.' Carder did as she asked. She spoke urgently to the boy who ran up and grabbed the sack and returned to the woman. She looked into the sack and pulled out what was left of Carder's rations.

'Where are you travelling to?' she asked.

'I'm headed for a place called the Village, if you've heard of it.' Carder replied.

'I know it. Why are you going there?' asked the woman, still pointing the gun at Carder's midriff.

Carder hesitated, and then decided his best course was to tell this strange woman all about London and Hugh's dying wish. When he'd finished the woman lowered the gun and simply said, 'Follow us.' With that, she and the boy turned around and started walking back towards the farm building.

Carder followed the woman and child into the house and was immediately glad of the warmth from the log fire.

'My name is Rosie Pemberton, and this is my son Charlie.' she said as she threw one more log onto the fire.

'Mine is David Carder and I'm pleased to meet you.'

'Sit down.' Rosie laid the gun down on the table in front of her, still within reach.

'Charlie, can you make some tea for us please.'

Carder marvelled again at the ability of these people to still have stocks of tea and basic comforts, but he knew from living with the old couple back near London that one day soon, all these stocks would dry up. He looked at Rosie and saw a strong jaw line and determined eyes. She had to be made of strong stuff to have got this far. She had streaks of grey in her black hair but Carder thought she was a good looking woman, probably in her early thirties.

'You can stay in the outhouse tonight and we'll give you food.' Rosie began. 'But in return, you could help us with some repair jobs. The roof is leaking and the fences are weak. Charlie and I can't do it on our own.'

'Thank you,' Carder replied. 'I'll do what I can to help. I'm grateful for your hospitality.'

Carder stayed a week. He worked hard during the days and ate well in the evenings. Both Rosie and Charlie also worked hard during the days as there seemed to be a never-ending list of chores to be done just to get by.

In the evenings, Carder was fascinated to listen to the stories Rosie read to her son. Adventure stories mainly, but always with a flavour of the past. Charlie always listened in silence the whole way through and then asked his mother questions.

As Carder listened, he realised that the mother and son bond was so strong and it was as if each night it grew a little stronger as they went through their little ritual of reading and questions. He listened with mixed feelings. He felt a sadness because he had never known the mother and son bond, but he knew he was witnessing something very precious and very human. He had never seen or heard anything like it in his life.

When Charlie and Rosie had gone to bed, Carder took the books with him into the outhouse and read himself. He found himself drifting off into a more deep and contented sleep than he had ever known.

On the fifth evening though, Rosie broke the spell.

'It is not safe for you to stay here much longer.' she began. 'They are coming. The Council are coming this way. They will leave me and Charlie be, but not you. You will be dealt with. Just like the other men.'

'The other men?' Carder asked.

'A year ago they came.' Rosie paused for several seconds. 'They came to see what we had and to recruit any men. They wanted our food-stocks, machinery, oil... anything that could be useful to them. Three men came in a van.'

'In a van?' Carder asked in astonishment. 'They have enough petrol to get out of here?'

'Yes.' Rosie continued, her face set hard against the amber glow from the fire. 'They can get petrol still but they use it sparingly. For special trips only... to forage for things. To steal from people who are just trying to survive.'

Charlie brought in the tea and sat down near the fire. Carder saw, once again, the strong resemblance to his mother as the boy turned his striking blue eyes on him.

Rosie continued. 'My husband resisted and argued with them, but it was no good. They dealt with him.'

'Dealt with him?'

'Threatened me and Charlie. Threatened to kill us both. Chris... my husband... he then said they could take everything. They then loaded up the van, laughing and shouting insults at us and...' Rosie's voice cracked a little.

Carder felt he knew what was coming next.

'When they'd finished loading their van they turned back to us and just... just shot Chris... right in front of us.'

There was silence in the room except for the crackling from the fire.

'I'm sorry.' Carder said quietly. 'Those men must be brought to justice; they must be punished for their crimes.'

'It won't bring Chris back.'

'No, it won't,' Carder said, 'but they must pay for it.'

They sat in silence again for a few minutes, with Carder allowing Rosie the time to gather herself again.

Then Carder asked how far it was to the Village and if Rosie knew of anywhere along the way where he could stay.

'Less than a week's travelling I think, if you are on your bike. I don't know of anywhere or anyone so you'll have to take your chances. We'll give you some food supplies to take with you on your journey.'

'No, you cannot spare them for me, Rosie.' Carder objected. 'I'll get by,' and he stood up.

'You haven't told me much about yourself.' Rosie said, watching Carder carefully. 'Maybe before you go you can tell me where you are really from.'

Carder slept uneasily that night. Rosie had referred to the Council. The same people that Hugh Hanson had talked about. It seemed like there was an evil shadow spreading slowly over the land. Carder had arrived in this place as a stranger, an outsider. And yet he sensed that he had a role to play. He just didn't know yet what that role was.

His mind went back to what Maldini had said to him. Trust your own decisions.

It was almost as if Maldini knew that Carder would end up like this. Stranded miles from home. Alone, and yet feeling that he would be called upon by the people of this place. Called upon to help them in some way. He had already made a few decisions, but he knew that he would have to make more.

The next day passed uneventfully with more hard work chopping wood and preparing a field for crops, and then the same evening routine. Carder managed to avoid having to explain where he came from to Rosie by offering to read Charlie's story. He felt guilty in that he had been evasive with Rosie, but somehow he didn't feel ready to open up and tell her.

Carder lay down on some straw and closed his eyes. After what seemed like seconds, but was actually an hour, he felt a tug on his arm.

'Mister, can you read me another story.' It was Charlie.

Carder smiled. Charlie had enjoyed his story-reading and it gave Carder a strange and unfamiliar warm glow inside. The boy was about to say something else but he heard a noise from outside, frowned and shot out of the door. Carder sighed, the boy was clearly still a little nervous of him.

He brushed himself down and then he heard some noises from outside, a laugh but also a shout. He then heard a scream. He rushed through the door of the barn and then froze. He found himself looking out upon a scene from hell.

CHAPTER 18

Three men were outside the farmhouse, one of them with a flaming torch in their hand. The house was alight with flames shooting out of the downstairs windows. At first, Carder couldn't see anything apart from the three men silhouetted against the flames. He started to move stealthily forward and then he saw Rosie.

She came screaming and running out of the front door. There was a flame on her right arm and as Carder moved closer, he saw her hair catch fire. Out of the corner of his eye and less than ten yards from the men, Carder could see Charlie. He held a gun but the men did not appear to have seen him.

Carder could see that one of the men had a gun and at that moment he started to fire it at the ground around Rosie's feet. She screamed louder and tried frantically to avoid the bullets.

A different shot rang through the air and the man with the gun fell to the ground. Charlie had fallen backwards with the recoil of his gun firing and Carder sprang forward. He bunched his fist and hit the torch carrier hard on the side of the head. The other man had gone for his partner's gun but Charlie had fired again, missing his target but frightening him off, running fast back to the van and then taking off with a screech of tyres.

Carder checked the man he had hit and could see that he was out cold. He then rushed to join Charlie who was at his mother's side where she lay on the ground, groaning. He could see immediately that she was not going to make it.

There was nothing either Carder or Charlie could do to help Rosie. She was in so much pain. Charlie held her hand 'Mum... please... please...' was all he could say.

'Charlie...' She croaked, 'Go with this man. Stay with him and go to the Village.'

Rosie then looked up at Carder. Her eyes pleading from the depths of her horribly disfigured face. 'Please...' She started.

Carder understood and nodded. 'Okay, Rosie, don't worry, I'll look after him.'

Carder thought he saw a small smile of relief in Rosie's eyes before she sank back and closed them.

'Mum.' Charlie cried. 'Mum...' The boy's voice trailed off and he just stared at his dying mother.

His young eyes had already seen far too much and Carder could not bear to see his distraught face.

Rosie made a final huge effort. 'I... I love you, Charlie... be strong.' She managed before she collapsed back. She was gone. She had survived for so long against the odds, but now the broken and violent world she had lived in had finally claimed her.

The house continued to burn all night.

Carder picked Charlie up and carried him to the barn. He was shivering as Carder laid him down and wrapped straw around him. He placed his coat over the boy to give him extra warmth. Charlie's eyes closed but Carder knew that it would not be for long. He was in shock, and the grief would hit him hard when he woke.

Carder went back to interrogate the man he had hit but it was too late. He had gone, vanished into the dark night knowing that he was up against two guns and that his friend in the van had deserted him. Carder feared that more men would return in the morning, so he resolved that he and Charlie had to move on before first light. First though, he had a burial to do and he carried out that gruesome work as Charlie lay asleep.

Charlie woke up yelling after an hour. Carder held him by the small fire and let him cry and sob until no more would come. He had no words for the boy. Nothing Carder could say could have any comfort for the boy. As Carder held the boy, he felt an anger stronger than anything he had experienced before. This was evil. A human evil. Why did these killers have to survive when so many good people perish?

Something inside Carder was changing. He wanted to do something. He wanted to help these brave people survive. He didn't know how or what, but he knew he was beginning to sense a purpose for being where he was. He was angry and he wanted to put the wrong right. He wanted to avenge the death of Rosie Pemberton and probably many others like her.

Finally he said, 'Charlie, I'm going to get some food and water for us and then we have to set off in an hour's time. Stay here and keep warm.'

Carder gathered what little provisions he could and then returned to the boy. To his surprise the boy was standing up by the fire holding a small bike. He felt a great admiration for Charlie. He had his mother's determination and survival instinct. It was a hard world and it was only the hard that would survive in it. Carder nodded to himself. The boy has what it takes.

Before they set off, Carder took Charlie to his mother's grave and they sat for some minutes. Carder knew no prayers and there was silence until the boy spoke softly. 'Sorry Mum, I should have stopped them... I... will find the others and they will be sorry too.'

Charlie's face was wet with the tears sliding down as he slowly stood up and just whispered, 'Goodbye, Mum,' before turning away.

The first dull glimmers of the new day's light were just beginning to show on the eastern horizon as the man and the boy set off towards the west. The clouds had dispersed and the half moon looked down on them and lit their way for the start of their journey.

CHAPTER 19

They made good progress and had seen no-one on their journey, until Charlie suddenly pointed ahead.

'There's someone there by the side of the road.'

As they approached cautiously, Carder could see that a man was lying on the grass, either asleep or dead. The man did not move as Carder stood over him, throwing a shadow over his face.

At first Carder wondered if it was the same man who had escaped from Rosie's place the previous evening, but he could see straight away that this was a different man.

'He's breathing', Charlie said, 'but he stinks.'

Carder nodded. It was a strong smell of alcohol. The man was a drunk.

Carder had rarely touched alcohol in his entire life and the smell in the crisp country air was making him reel.

'Are you alright, mister?' Charlie touched the old man with his shoe.

'Get away, Charlie,' Carder said, but he was a fraction too late.

The man on the ground had grabbed Charlie's ankle and was tugging him towards him.

'Get off!' Charlie shouted as he tried to get away. 'Get...' He broke off as the man pulled a long rifle out from under his filthy coat.

Carder leaped forward and crashed his foot on the rifle. It fired as it fell away onto the ground.

Charlie had wrenched himself away but the man was up off the ground though, glaring at Carder and Charlie.

He was rough looking. Unshaven and with long, unkempt hair. His small eyes were wild and almost feral.

'I want food,' he snarled. 'You must have some food for me.'

Carder could see that although the man had a feisty attitude, he was very weak and ill looking. The drink was taking its toll and he seemed to be having some trouble focusing on Carder.

'Sit down and let's talk,' Carder said.

The man did not move so Carder pulled his gun out to encourage him.

'Okay' he said 'we'll do this the hard way. Sit down.'

The man's wild eyes glanced down at Carder's gun.

Slowly he sat down. When he hit the ground a change came over him. His expression crumpled and he broke down in sobs.

Carder just stared at him for a few moments, unsure of the next move.

The man recovered a little and looked up at Carder 'Please... don't shoot me... please... I have lost everything. I... had a wife and children... they have gone... all gone... please.' He spoke before breaking down again.

Carder said nothing for a minute and then he pulled out some bread and fruit and put them down on the ground next to the man.

Charlie looked across anxiously as he knew that their supplies were sparse.

'Eat these,' Carder ordered.

The man pulled himself together and looked at the food offering. He looked up at Carder and then back at the food. For a moment he paused, and then he started to eat hungrily.

Carder sat down opposite the man with his gun still trained on him and he tried to talk to him. He had no success though. The man just tore into the food, occasionally looking up to glare at Carder and Charlie.

Eventually, Carder sighed and stood up before walking over to the man's discarded rifle on the ground. He thought for a moment before emptying the bullets from the gun and putting them in his pocket.

'You'll find them down the road about a hundred yards.' Carder said. 'Don't go and get them until we are out of sight.'

He tossed the man another apple and then motioned to Charlie that they were moving on.

As they cycled onwards together, Charlie shot a puzzled glance across at Carder.

'Why did you do that, mister? Why did you give the man food?'

Carder looked across at the boy and paused before saying, 'He was a very ill man, Charlie, and he is not going to last long. We couldn't bring him with us. It was all we could do for him.'

Charlie said nothing but shot another glance across at Carder.

CHAPTER 20

That night they stayed in a church.

It was very cold in the old stone building but it was dry and Carder soon had a small fire going at the back of the church. The glow from the flames cast strange shadows and Carder looked around in wonder. He had heard of these places but had never imagined them to be so atmospheric, even many years after they had last been used and even with most of the colourful stained glass windows cracked or broken completely.

One of the windows was intact though and Carder stared up at the picture of the pale faced woman holding a baby close to her.

How many people over the years had looked up at that window? He tried to imagine the villagers walking from their homes to the church on a Sunday morning, and singing their hymns and saying their prayers.

Tom and Trish had told him about this weekly ritual and how they loved it so much, and found so much comfort and togetherness at their village church.

Carder walked slowly around the church and sat on one of the long benches facing the front. This was such a different world to the one he knew and as he sat there reflecting on this, he had a feeling of loss and emptiness. His life had been so structured, so focused and so constrained by boundaries. Maldini's boundaries. He didn't understand how but he could feel himself beginning to push on those boundaries.

Charlie was sleeping fitfully. He woke at one point crying and sniffing quietly. Carder put his own coat over the boy to keep him warm, and only drifted off to sleep when he was sure that the boy was asleep also.

A slight noise in the early hours woke him though. He opened his eyes and peered through the gloom. The fire had died down to just a red glow so it was much darker in the church, but he could see the small figure illuminated on the other side of the fire from him.

Charlie was standing there. He was making a small and low sound, almost guttural.

At first, Carder couldn't understand why he was doing this but then he saw them.

The dogs were all bunched up together. Carder could see three of them. Thin, rangy dogs just standing there in front of the boy.

Carder's first instinct was to leap up and protect Charlie but then he realised that would be foolish. It was Charlie who was protecting him.

The dogs must have crept into the church somehow and by the looks of them, would have attacked Carder and Charlie whilst they slept. But Charlie had them under his control. Almost under a spell, Carder thought. He seemed to be communicating with them somehow.

He watched motionless as Charlie threw some small morsels of food down onto the floor which the dogs ate hungrily.

He then heard Charlie saying something very quietly and the dogs all slowly disappeared into the darkness and away from them.

Charlie stood there watching them go before he came back to put some more wood on the fire and fan the flames.

Carder said nothing as he watched the boy settle back down and close his eyes.

The next day's travelling passed quietly. Carder did ask Charlie how he had dealt with the dogs but the boy just shrugged, and said they were just frightened and needed food.

Just after the weak sun had reached the high point in the sky, Charlie suddenly pointed excitedly over towards a field.

Carder could not see anything at first and had to line himself up exactly with where Charlie was pointing.

Up in the sky there was a small dark speck. Just hovering there.

'What is that?' Carder asked.

'Watch it, mister. You keep watching it.' Charlie replied.

Carder did and for a minute or two nothing happened. And then suddenly the speck changed shape slightly and plummeted fast towards the ground.

Carder could now see that it was a bird and that it must die if it hit the ground at that speed.

Without slowing though, the bird came right down to the ground and then in the same motion climbed back up again, this time more slowly and with something held in its talons.

'A hawk, mister.' Charlie cried. 'That's a hawk. I've only ever seen one before. My dad said they were coming back. He said it was a good sign…'

'A good sign.' Carder looked at Charlie's excited face. 'That's just what we need. A good sign. Come on then, let's keep heading west. Maybe we'll see some more good signs.'

CHAPTER 21

Three days later.

They cycled over the crest of the latest one of the rolling hills they had come across and stopped to look down upon the scene below.

The sun was low in the west and casting a warm glow over the countryside. Carder's eyes were immediately drawn to the strange ring of stones perched on a low hill. The stones were bathed in the red light and to Carder; it was almost as if they sent out some sort of a force to the surrounding area. He was transfixed by the sight of the ancient stones, but then he let his eyes slide down the slopes to what was clearly a community nestling below. There were wooden buildings, huts and some tents and everywhere there was activity. Men and women were walking around purposefully, some of them carrying things or pulling along carts behind them. There were also children. Some of them seemed to be in groups, running and playing but some of them were walking with the adults and helping them carry things. There were animals in enclosed pens and as Carder's astonished eyes took in more, he could see carefully tended and fenced-off areas where crops or vegetables of some sort had been planted in neat rows.

Carder looked across at Charlie who was wide-eyed at the scenes below him.

'We've made it, Charlie. Now let's go and see who these people are that live here.'

The setting sun was providing a riot of colour in the sky as the man and the boy cycled slowly down the hill and approached the Village. The people looking after the crops were the first to notice them, and then gradually more and more faces turned towards the strange couple as they made their way towards the front gates. There was a calm about these people Carder thought, and they obviously felt confident and secure because there seemed to be no open alarm or hostility towards them as they came close and got off their bikes to walk the last few yards.

They were stopped at the gates however.

A giant of a man stepped out onto the road in front of them and watched them approach with his arms folded across his massive chest. His untidy long, brown hair was complemented by a thick beard and Carder could sense the enormous physical power he possessed.

Carder and Charlie walked slowly up to the giant at the gates.

'We are looking for a place called the Village,' Carder said.

The giant spoke in a deep, rumbling voice. 'This is the Village. Why do you come here?'

'I have travelled from London,' Carder said, 'and I am looking for someone by the name of Sarah.'

'London, you say?' replied the giant, and Carder had noticed a slight uneasy murmur amongst the onlookers.

'Why does someone from the City want to come all the way here?'

Carder hesitated, but then decided on the course he would take.

'I could not live there any longer. Too much thieving, too little food left. I had to get out and find somewhere where I could live in peace.'

'Why do you look for someone called Sarah?'

'I met a man in London who said he had a daughter here called Sarah. He knew I was leaving and asked me to find her.'

The giant look puzzled. 'And why would he do that?'

Carder hesitated and looked round at the crowd that had gathered. There were children in the crowd and he did not want to create any panic amongst them. He had to speak in private with the leaders of this place.

'It is a message only for Sarah.' Carder said.

The giant man paused, and looked first at Carder and then at the boy. He shrugged. 'You can come in but we will search you first,' and he beckoned at two others to come forward and carry out the search.

The boy was searched first and then it was Carder's turn. Before the search started, Carder said, 'Wait, I have a gun to give to you.'

The men backed off and the giant sprang forward with surprising speed and pushed Carder to the ground before pinning him down. 'A gun, eh? A man of violence are you?' Carder could barely breathe let alone speak, and was helpless as one of the giant man's helpers found the gun in his coat pocket. 'Tie him up boys and put him in the cold house. I'll have a little chat with him later.'

'No!' Charlie cried out, lashing out at the bearded giant.

'What have we here?' Came the rumbling laugh from behind the beard. 'You've got a lot of spirit,' as he easily swept up the boy in one arm and kept his little flailing fists out of reach. 'Sean, take this boy over to Miss Hanson. She'll get him washed and start teaching him some manners.'

Carder picked up the name. Miss Hanson, that had to be Hugh's daughter. 'Miss Hanson?' he asked, 'is that Sarah Hanson?'

There was no reply from the giant as Carder was taken away and the crowd of people dispersed. One-by-one they went back to the jobs they were doing and, as it was dusk now, most of them had their evening supper on their minds after the afternoon's entertainment.

A woman had stepped forward from the crowd though. Her voice came through the clear evening air.

'Let him go, Connor. Let me speak to him.'

Carder twisted his head sideways towards where the voice came from. He could make out a slim figure in the shadows. The rough hands eased their grip on him and Carder was pulled to his feet. Connor the giant reluctantly let go of him but stayed within arm's reach. Carder gave him a glance before turning to face the woman. And something inside him jumped.

She was very beautiful. Carder held her gaze for a long moment before she spoke. 'I am Sarah,' she said. 'Why do you wish to speak to me?'

'I met your father in London' Carder replied. 'He asked me to find you and tell you some things. Can we speak privately?'

Sarah Hanson studied Carder. She looked over at Charlie and then back at Carder.

'Connor, bring this man and the boy to the schoolhouse in an hour please. Give them some food and water. It looks like they need it.'

'But Miss Hanson…' Connor started.

'It's alright, Connor. Please bring them. I will talk with them and then we can talk afterwards.'

Connor did not look at all happy and when Sarah had disappeared into the darkness, he turned to Carder. 'If you cause any trouble to that lady you will pay for it immediately. Do you understand?'

Carder nodded. He understood. The people in the Village looked happy and secure but he could see that they depended on Connor and his henchmen to keep that security. The giant had a job to do and he was doing it well.

CHAPTER 22

An hour later Carder and Charlie walked up to the door of the schoolhouse and stepped inside. Connor told them that he would be waiting outside and he repeated his earlier warning to Carder.

It was dark and very cold outside and Carder and Charlie were glad to get inside where candles and a small fire were giving light and warmth.

Carder had never seen a room like this before. Rows of desks with chairs behind them faced towards the front of the room, where the wall was dominated by a large blackboard with lots of numbers chalked on it.

In front of the blackboard was another desk, with the chair facing out to the rows of desks.

Sarah Hanson was sitting in the chair, carefully watching the man and the boy as they walked down the centre of the room.

'Take a seat,' she said, pointing towards the chairs on the front row, 'and please tell me how my father is.'

Carder coughed. This was not going to be easy. He sensed that Sarah would know if he spoke any half-truths, so he would have to tell it all as straight as he could.

'Okay, Miss Hanson,' he began. 'First of all, my name is David Carder and this is Charlie Pemberton.'

Carder then explained how he had met Hugh Hanson in London, and then the capture and escape from the Council. Sarah just listened, her huge green eyes fixed on Carder. She listened intently and without any expression, but she had started to sense the worst.

Carder was finding it very difficult. 'Miss Hanson, your father... the injuries your father suffered... the injuries were very severe. I'm very sorry but... but he did not survive them. I am very sorry but your father has died.'

Sarah sat motionless for a long minute and then she stood up and walked slowly to the small fire. She sat down by it and buried her face in her hands. Carder put an arm round Charlie and motioned to him to be silent.

After several minutes, the schoolhouse door opened and Connor peered in.

'Are you alright, Miss Hanson?' he enquired.

Sarah looked up from where she sat. Her face was grief stricken and her tears had left her cheeks glistening in the firelight. 'Connor, please show them to the guest house. We can all talk tomorrow after the morning lessons.'

'I'm sorry, Miss Hanson. I'm sorry to bring you such bad news.' Carder said as he stood up. Sarah did not look up or reply, but went back to watching the flames flickering at her feet.

CHAPTER 23

The following morning brought clear blue skies and bright sunshine.

Carder had stepped out of the guesthouse and was immediately met by Duke, one of Connor's henchmen. He had brought bowls of a grainy cereal and milk for the two guests. He also had a warning.

'The big man is not happy with you,' he said gruffly. 'You've gone and upset Miss Hanson, just like he warned you not to.'

Carder shrugged. 'I had to give her some news. Bad news.'

After their breakfast they had another visitor. Two young boys came sheepishly up to them and pointed at Charlie. 'Miss Hanson says you should come with us and meet everyone at the school,' they said.

'No,' Charlie said, 'I'm not going to the school. I...'

'Charlie, please go with them.' Carder said. 'They don't know yet whether we are friends or enemies and for now, we have to do as they say. Please go with them.'

Reluctantly, Charlie walked off with them. Carder watched him go fondly. The boy had shown great strength already and had seen such terrible things. He needed something different and he needed companions of his own age. He called after him 'Charlie, I'll come and see you later. Just do as everyone asks and no harm will come to you.'

One of Charlie's companions called back to Carder. 'Oh... and Miss Hanson asked for you to come to the schoolhouse at midday, mister.'

Carder stood up and surveyed the scene around him.

Everywhere there was bustling activity. The Village was going about its routines for another day.

It was bigger than Carder thought it would be and he could see that the people were happy. There were lots of chatter and a lots of smiles. And over in the distance, looking down on it all, were the stones. Once again, Carder cast his eyes up to the strange circle on the hillside. There was something about them that Carder could not place. He could sense something but he was not sure what. He decided to set off to walk towards them but Duke called him back.

'You're not to leave this area,' he said. 'You can wait here until midday and I'll then take you to the schoolhouse.'

So Carder had to sit there and wait. He also had to think about what his story would be to these people. To Sarah. He had told them the story in London and he would tell them about how he had met Charlie, and he would tell them what he had heard about the Council. He had to warn all these people that their way of life was threatened. And yet, he couldn't tell them who he really was or where he came from.

He sighed and rested back against the guesthouse wall. He had brought nothing but trouble to anyone he had met. He was about to bring more trouble.

CHAPTER 24

At midday, Duke escorted Carder to the schoolhouse. A bell sounded from within the building and several children came out and dispersed in different directions. There was no sign of Charlie though, and Carder started to worry if he had been rash in letting him go off with the two other children earlier.

Connor joined the two men as they stood in the sunshine outside the schoolhouse. He looked menacingly at Carder again, but said nothing. Other men and a woman gradually joined them and waited a few yards from the door to the building.

After five minutes, Sarah appeared at the doorway and called them all in. She looked pale and tired, Carder thought. She had probably lost a night's sleep after his terrible news.

As they filed in to the schoolroom, it was clear that one of the group was taking charge.

An elderly, grey-haired man was ushering people to their seats and handing out papers with lists on them. He introduced himself to Carder. 'My name is Benjamin,' he said, stretching his hand out to Carder, 'and I am the Chairman of the Village community.' Carder introduced himself and sat down where the old man was indicating. Right at the front, facing the others.

He caught Sarah's eye. 'Miss Hanson, have you seen Charlie?' He enquired.

'Yes, he came to lessons this morning and is now round at the back with some other children gathering some wood for me. He's fine. And you can call me Sarah.'

She held Carder's eyes for a moment before sitting down at the side of the group next to Benjamin.

The old man began proceedings by welcoming Carder to the Village and asking the others to introduce themselves to him.

Apart from Sarah, Benjamin, Connor and Duke, there were two others.

Eleanor looked almost as old as Benjamin. Her wispy grey hair framed a strong and determined face and her piercing blue eyes seemed to delve deep into Carder's soul as she was introduced to him.

Eleanor then, in turn, introduced Carder to the priest.

Tobias was a tall olive-skinned man with a thick mop of black hair, which Carder thought made him look younger than he probably was. The wrinkles around his eyes and mouth suggested to Carder that he was at least in his forties.

Tobias seemed very wary of Carder. It was if he could tell that Carder had not been brought up with religious beliefs. Carder could not help wondering how Maldini would have fared in this meeting.

Carder took a deep breath and prepared himself. He was a stranger in the midst but he was beginning to get used to that feeling.

Benjamin waited impassively for the introductions to be completed and the chatter to die down, before eventually he could start.

'David, we have a few routine matters to run through and then we'll hear your story. Your news of the world beyond our boundaries will be of great interest.'

It took over an hour for the routine matters to be dealt with, and Carder was struck by the energy and enthusiasm that these people had summoned up.

There was a simplicity about their life in the Village but this was necessary, given the times they lived in. However, there was also a sense of order and strong values which he could pick up. They were together this community; they were pulling together as one. There was a strange innocence about these people but at the same time, it seemed they were earnestly trying to build a future. There was talk about crops, animals, schooling and even the weather before Benjamin finally wrapped up the session and then slowly sat back and folded his arms. All eyes turned towards Carder.

'David, I understand that you brought some sad news for Sarah last night?' Benjamin started. 'And I also understand you mentioned a warning from Sarah's father. We need to understand the nature of this warning.'

Carder drew a deep breath and then started to relay what Hugh had told him about the Council. He told them about Gorman and his henchmen, he told them about the way they were hijacking all the food supplies and building their power base through stealing and intimidation. He told them about their ruthlessness and the way they were dealing with people who got in their way, and finally he told them that it was likely that they knew about the Village.

There were a couple of moments before anyone spoke in the schoolhouse. It was Connor who broke the silence.

'So, what evidence is there of all this going on?' he asked. 'Apart from Mr Hanson, did you see other things in the city?'

Carder relayed a tale of escape from the city. He had constructed this in his mind overnight as he knew that the truth would be impossible for these people to believe. They would lock him up and throw away the key.

Carder told them how he had fled London and then found shelter with an elderly farming couple, before setting off for the Village – no lies there, he just omitted the details about his journey with Scott and the horrifying vaporisation scene. He then went on to describe how he came across Charlie Pemberton and his mother on his journey to the Village. He spared no details about what Rosie had told him, and what then happened on that awful night the men came.

Benjamin looked across at Sarah and she nodded. She had clearly heard something similar from the boy that tallied with Carder's story. The old man looked at Carder and spoke softly. 'It seems to me, David, that you and trouble go hand-in-hand... and now you say it may follow you here.'

'I am sorry, sir' Carder replied. 'Mr Hanson wanted me to warn Sarah and from what I've seen, these people do mean business. You need to prepare the people here so that they are ready to deal with the Council if they come to the Village.'

Again, there was a brief silence. Sarah then spoke. 'And what about you, David, what are your plans? Where are you headed next?'

'I haven't really thought about that,' replied Carder, and then after a small pause. 'If there is work I can help with here then I'll do it. If you want me to move on, I will... but I would need to know that Charlie is alright first.'

Benjamin stood up and walked slowly to the front of the room. 'David, we are trying to build something here. We do need help but we only need it from people who will abide by our rules. This is a community here and our goals are to bring forward the community as a whole, and not to see any individual gaining at the expense of others.'

One-by-one the others in the room spoke. Connor spoke of the need for the men in the Village to work for the community only. Money was meaningless so, in return for work, the men would receive basic supplies in proportion to the number of mouths they had to feed. He ended by saying that the men would have to be organised and trained somehow, if they were to be capable of repelling unwelcome visitors. Carder agreed and said he could help.

Tobias looked concerned and spoke up. 'If we speak of violence we will surely bring it to our own doorstep. This man is a stranger with strange tales from the City. Why would anyone come all the way out to here to harm us?' He paused and looked round the table.

'We should keep our faith. We should keep our peace. The prayers we make every day are protecting us and allowing us to grow.'

He then turned directly to Carder. 'You are a man that attracts violence. I am not that sure you are a good person for our Village.'

It was then Eleanor's turn. She had been quiet throughout the meeting and Carder knew that she had been scrutinising him, trying to work him out.

'I share Tobias's concerns. I am not sure that you are the sort of person we should welcome to our Village.' She paused, and then sighed. 'But I fear that the times are changing. We have been isolated here for a long time. We have been lucky so far, but the day will come when we will need to protect ourselves.'

She turned to Benjamin. 'I agree with Connor. We should organise our defences and give us all more comfort that when that day comes, we can protect ourselves and preserve our way of life.'

Carder nodded. Eleanor had not endorsed his presence in the Village, but she had listened to what he had said. She had made her judgement of him and she had believed what he had said.

Sarah spoke of the need to put the children first always. They were the future. Their education was important and their values as they grew up had to be taught carefully. But they had to be able to do this in a safe, protected environment. Otherwise it could all come to nothing. She made no direct reference to Carder, but it was clear that she agreed with Connor and Eleanor.

Benjamin stood up. 'I feel this is an important day. An important day for all of us. We recognize that there is an outside world and we cannot isolate ourselves totally within this Village. Not for ever.' He glanced at Tobias before continuing. 'We have heard news of this outside world from David and we would be foolish to ignore those words. We need to adapt a little if we want to be confident that we can always say our prayers in peace and safety, knowing that we have done all we can to protect ourselves.' He paused for a moment, before turning towards Carder and smiling. 'I am sure that there will be work that you can help us with in our Village.'

So Carder was accepted into the Village that day. He knew that there were reservations about him and he knew it would take some time before he could be fully trusted. He was told that he would sleep and eat in the great central hut that was known simply as the Village Hall, and that Charlie would stay with him.

As he was being shown to the Hall, Carder couldn't work out whether he was happy at having been accepted or full of foreboding about what he sensed was to come.

CHAPTER 25

The late winter months passed by and the spring brought back the colour and warmth. Carder was busy every day, teaching the men of the Village the basics of self-defence and organising them so that they could provide some resistance and protect their Village.

They had few weapons though, half a dozen guns was the sum total.

In the early evening, Carder would often sit with Charlie and hear about his day at school. Initially, he had felt a responsibility to the boy but now he just enjoyed his time with him, hearing about the things that he had learnt about that day at school. Charlie would occasionally want to show Carder something that he had made at school and Carder gladly went with him, as this also gave him an excuse to see Sarah.

One afternoon, Sarah was talking to Charlie about the ancient stones up on the hill and Carder asked if he could join the school children's' trip to see them close up the following day. Sarah was hesitant, but eventually agreed that Carder could come with them.

They set off early the following morning and climbed the small hill up to where the stones stood.

Sarah said that there was once a protective fence around the stones to stop people vandalising them.

'Vandalising stones?' he asked aloud. 'How could people do that? How had the world come to that? Where you had to protect some stones from people who just wanted to destroy them.'

Carder could see the remains of what long ago must have been a car park and buildings, and asked Sarah why they had been placed there in the middle of nowhere.

Sarah looked at Carder strangely. 'You mean, you don't know about these stones?' she asked. 'David, where have you been all your life? This is Stonehenge, one of the most famous ancient historical landmarks in the world. People used to travel from all over to see these stones. Where have you been to have not heard of Stonehenge?' The children all laughed at Carder's discomfort, but Sarah looked puzzled.

They walked up to the stones and Carder looked at them more closely. They were gigantic. Huge heavy stones that must have taken many men to put them there.

The children ran around excitedly as Carder and Sarah walked slowly around the ancient ring, with Sarah filling Carder in on the history of the place. Carder was still worried about showing his ignorance about the stones, but managed to ask Sarah a few questions without apparently arousing further suspicions from her.

She told him about how, originally, there had been a circle of wood and then the area had been left deserted for a long time before the stones arrived. She told him that some people had said that the some of the stones came from the Welsh mountains, but she couldn't see how they could have transported them over such a distance.

'They must have really wanted to build something important here to do that. They must have had a good reason.' Carder said.

Sarah then gathered all the children together and started their brief history lesson.

Carder watched her as she drew a diagram with a stick in the Earth showing them what the huge wooden circle would have looked like, and then she drew the stone circle inside it and described the huge lintels that would have once run around the top of all the stones.

She drew a pathway. She called it an avenue that ran from the centre of the stones to the edge, and then down the hill all the way to the river.

She told them all about how the stones were aligned with the position of the sun and the moon.

As she stood on that hill with the breeze blowing through her dark hair, Carder thought that he'd never seen anyone more beautiful. And he felt sad because he knew that she totally belonged here. She was of this Earth. And he was not.

After they had walked back down to the Village and the children had all run off in separate directions to their homes, Sarah invited Carder to join her for supper.

Carder had never been in Sarah's lodgings above the schoolroom, and he looked round in fascination at the pictures on her walls and the books on her shelves. As she came into the room with a glass of home-made wine, Sarah caught Carder looking at a picture of her as a child with a younger Hugh Hanson holding her hand.

'He was a good father,' she said, offering Carder the glass. 'We had such fun together. He showed me round London and tried to explain how it all used to be so exciting, with all the people and the traffic and the boats chugging down the river. It really must have been something else. He loved London so much, which is why he couldn't leave the place with me when I decided to come here.'

'What made you come here?' Carder asked.

'It was like a new beginning,' Sarah said. 'I needed to find a purpose and I thought I could do something for the children... I could help them along with their learning and give them something to aim at.'

'You are great with the children,' Carder said. 'They hang off your every word.'

Sarah smiled. 'You weren't so bad yourself today. I saw you helping them and playing with them. You were very patient.'

Sarah walked back into her kitchen and left Carder alone with his thoughts for a few minutes. He wondered what Carla was doing at that moment. Had she forgotten him? She would certainly believe that he had perished. Had she found someone else? He couldn't blame her if she had.

The meal was wonderful. Carder had not eaten so well for a long time and the wine was also getting to him. He was not used to feeling so full and at ease so he wasn't ready for Sarah's next question.

'So David, what about you. Did you always live in London? I really don't know much about you before you bumped into my father.'

Carder looked at Sarah and had another sip of wine. 'No, Sarah I didn't live in London. In fact I had been there less than a day when I met your father.'

Now Sarah looked very puzzled.

'I told your father where I was from.'

'Will you tell me?'

Carder did not want to be thrown out of the Village and he didn't want this wonderful evening to end. But he knew he had to tell her. Tell her everything. He had known for some time that this moment would come along one day.'

'Yes, Sarah, I will tell you. I will tell you but I need you to keep it to yourself.'

Sarah shifted uneasily in her chair. 'I can't promise that, David, you know that. We are a community here.'

Carder looked into her beautiful eyes and decided to tell her his story.

'Sarah, did your father ever tell you anything about... anything about a moonbase?' he began.

'Er... yes, he did say something... a little bit.' Sarah replied with surprise at the question. 'Just that there was some sort of international base set up there and that, according to some people, a selected group were evacuated there. I imagine it is all pretty much mothballed now because, if it was true, no-one would have survived this long.'

Carder sighed. He had hoped that Sarah would have known more. Her father had suspected that a new generation had grown up there. But he had chosen not to tell his daughter.

'He didn't tell you everything he knew then.'

Sarah stared at him. 'Go on,' she said.

'The moonbase is still very much alive,' Carder said, 'and it has been monitoring the progress on Earth for over fifty years now.'

'Monitoring? What do you mean monitoring?' Sarah asked, incredulous. 'Do you mean to say there's been people up there watching everyone suffering here and just monitoring how we're all surviving? For all that time?'

'More than that, Sarah,' Carder paused, seeing her outraged expression. 'They plan a return here when it's safe to do so.'

'When it's safe?' Sarah shouted. 'What sort of people are they? Watching people die here and doing nothing to help?'

Carder had feared this. Sarah was becoming more and more angry.

'Sarah, the original moonbase people were chosen. Chosen to be a lonely outpost for the human race. Chosen so that maybe, just maybe, humans would survive and not be completely wiped out. It can't have been easy for them to be hurled out into space and asked to live their lives, cut off from their home and indoors in a sterile world.'

Sarah's eyes were blazing. 'True enough, but then to spend all those years monitoring us and not helping and… wait a minute though… how... how have they done that? They would be too old. I can't imagine that there were any babies evacuated, no children… oh god, they didn't evacuate babies as well did they?'

'No, Sarah, they didn't,' Carder replied. 'But some have been born there.'

'No… I don't believe that.' Sarah was shaking her head in disbelief and horror.

There was a moment's silence whilst Carder summoned up his courage.

'Sarah... Sarah, you are looking at one of those babies born on the moonbase.' Carder said, as gently as he could.

Sarah stood up slowly and took a deep breath.

'David, do you really expect me to believe you?'

'It's the truth, Sarah, I swear to you.'

'So let me get this straight. I want to know where you come from and you tell me you are from the moon!' Sarah's voice had an angry edge on it now.

'I have lived there all my life and there are others like me. There are around five hundred people on the moon right now. No children now though, none at all. But there are men and women who have lived there all their lives.'

Sarah studied Carder carefully. She walked backwards away from him and then paced around the room. She came back and stood in front of him. After a moment she said, 'Come through and eat David. Come through and convince me that you are not completely mad.'

It was at that moment that Sarah Hanson claimed a piece of Carder's heart. This beautiful, brave, clever woman was prepared to listen to him. She was giving him time to explain himself.

As they ate, Carder described his life on the moon. He talked about everyone and everything there from his earliest memories as a boy and his days at what they called the school, although he added that he would have rather been at Sarah's school. He mentioned Carla but said that she would believe him to be dead now, and would have found someone else by now. Finally, he came round to telling the story of his landing on Earth, his capture and subsequent escape with Sarah's father. He then told her about the terrible massacre after his run through the woods back to the ship, and how he realised that he could not return in the ship to his home.

Sarah was captivated. 'What do we look like from up there?' she asked.

'What do you mean?'

'The Earth... what does it look like?'

Carder thought for a moment. 'Beautiful... delicate... and I think lonely... it looks lonely.'

'Lonely?' Sarah asked.

'Yes, the Earth is a tiny blue ball in a huge black blanket. It just looks very vulnerable hanging there in space.'

Sarah closed her eyes for a moment, lost in thought. When she opened them they were once again fiery.

'What do your people plan to do, David?' she asked. 'Come back here when it's safe? It will never be safe for them to return. There will be anger. People here will not take kindly to them.'

'They cannot stay up there forever, Sarah.' Carder replied. 'They will run out of supplies and life support in about two years. They must come to Earth.'

'Five hundred people.' Sarah continued. 'How are they going to do that? All in one country or spread around the world?'

'I don't know/' Carder replied, honestly. 'There are some parts of the world where the virus is still active – North America, parts of Asia, parts of Europe…'

'You mean…' Sarah started and then put her head in her hands. 'You really have been watching us… watching and waiting…'

'Sarah, it has been my life.' Carder replied. 'I know no other way. I was brought up there and never knew of any other way, just like everyone else that has never been on Earth.'

Sarah looked at Carder with those alluring eyes. 'I'm sorry, David,' she said simply. 'This is just so much to take in. I'm just shocked and angry and…'

'I don't blame you,' Carder said softly. 'I'm just grateful you have listened. I didn't think anyone would. I have wanted to tell you for a long time, but any time I had a chance I didn't have the courage to take it.'

Sarah smiled grimly. 'Come to think of it, you do speak a bit strangely,' she laughed.

After a moment's further thought, Sarah abruptly stood up and started collecting the plates to take back to the kitchen.

'So, when do you go home?' she asked.

Carder stood up and accidentally touched her arm briefly, feeling an electric sensation as he did so. 'Sit down, I'll take them and clean up, it's the least I can do. The food was delicious.'

They cleaned up in the kitchen together. There was a nervous tension between them as they chatted and Sarah became quiet again, withdrawing into her shell, and Carder knew that she was trying to make sense of all that she had just heard.

After they had finished tidying up, they both clumsily tried to get through the kitchen doorway at the same time. Their faces were inches away from each other and their eyes met. They stood like that for a moment and Carder felt awkward. He tried to move on but Sarah touched his face gently and he stayed where he was.

Slowly, Sarah leaned forward and kissed Carder very gently on the lips before withdrawing again.

Carder needed no second invitation. They kissed long and tenderly before Sarah broke away again. She took a step back and David could see that her cheeks were flushed. He was worried that she was regretting kissing but then she spoke again... she was flustered as she said, 'follow me David,' before walking through to her bedroom.

The Village slept under the dark blanket. The wind howled around the huts and houses nestled on the slopes, whilst a little higher up, as ever, the ancient stones looked down on them all.

CHAPTER 26

A week later the men from the Council arrived.

Connor was the first to see the pickup truck driving slowly down the hill. He gathered three of his men to greet the visitors at the Village gates.

Two men stepped out of the truck and Carder's heart sank. He recognised Stein, the man who had been his captor in London. This was worse than he had feared.

There was a silent stand-off for a minute and then Stein spoke. 'It is important for the survival of us all that all fuel, food and water supplies are placed under the central control of the Council. For that reason, I am bringing this letter from Chief Councillor Gorman for the head of this community.'

'Central control?' Connor grunted. 'The supplies we have here are for this Village. We are not going to hand them over to anyone.'

Stein looked impassively at the giant and slowly looked at each of the Villagers standing at his side. His eyes rested on Carder for a moment and he frowned, but said nothing.

'Tell your leader...' Stein began

'I am the Village leader.' Benjamin had joined the group and the old man was leaning on his staff as he continued. 'You are welcome here as visitors and we will feed you before you go on your way. You must understand though that what we have here is ours. We have worked hard for it and we are self-sustaining. We do not need your Council's control.'

'I'm sorry you take that view old man,' Stein replied, 'but you should think about it some more because you have a deadline.'

'A deadline?' Benjamin asked.

'One week from today we will return to take control of your supplies. You will hand over control or...' Stein looked around at the Village... 'or all of this will no longer exist.'

Connor moved forward but was restrained by Benjamin's staff.

'Go back to your Council,' the old man said, 'and tell them that we do not accept their ways and that you should not bother coming back. In a week, our view will not have changed.'

Stein spat on the ground at Benjamin's feet. 'You will regret that old man,' he said and beckoned to his henchman to get back to the van. As he turned, he gave Carder a long, malevolent stare.

Connor, Carder and Benjamin said nothing as they watched the van disappear over the hill.

'So young man,' Benjamin turned to Carder, 'it seems your warnings were right. We have trouble headed our way.'

Benjamin glanced up at the ring of stones before turning back to the group around him.

'We will have a Committee meeting in one hour's time at the schoolhouse. David, you will join us.'

116

As the group dispersed, Connor turned to Carder. 'He recognised you. You should leave because I don't think they're going to be gentle with you.'

'I'm staying Connor' Carder said simply.

CHAPTER 27

The Committee gathered at the schoolhouse and Benjamin stood up to address them.

'My dear fellow Villagers,' he began. 'As you will all know by now, we have had some unwelcome visitors this morning. As we had been warned, our way of life here is under threat.' There were some murmurs and frowns before Benjamin carried on. 'The warning, which our friend David here gave us, has unfortunately come home to roost. We are grateful to David that we have had some time to prepare for this, but we now have to put all that preparation into action.'

The meeting went on for much of the afternoon, with everyone getting to have a say and eventually everyone being allocated tasks over the coming week. Carder feared though that they would be heavily outnumbered when the Council thugs arrived back, but his suggestion that the whole Village moved on to somewhere safer was turned down by everyone else. No-one wanted to move.

After the meeting, Sarah came up to him.

'David, we can't leave here. It has taken so long to build this place up. We can't just run away.'

Carder nodded. 'I understand, Sarah, but I also fear for everyone. I have seen these brutes in action.'

'We'll be alright.' Sarah replied. 'The Village will stick together and hold strong.'

Carder kissed her gently and said he would see her later. Right now, he had to address the men of the Village and start putting the defensive positions in place.

Charlie ran up to Carder as he walked through the Village. He had heard the news. 'I can use a gun,' he said, 'let me help defend this place.'

Carder looked at the boy with admiration. He had become part of the Village and found some kind of normal life, having been adopted into a family and having a few friends of his own age.

Rosie would have been proud of him, Carder thought.

'No, Charlie, I've got a more important job for you.' Carder said.

The boy looked disappointed as Carder put his arm round his shoulder and told him what he needed.

'But I can fight them with you.' Charlie said.

'I'm hoping there will be no fighting, Charlie,' Carder replied, 'and I need to you to organise the children and make sure everyone gets food and water.'

Charlie looked unimpressed as he went back to his adopted family's house. Carder smiled grimly after him. He did not want that young boy to witness yet more horrors, but he feared the worse.

He walked on to the area that had been marked out as the practice ground, where Connor and his men waited for him.

In total, there were twenty-one men including Carder himself. They had six guns between them and a variety of axes and knives.

Apart from himself, Connor and two others, all the men were at least fifty years old and none could be counted on for heavy physical exertion. Still, Carder thought, with some careful planning and organisation they could at least provide some resistance to the Council thugs. He was not optimistic though.

When he had finished giving the men their instructions and arranging the training sessions for the week ahead, Carder returned to the schoolhouse to see Sarah.

She was clearly worried by the visitors earlier in the day but Carder marvelled at her determination and energy. She had spent the day talking with the parents and agreeing that this week's school lessons would carry on as normal. Everyone felt it was important for the children to not be alarmed. She had also discussed with the parents ways of stock-piling supplies and hiding some of these outside the Village, so if the worst came to the worst, there would be some reserves to fall back on.

After their evening meal, Sarah talked to Carder some more about her life and her memories of being with her father in London. She stopped often to wipe tears from her eyes as she recounted those days. At all times, it had been a struggle for the father and daughter just to survive in the big City, but Sarah had been too young to remember the immediate impact of the virus and the speed with which it swept through the countless millions. She recounted to Carder what her father had told her.

'He said, at first there were isolated cases where the more vulnerable people got sick and then died within a week. In less than a year though, the virus had affected nearly every family. Doctors on the television said it was gathering in strength. The government kept denying this, but everyone saw through that as an attempt to prevent anarchy and a complete breakdown of any authority. Dad said that he and Mum were constantly trying to keep me isolated and away from any other people. I was just one year old. Then Mum got it.' Sarah paused. She couldn't remember but she could see her father's face as he told her how, within the space of five days, he lost his wife and my mother. 'It was quick,' she said, 'it just showed no mercy…'

Sarah had a photo on her shelf which Carder had often looked at. Sarah as a tiny baby being held by a beautiful woman, her mother, with her father standing proudly at her side. The joy inside the two parents hearts and eyes leapt out at Carder, and filled him with a sadness that they had enjoyed so little time together as a family.

'Sarah… I'm so sorry.' He said quietly.

Sarah carried on grimly. 'Dad said he saw television pictures from all round the world. Bodies everywhere. Deserted towns and cities everywhere. Then the television pictures just stopped. Dad said that was a terrible moment… when suddenly he felt cut off and alone. Alone with a one year old to care for and protect.'

'That must have been very frightening.' Carder said. 'I can't imagine how difficult it must have been at that time.'

'He didn't tell me too much about how he coped. It must have been desperate for him trying to get hold of fresh food and water. I think he said that at first there was some organisation, somewhere people could go to get fed… I think he said Southwark Cathedral was a meeting place... but eventually that must have stopped. There were just less and less people around.' Sarah paused and Carder could see that this was draining her.

Sarah took a deep breath and carried on.

'Of course, there was looting. Dad must have done some too just to survive. Bottles of water, stuff like that. How he survived and how he kept me alive I just don't know... I'll never really know.'

Carder felt uneasy. All the time this desperate man and others like him were scraping a living and clinging on to their lives, the people on the moonbase were safe, well fed and doing nothing to help.

Sarah must have read his thoughts. 'David, I don't blame you. You couldn't have helped then. You were just a young boy. But there were people up there who maybe could have helped... maybe saved lives...' Sarah trailed off.

They carried on talking and the topic moved on to the threat to the Village. Carder didn't want to worry Sarah, or any of the other Villagers unduly, but he felt they were under-estimating how ruthless the Council would be. Eventually, they became tired and Sarah rested her head on Carder's shoulder and dropped asleep. Carder looked into the flickering embers of the dying fire and thought about the week ahead, and what would happen when the Council thugs turned up.

CHAPTER 28

They came on the morning of the seventh day. Connor was the first to hear a distant rumble of engines and he mobilized the Village by hammering on the huge gong several times.

Carder had already been organizing the men into their defensive positions around the front perimeter of the Village, facing to the east from where the sound of engines was now much louder.

Sarah stood at the entrance to the schoolhouse taking a look at the activity around the Village, before going back inside to supervise the children who were preparing some food.

One-by-one, the vehicles appeared over the brow of the hill half a mile away. Carder counted them and cursed. Fifteen vehicles and some of them were trucks which could carry many men.

The vehicles parked and the engines cut off. Suddenly there was a silence hanging over the Village. The still-early summer heat seemed to shimmer off the vehicles for long moments. No-one spoke in the Village.

Then the men started coming out of the vehicles and gathering together. Carder could see that most of them were armed. Again, he started counting but stopped when he got past thirty. When all the vehicles were empty, Carder estimated sixty men in total. They were easily outnumbered in fighting power.

Carder could make out Stein who was clearly the leader. He stood in front of the men issuing instructions. He saw Stein and two others break away from the group and start to stride down the hill towards the Village.

'Let's go and meet them, Connor.' Carder muttered, and the Village was quiet behind them as the two of them walked out of the gates to meet Stein and his henchmen.

The two parties stopped, facing each other about ten yards apart. Carder momentarily glimpsed the ancient stones over Stein's shoulder before re-focusing back onto Stein's impassive face.

'Good morning, gentlemen.' Stein began with an undisguised sneer. 'We hope you have had time to reconsider our conversation last week, and you have got the food and supplies ready for us to collect.'

'We gave the matter considerable thought,' a wise old voice came from behind Carder and Connor. Benjamin had walked out to join them and he continued, 'and we came to the conclusion that we must hold on to what is rightfully ours. You have no authority to take our possessions.'

Stein looked at Benjamin. 'So you have made your choice.' He pointed at him and shouted. 'We will take your food and supplies old man, and if anyone resists they will be dealt with.'

Connor moved a step closer but paused when one of Stein's friends raised his gun up. The giant was fuming. 'I will look forward to dealing with you personally,' he said to Stein. 'You come barging in here and...'

'Good' Stein interrupted. 'I didn't want to bring the Council's security forces all the way out here for nothing. I am glad to hear that their trip will not be wasted. You have one hour to change your mind and then we will come into the Village.'

Stein turned and walked up the hill with two others.

Benjamin turned to Carder and Connor. 'Maybe we should negotiate with them,' he said. 'We might let them have something and then we can avoid any violence.'

Connor was indignant. 'No, Benjamin, we can see them off. They need teaching a lesson.'

Carder looked at the Council's men up on the hill and then back at his two companions.

'I don't think it's going to be like that, Benjamin,' he said. 'These men have come for a fight. If we offer them something it won't make any difference. They want total control.'

Benjamin thought for a moment. 'Wait here,' he said and started walking up the hill towards Stein and his men.

Carder and Connor both protested strongly but Benjamin was adamant. He turned to them. 'No, I will go alone. I need to test them. See if they will discuss a reasonable compromise. I must go alone because I am unarmed and old and they will know I pose no threat. If you come it will be hostile and there will be no chance of any talking.'

Reluctantly, Carder and Connor let the old man go. They knew it was a last chance for a peaceful outcome.

Benjamin set off slowly up the hill, pausing every now and again to catch his breath. Eventually, he arrived at Stein's group on the hill where all the men had turned to face him.

Carder and Connor watched the old man making his case, arguing for the Village. He occasionally turned round and waved his staff at the Village as he made his point to the men who faced him. Then, without warning, a shot rang out and Carder could see the trail of smoke from the gun Stein held. For a second nothing happened, and then slowly and horrifically the old man crumpled to the ground.

Carder and Connor yelled and ran forward bounding up the hill. They had to stop though as a hail of shots rang out. The bullets fell just short but the two men knew they were helpless. They had to get back to the Village and fast. Stein was leading his men down the hill in a charge. Connor was in a blind rage and he was shouting at Carder as they got back to the Village gates. 'Let me have him. Let me have him. I'll tear him limb-from-limb.'

Inside the Village it was pandemonium. Women were crying. Eleanor was staring stony-faced and in total shock, up to where Benjamin had been shot. She just kept repeating 'No... no... no.' As she stood frozen on the spot.

The men were looking stunned and Carder had to push some of them towards their pre-planned defensive posts.

Connor had gathered his gun and was taking aim at the advancing horde.

Sarah ran up to Carder. 'Benjamin?' she asked breathlessly.

'I'm sorry, Sarah, they shot him.' Carder replied. 'Get inside now,' he shouted as bullets whistled past them. A woman cried out, hit in the shoulder and Sarah ran to her to help her get inside.

The Village started to fight back. Carder had placed the men expertly and they were cutting down some of Stein's men. One of the thugs tried to barge through the gates but Connor was there to shoot him between the eyes at close range. The giant bellowed as he saw Stein pull his men back to re-group. He took aim and fired. Stein cried out and clutched his side. He was hurt but not fatally and

Connor wanted more. He rushed out of the gate to finish the job, yelling with the bloodlust. Carder ran to join him to give him covering fire. Once again, though both men were met with a hail of bullets and this time Connor was hit, the giant continued to stagger a few yards yelling obscenities at Stein. The bullets kept coming until Stein yelled, 'Stop!'

The silence was immediate as the smoke and dust swirled around Connor. The giant sank to his knees but still he held his gun. Slowly he raised it and started to point it towards Stein. The effort was too much though and he fell forward heavily, face first into the ground. Through the haze Carder could make out Stein's face. He was looking directly at Carder and he pointed at him as he yelled, 'You next!'

There were men lying and groaning on the ground. Some were motionless. Carder's defenders had done well but he knew Stein and his thugs would be back as soon as they had seen to his wound and re-grouped. They were returning up the hill now and that gave Carder the chance to rush over to where Connor lay. With a huge effort he turned the giant over. He could see he had taken several bullets in his massive body but he was still alive, just.

CHAPTER 29

Connor's wife Mary came running out through the Village gates. She was distraught as she fell to the ground beside her husband and looked at the wounds he had suffered.

'We need to get him inside,' Carder said softly. 'I'll get some men to lift him up on a stretcher and get him to the doctor.'

The Village doctor, known as Asif, had lived a quiet, relatively peaceful life up until now. Apart from Benjamin, two others, a man and a boy, had been killed by Stein's men but Carder could see at least a dozen injured as he walked into the small Village hospital. The sparse medical supplies were stretched to the limit and Doctor Asif was rushed off his feet as he looked at all his new patients.

Connor was lifted onto the main table in the middle of the room. There was no privacy for him as the doctor examined his bullet wounds. All around there were groans and sobs from the other injured Villagers. Two women were assisting the doctor and trying to provide comfort to the injured.

Carder looked around at the carnage, and once again was consumed by guilty feelings that it was him who had brought this horror to the Village.

Sarah had come up beside him and she gently touched his arm. 'You must get back to organising the defensive posts, David. The men are in disarray and are shocked that Connor has fallen.'

Carder looked across at Sarah. She looked very frightened and grief stricken. She had been very close to Benjamin and must have been in shock about the way he had been brutally gunned down. He held both Sarah's hands. 'I'm sorry, Sarah. Maybe if I had never come here this wouldn't have happened. Maybe...'

'No, David,' Sarah interrupted. 'This was going to happen anyway. You warned us. You gave us a chance to get ready.'

Charlie rushed in shouting. 'Mister Carder, come quickly. All the men are leaving!'

Carder shot out of the door and followed Charlie, running through the Village to the west perimeter of the Village. His heart sank as he got closer.

Six of the Villagers were deserting the cause. He could see them disappearing into the gathering dusk. Moving as fast as they could, carrying their belongings and with women and children in tow, they were headed for the west woods. They were deserting the Village and were not going to risk their lives.

'What are we going to do now, Mister Carder?' Charlie asked.

Carder looked at the boy. He was not frightened. He had seen so much already in his life and he was hardened. Carder knew at that moment that Charlie could be a leader of men. He had a spirit about him and he had courage.

'I don't think they'll attack again today, Charlie. They're running out of daylight now so I think they'll come again in the morning. That gives us the night to come up with a plan.'

The moon was rising to the east as Carder and Charlie walked slowly back through the Village. Charlie gave Carder a strange look as he stared up at it for a long moment.

The grief at the loss of Benjamin hung in the air of the schoolhouse as the remaining Village leaders gathered once more.

Carder had assessed the defensive positions and knew that the Village could not hold out against another attack.

'The odds were never in our favour,' he said. 'But now they've tipped too much. We don't have the men and we don't have the guns.'

It was unanimously decided that the Village had to yield. Three cartloads of supplies would be made ready to give to Stein's men, and they would also be given access to the Village. There was no other choice.

There was little sleep for anyone in the Village that night. The loss of loved ones was hitting hard, as was the realisation that their way of life was coming to an end.

'We have to start again somewhere else,' Sarah said to Carder as they stood outside the schoolhouse. 'These men from the Council are evil. We cannot live under their rule.'

Carder nodded. 'I think a new location is best now that they've found the Village.' They both fell silent again.

'What are you thinking?' Sarah asked.

'I'm thinking of revenge,' Carder said. 'Greed and cruelty should not be allowed to rule this place. Somehow the Council have to be stopped.'

'I wonder if this is happening all over the country... all over the world?' Sarah said, looking at Carder as he kicked some stones around angrily.

Carder was wondering the same thing. The moonbase would find it difficult to settle back on Earth if the Council got a real grip. The moonbase... Carder's thoughts went back there. Maldini, Carla... what were they doing now? What were their plans for new landings? Maybe, after his disastrous mission, they were putting back the timetable.

He turned back to Sarah. 'Sarah, what you have started here in the Village is the right way forward. Eventually, places like this will grow and merge and become towns. But you had the basics right. Everyone supported each other.'

Sarah then started sobbing. She leant against Carder. 'Benjamin... why did they shoot him? He was such a good man. He harmed no-one.'

Carder had no answer, but just held Sarah. She had to cry all her tears and let her grief come out because in the morning, she would need to be strong.

CHAPTER 30

The red glow in the eastern sky heralded the start of another hot June day. Carder had not slept, but had been glad to see Sarah get a couple of hours as she lay beside him. He got out of the warm bed and let her carry on sleeping.

As Carder walked through the Village he could hear the first signs of stirrings. He talked to the three lookout men he had posted. They had seen nothing during the night.

Gradually the sky brightened and Carder could see Stein's men beginning to move about up on the hillside. The ancient stones were cast in a pink glow and caught Carder's eye. On another day he would have taken time to absorb the beauty of the scene, but this day was never going to afford that.

The cockerels were in full song as Carder walked back through the Village and helped with the lifting of supplies onto the three carts. There was a sombre air amongst the Villagers. Their world was changing.

The three carts were ready and most of the Village was now awake. Carder could see Sarah getting the youngsters together and helping bring some food and water into the main Village hall.

Carder went to see how Connor was faring. He was fearing the worst but was pleased to see that he was sitting up. Asif looked worried though as he hurried over to Carder.

'He's as strong as an ox and as stubborn as one too. It's as though he is willing himself back onto his feet so that he can fight again. The effort of that will kill him.' The doctor pleaded with Carder to make Connor see sense and keep rested in the hospital.

Carder walked over to the giant and smiled. 'It's not easy to put you down then?'

Connor grinned. 'I'll be ready when they come again,' he said, but grimaced in pain as he spoke.

Carder looked at him and shook his head. 'We're not fighting them today, Connor. We have to yield. Several of the men have deserted us so we have far too few men fit enough to fight.'

'Cowards.' Connor spat on the floor. 'How can they leave us? Wait till I catch them… wait…' But the effort and anger had drained him and he had to fall back on his pillow.

'Stay here, Connor. We will re-build and find somewhere new. Stay here and get fit. The Village will need you.'

Charlie had come in silently and was at Carder's side. 'Come, please, Mister Carder,' he said simply and Carder knew what that meant.

Carder and Charlie walked out of the hospital and over to the front gates, where the three carts were being slowly pulled out of the Village. Stein and his men were approaching. Stein looked to have recovered well but had his arm in a sling. Carder noticed that it wasn't his shooting arm.

Stein and his men inspected the carts which had been left a few yards outside the Village gates. Carder made sure that the few fighting men the Village had left were all taking up defensive positions in the wall. He didn't want Stein to realise that the Village's fighting force was decimated, and that there had been deserters.

Sarah had walked up to the Village gates. Without Benjamin and Connor, and with Eleanor in shock, she was taking the leadership role. Carder hurried up to join her as she called out to Stein.

'We will give you these supplies now and then give you the same a year from now,' she began. 'The people of this Village do not want anyone else injured or killed. What you have done is wrong but we will not see more suffering. Take our supplies and leave in peace.'

Stein turned his dark eyes on Sarah, then to Carder, and back to Sarah. Slowly he smiled, a chilling smile.

'We will take your supplies and we will take him also,' he said, pointing at Carder. 'We have some unfinished business with him back in London.'

Sarah turned to Carder horrified. 'No,' she whispered. 'They will kill you.'

'I must go with them', Carder replied. 'Otherwise they will not leave and the whole Village will be destroyed.'

He turned to Stein. 'Give me one hour. I will come to you then.'

'One hour,' Stein replied, 'that is all. And in the meantime you can have this old fool back.' He beckoned to one of his men who lay Benjamin's body down on the path.

The men retreated back up the hill with the three carts but not before Stein had given Sarah a long, leering look that made her blood run cold.

Sarah went over to Benjamin's body and looked down at the dead man who had been such an inspiration to her, and she stayed there in silence for several long minutes. She then returned to Carder.

'David, no... they will kill you,' Sarah said quietly 'You must not go with them.' But her voice trailed off as if she realised that Carder had no choice.

'They want information from me, Sarah. They have to take me back to meet Stein's boss. That will give me time. Time to think. Time to escape.'

'They will be more careful this time,' Sarah replied. 'You won't be able to get away.'

They walked back to the schoolhouse as some of the men gathered up Benjamin's body.

Carder sat Sarah down, and then sat down opposite her as he had done so often in their short but wonderful time they had shared together.

'You must tell Charlie once I have gone,' Carder said. 'He will understand why I had to go. Please take care of him, Sarah. He is a good boy and he will grow strong.'

Sarah nodded.

They wanted to say so much to each other. They had been thrown together for such a short time but they had found such a deep happiness. Now, they were being wrenched apart and neither of them had the words to express their sorrow.

They both stood up. Carder held Sarah tight. Tears were streaming down her cheeks as he took her face in his hands and kissed her lips gently.

'I will go now, Sarah.'

Sarah wiped her eyes and looked into his. 'Come back, David Carder,' she said.

'I will. I promise,' and Carder turned and walked through the door without looking back.

CHAPTER 31

The walk up the hill was a forlorn one for Carder. He had found something special at the Village and that was now being taken away from him.

Two of Stein's men came to meet him and immediately they searched him, and then tied his hands behind his back. He was led to a red van and told to sit on the floor. The back doors of the van were left open, and Carder could see Stein gathering his men around him and looking at the contents of the supplies carts taken from the Village.

Down below and in the distance, the Village lay nestled in the valley and over to his right, the great Stonehenge stared out solemnly over everyone.

The day was getting hotter and Carder grew increasingly uncomfortable as he sat in the van looking out and feeling helpless.

Eventually, Stein walked over to him.

'So, we meet again,' he began. 'You are going to have to tell us what happened that day in London. A lot of our people died and we need to know who was responsible for that. Mr Gorman is very interested in seeing you again.'

'You kill and you steal,' Carder replied evenly. 'I don't need to tell you anything.'

Stein smashed the butt of his gun across Carder's face. 'You will talk. I would like the pleasure of extracting the information from you myself, but Mr Gorman wants to do that personally.'

Carder felt some blood trickling down his face. His nose felt dreadful, probably broken, and his vision was blurred. The pain was intense but he steeled himself.

'How many people are in that Village down there?' Stein asked.

'About three hundred,' Carder said, 'most of them armed.'

Stein smiled. 'I think not. There are a lot of women there, and I think we must have seen off most of the men who were foolish enough to try and fight us.'

Carder shrugged. 'They will give you supplies each year, just as the lady said.'

'Ah, yes, the lady…' Stein paused. 'She was a pretty one, eh?' He looked into Carder's battered face. 'I think I'll have her for myself.'

Carder said. 'Leave her alone. Leave them all alone. They will give supplies to your damned Council. Leave them in peace.'

'Leave them? So that they can run away and hide from us… I think not,' Stein sneered. 'Tonight we will finish the job… and give the women a good time. I've chosen mine already, and the other boys deserve a good woman as reward for a job well done.'

Carder was chilled. 'Rot in hell, Stein,' he spat at Stein's feet. Stein swung the butt of his gun again and this time caught Carder on the temple and knocked him out cold.

CHAPTER 32

Sarah and the remaining Village leaders were in the schoolhouse. The talk at first was of moving on and finding somewhere new, but they couldn't reach agreement. Sarah led the argument for moving on, but the other three wanted to stay put and yield supplies to the Council each year.

'We must stay,' Tobias said. 'If we share what we have then we will live in peace. You all know that in our prayers we talk of sharing and giving. That is what we are being called upon to do.'

'We should stay. Connor will be up on his feet again soon and we can fight them here.' Duke chipped in.

Eleanor was looking shocked by what she had seen and looked ten years older. 'I think if we run then they will just come and find us. They have vehicles. They could chase us all over the country.'

Sarah knew it was hopeless trying to convince them, but she would keep trying whilst she had time.

As the dusk fell up on the hill, Carder had regained consciousness and was sitting up again. His head was thumping but he could see and think clearly enough. He was being guarded by one man with a gun. The gun was pointing at him and behind it was a vicious looking face. Cold, black eyes stared back at him and the man's grin showed cracked and missing teeth. The grin widened as the shrieks and screams from the Valley below reached up to Carder.

He could see flames taking hold of the Village buildings and he could just make out some figures running around. There were some shots and more screams. The Village was being ransacked and he could only sit there, helplessly and watch. Sarah... please run, please get out of there he thought, as he tried to push out of his mind vivid pictures of what Stein might be doing to her.

Outside the schoolhouse, Sarah stared out in shock at the mayhem around her. Buildings were on fire. People were screaming. Animals were also screaming and shots were ringing out. She held her hands to her face in horror.

It was a dark night with no moon, but there was light flooding out from the room behind her and that allowed Stein to catch sight of her. He ran over shouting and whooping with crazed and lust-filled eyes.

Sarah tried to get back in the schoolhouse and bolt the door but she was not quick enough. Stein's foot jammed in the doorway and he barged into the door, flinging it open and sending Sarah tumbling onto the floor. She tried to get up but Stein slapped her face and pushed her back down.

'No,' Sarah cried. 'Please no!'

Stein had stepped back and was panting heavily 'You're mine, little lady, and I want you right now,' he growled as he moved forward again towards her.

A deafening crash rang out and for a moment Stein just stood there with a surprised expression on his face. Then his eyes froze and he fell forward. He was dead before he landed heavily on top of Sarah.

When Sarah opened her eyes and tried to push Stein off she saw Charlie, standing there, grim-faced with the smoking gun.

'Its okay, Miss Sarah,' he said. 'He can't hurt you now.'

Sarah was frozen in shock as Charlie pulled Stein's body away. He hugged Sarah as she wept and then gently helped her get on her feet. She had Stein's blood all over her front as she just stood there, hugging Charlie and thanking him for saving her.

'We must get away,' Charlie urged. 'Quickly, no time to get anything. We must run for the woods.'

The shouts and screams were still raging outside and they brought Sarah back to her senses.

'Yes, Charlie... we must go... but not the woods. Follow me.'

Through the chaos in the dark, the woman and boy slipped quietly and unnoticed out of the Village, and they then made their way up towards the great stones.

Sarah stumbled a few times, but each time Charlie helped her up and they carried on up the hill. They reached the stones and looked back.

The whole Village was ablaze and now the surrounding fields were lit up in a red glow. Sarah and Charlie could see people running to the woods and animals bolting in all directions.

'Quick,' Sarah said, 'we don't have long.'

Silently they made their way over to the vans where Stein's men had camped. Their eyes were now accustomed to the dark and the glow from the Village below was continuing to cast its eerie light. They could see that no-one was around.

'They must have left someone though... to guard David.' Sarah whispered. 'Keep quiet.'

Charlie tugged on Sarah's arm and pointed. 'Over there... look,' and Sarah followed his gaze.

She could see a bearded man with a gun pointing inside the back of a van. The open doors hid her view but she knew it had to be Carder inside that van.

Charlie motioned to Sarah to stay silent and still. Very slowly, he crept up behind the bearded man and when he got within ten yards, he took aim.

In the van, Carder had seen Charlie and deliberately kept his guard talking to keep him distracted.

Charlie's foot caught a small stone which moved a little. The guard span round but only in time to receive a bullet between the eyes. Charlie's aim had been steady and the man fell to the ground face down.

Charlie sprang forward.

'Are you okay, Mister Carder?' Charlie asked.

Carder laughed grimly, even though it was agony to do so. 'Thanks to you, young man, yes.' He continued, 'we must get down to the Village and save Sarah...'

'I'm here, David,' came a voice from behind Charlie, and the relief flooded over Carder.

'Sarah... are you okay?' Carder asked.

'I'm fine, now let's get these ropes cut and get out of here quickly.'

Charlie cut the ropes and Carder stood up groggily, and embraced them both.

'The Village has been destroyed.' Sarah said bitterly. 'We must run now.'

'Quick,' Charlie said, 'they are coming... they must have heard my shot.'

They turned to see a dozen or so men running up the hill.

Sarah pointed and said, 'This way,' and the three of them ran off into the night.

They paused behind one of the giant stones and listened to the angry shouts of the men as they discovered the guard's body.

Then Sarah guided them silently away from the stones, down into the fields below which she knew so well, away from all the carnage and the horrors which would live with them all forever.

A breeze had sprung up and it had started to drizzle. After a while the rain became heavier and then it poured for the rest of the night, dousing the flames so that by the time the grey morning arrived, trails of smoke wisping out from the collapsed buildings and rubble was all that was left for the great stones to look down on.

CHAPTER 33

Gorman was incensed. 'Find them,' he roared. 'Hunt them down like dogs and bring the one called Carder to me. I want him alive.'

'I will bring him here for you,' replied Bedrossian, the man promoted into Stein's job. He made Stein look soft and compassionate by comparison. An eye patch, an ugly scar down his left cheek and badly pock marked skin seemed at odds with his slightly high-pitched voice, but Gorman knew him to be a remorseless killer who had done a lot of Stein's dirty work. He worried though that Carder might not survive the journey back to him.

'I want Carder alive, Bedrossian,' he said. 'The others are yours,' but bring me Carder alive.

Bedrossian nodded and left the room.

Gorman was left alone and he sat heavily down at his desk rubbing his chin thoughtfully. It was nearly time, he thought. The time of reckoning when the new settlers would arrive. The coded message he had received a week ago told him to expect the ships to arrive soon. Then the new world would be ushered in quickly. So far he had done his job well.

He had controlled and contained the people. He had created the fear. He had prepared the ground for the new order. He had given the man he had only met once everything he had asked for. Pirrin. The only man he had ever feared.

Carder was not that important to Gorman. He was an irritant who had embarrassed him by killing Stein and escaping. Gorman wanted revenge, but Pirrin wanted Carder much more. Pirrin wanted to get to Carder before anyone else did. What Pirrin wanted, Gorman had to deliver. Or risk everything.

CHAPTER 34

Two days later.

Carder, Sarah and Charlie were hungry and thirsty. They had been on the run without shelter and Carder could see that his two companions were tiring badly. They had met no-one since escaping the Village, but Carder knew that they had to get help and shelter. It was a risk because he knew that the Council would come after them. They had all witnessed an atrocity and also killed one of the senior men in the Council. They would surely be hunted down.

Carder estimated that they were about fifteen miles north of the Village. It was not far enough but they had to rest and get food and water that night. He looked across at Sarah and Charlie as they nibbled on their stale bread and sipped at the nearly empty water bottles.

It was a still night with no breeze. The stars were out and Carder looked up, on impulse once again, at the nearly full moon. It seemed huge in the sky and close enough to reach out and touch. He could easily make out the Sea of Tranquillity and some craters and ridges. He started to wonder what Maldini and the others were doing right now up there, but then his thoughts were interrupted.

'Listen,' Charlie said. 'What is that noise?'

Carder and Sarah strained to hear and they could just pick up a distant low humming noise cutting through the silent night. It was coming from the north and for a moment, Carder thought it was almost as if the noise was coming from the moon itself.

Sarah saw them first. 'Look,' she said pointing. 'What...' She broke off in astonishment as she could see that what had started off as one bright moving dot in the night sky, turned into two, then three, four... she lost count as the tiny dots moved across the sky, all heading in the same direction. As they slid across the shining orb of the moon, they turned into black shadows and at that moment, Carder realised what they were looking at.

'They have come,' he said softly. 'They have come here... to Earth.'

Sarah and Charlie looked at him with wide eyes. 'You mean...' Sarah began.

'Yes, it's the moonbase. They have left the moonbase and are coming here to Earth.'

There was a moments' silence before Charlie asked, 'Mister Carder, you have known about them haven't you? I've seen you looking up at the moon...'

'Yes, Charlie, it's a long story and I think now is the time to tell you about it.'

And as they finished their meagre rations and watched the ships disappear over the horizon, Carder told Charlie what he had told Sarah.

The boy listened without interruption and then, when Carder had finished, he thought for a moment and then smiled. 'Maybe now we will be alright. The Council will get taught a lesson!'

Carder smiled at the boy, and then spent the next hour answering all his questions about what life was like on the moon.

Sarah smiled for the first time in two days, and Carder thought there was perhaps just the beginnings of a renewed hope and energy in her and in Charlie. None of them realised though that things were about to get much worse.

CHAPTER 35

Gorman had been driven out to meet them. They had all landed on the vast, empty runways at Heathrow. Forty-two ships with nearly five hundred occupants. About three hundred men, two hundred women and no children.

It was an eerie sight as the moonbase migrants slowly walked from their ships over to the huge hangar where Gorman and his small party were waiting, standing on a raised platform.

Eventually, everyone was in the hangar. Chairs had been set out for the new arrivals, and abundant food and drink were displayed on long tables along the sides of the hangar.

Gorman stood at the centre of the platform and held his arms out. Maldini and Pirrin had joined him.

'Welcome to Earth,' Gorman announced. 'Welcome to England and welcome to London.' Gorman looked out over the seated audience and continued. 'We are now ready to start a new stage in the re-development of our people and our lives. Much work has been done to make the place ready for you, and you will find everything you need to start the re-building. I say to you once again, welcome... welcome to your new home.' There was loud applause for Gorman as he then beckoned to Maldini to take centre stage.

'Thank you, Councillor Gorman. On behalf of everyone here, I thank you for all your hard work and for giving us such a warm welcome.'

If only you knew, Gorman thought.

Maldini continued. 'Our community on the moon has looked forward to this day for many years. We have looked at this beautiful blue marble in the sky and longed to be here. Now, all our dreams have come true. We are home. We are Earth people. We will look back at the old home from the warm safety of Earth. And now, if you all have a glass, please join me in a toast... to the New Earth.'

Everyone roared out the toast and shook hands. Maldini glanced across at Pirrin who moved forward across the stage. Gorman felt a distinct chill.

Pirrin was a short, thick-set man with a neatly trimmed moustache and beard. He looked supremely confident and fit. Gorman thought he must be at least in his early sixties but he looked many years younger.

'My friends here on New Earth.' his deep voice cut through the air in the hangar, commanding an instant authority. 'We have much work to do, but first we shall refresh ourselves. Councillor Gorman invites you to eat, drink and enjoy yourselves. Afterwards, you will be taken to your overnight accommodation and in the morning, we will have a briefing back here.'

Gorman felt his power and position usurped already. When Maldini had moved away out of earshot, Pirrin asked him quietly, 'what news on Carder?'

'We've not located him yet, Sir, but it will not be long. He is on foot and we have vehicles,' Gorman replied.

'I need him brought to me... privately. No-one else from the moonbase must see him,' Pirrin said.

'Understood.' Gorman moved off uneasily to join the throng. He hoped Bedrossian was making progress.

As the night drew on, silence hung over the dark and nearly empty land.

In the city, the new arrivals settled in for their first night on Earth, whilst out to the west, deep into the countryside, the hunting party had reached their first destination.

Bedrossian and his team of six heavily armed men had started at the remains of the Village. The burnt-out homes and decaying bodies didn't offer any clues, but Bedrossian wanted to try and retrace the steps and guess which way Carder went.

One of Stein's men had briefly seen the three figures disappearing into the darkness, and thought that it may have been Carder with a woman and a child.

He set his team to work on burning the bodies whilst he walked up the hill, alone, to where Stein had set his camp up. Looking around he started to formulate in his mind a picture of where the three would run to. Not to the road and open fields to the south, they would have been picked up easily there. The dense woods to the west of the Village would have been ideal, but they would not have gone there as it would have meant going back past the Village where Stein's men were. So he looked to his right, to the north and gazed upon the stones. Slowly he walked across to the great circle and made his way into the centre.

This was it, he thought. Over to the stones first and then down the gentle slope into the valley below. He could see the undulating low hills, and the strange humps which were ancient burial grounds stretching for miles ahead of him. Yes, they had headed north, he was convinced and he set off back to join his team.

CHAPTER 36

Carder decided they had to take a risk and seek food and shelter from the farm he could see in the distance. He could see a few goats and pigs in the yard, and a man tending to them. It would be a risk making contact with anyone but looking at Sarah and Charlie, Carder knew they could not go any further.

The farmer looked up and stared in surprise at the man, woman and child emerging from across the fields.

He ran back inside to fetch a gun and then came back outside, and approached the bedraggled visitors.

Sarah spoke first. 'We need help. We have run out of food and water. Can we stay a day and a night, and then move on?'

Carder studied the farmer and could see that although he was tall and muscular, he also looked very tired and overworked.

'We'll do work around the farm for you,' Carder offered.

The farmer could see the woman and child were in a sorry state. He slowly lowered his gun. A woman had come out behind him.

'Let them come in, Greg,' she spoke. 'We have enough food for them.'

She was a striking looking woman. Tall with cropped red hair and when she spoke, Carder thought it almost sounded like she was singing softly. He had never heard an accent like it before.

Greg and Caris were warm hosts, and Carder was relieved to see the colour and life returning to Sarah and Charlie's faces. They ate enormously and talked between mouthfuls. Then exhaustion set in, and Sarah and Charlie were led off by Caris to rooms where they could get a wash and then some sleep.

Greg wanted to talk with Carder some more so he told Caris that he would join her later.

CHAPTER 37

When Bedrossian got back to the Village, he found that his team had found a survivor.

Tobias had hidden during the ransacking and somehow managed to avoid being seen.

Bedrossian asked him about Carder.

Tobias was terrified. 'He was taken up onto the hill up there. The men wanted to take him up there. And good riddance to him, I say. I didn't like him and he should never have been allowed to stay in the Village.'

'So where is he now?' Bedrossian asked.

Tobias shook his head. 'I don't know.'

One of Bedrossian's men placed his gun against Tobias's temple. 'Please, I don't know... please.' Tobias begged.

'Was he alone?' Bedrossian asked.

Tobias was wild-eyed with fear. 'He... he was taken up the hill on his own. But...'

'But what...'

'But I think they went to find him.'

'Who went to find him?' Bedrossian asked, placing his face very close to Tobias.

'S... Sarah and the boy. Sarah and Charlie.' Tobias spluttered. 'I saw them sneaking out of the Village... I think they got away.'

Bedrossian paced around for a bit, looking thoughtful. After a while, he smiled and said, 'You have been very helpful, thank you' before turning round and walking away from the distraught Tobias. As he did so though, he gave a very slight nod to one his men who nodded back in understanding.

Bedrossian walked out of the burnt-out hut and stared back up at the stones. As he did so, the single shot rang out loudly behind him.

After a while, Bedrossian's team gathered round him and they started to walk silently up the hill towards the stones.

'Put yourself in their shoes and in their minds,' Bedrossian said as his team tracked through the fields. 'Get a feel for the contours of the land and think as they would be thinking. What route would they take as they try to put as much distance as possible between themselves and the Village?'

He was pleased with the team he had been given. They were all hunters and all killers. And they were all terrified of Bedrossian.

They weaved their way along the country paths and natural contours through the rest of the day and the night, and only rested in short intervals. Bedrossian was confident that they were rapidly closing in on their quarry.

CHAPTER 38

Pirrin held centre stage again for the morning briefing with Gorman at his side. He explained to the moonbase settlers that London would be the centre of operations and that his 'units of six,' as he called them, would radiate out from Central London to look at the infrastructure and the resources available across the City. Councillor Gorman would provide men to accompany the units.

Pirrin then spelt out his initial plans for food and water control, then for the transport and fuel policy, but he caused the biggest surprise by announcing that Maldini had already returned to the moonbase to complete the closing down procedures there.

In the second row, the woman with the tumbling red hair looked astonished. Carla Maldini knew that her father had to return to the moonbase to work with the few remaining staff there to safely close down the moonbase, before returning to Earth in about three months. Why the rush though? Why hadn't he said anything to her?

As Gorman started outlining the detailed plans and who was assigned to which unit, Carla checked her communicator. She had one new message and it was from her father. She clicked to open the message. This must be the explanation from him she thought, perhaps he had a good reason to rush off and he hadn't had time to see her face-to-face.

The message opened up and Carla looked at it and blinked. She caught her breath and her head started swimming. The message was short but it took Carla some time to recover from the impact. 'DAVID IS HERE. FIND HIM BEFORE THEY DO' was the blunt sentence her father had typed out.

She took a step forward and staggered a little.

'Are you alright, Carla?' Peter Straker asked her, looking concerned. 'Is the Earth air getting to you?'

'No, no... It's okay,' Carla said. She flicked off her communicator and recovered her poise. Now was not the time to talk to Peter. She had to think straight. Her mind was whirling... David... her father... what was going on? For now she had to keep her father's message to herself and trust no-one.

She walked over and consulted the large screen to find out what unit she would be leading. She had to act as normally as possible and watch everyone around her. She knew something was terribly wrong.

Pirrin cursed. He had overlooked the daughter. He had dealt with Maldini but had not found his communicator. Had he got a message to his daughter?

Maldini had overheard Gorman talking about Carder. That careless idiot, Gorman. Maldini had heard him and then come straight to Pirrin. It had left him with no choice. All his plans were at risk.

Maldini knew that Gorman was after Carder, and that Gorman took instructions from Pirrin. His already weakened trust in Pirrin had evaporated in that moment. And Pirrin had seen the change in Maldini's eyes and told Gorman that he had a job to do without delay.

Maldini had time to send one message. Then he saw Gorman coming for him and managed, unseen, to drop his communicator down an old unused drain. He had to warn Carla but somehow keep her safe. It was the last thing he ever did.

CHAPTER 39

Bedrossian and his team had fanned out in different directions, hunting in pairs but keeping in touch through walkie-talkies. It was a painstaking process but Bedrossian was convinced that they were near.

They had found the remains of camp fires and footprints suggesting a man, woman and child were making their way through the countryside. He felt the buzz of adrenalin coursing through him. He was disappointed though that he had to keep Carder alive, but found consolation in knowing that he could force him to watch the woman and child die slowly.

'Come on, Dexter.' He urged his sidekick to keep up the pace. 'I want them at first light.'

His walkie-talkie crackled into life and he heard the words he had been waiting for.

'We've found them, boss. Holed up in a farmhouse. I can see them in the light through the window.'

'Stay out of sight.' Bedrossian ordered. 'We will join you.'

Inside the farmhouse, Carder went to sit down in the living room to talk things through with Greg but before he did so, he walked over to the window.

'Do you mind if I draw the curtains, Greg?' he asked.

'No, that's okay. You seem nervous,' the farmer replied.

'I just don't want to advertise the fact that we're here, Greg. I don't want to bring trouble to your doorstep. You have made us very welcome but we will move on at first light.'

Carder returned to his seat and relayed to Greg all that had happened at the Village.

Greg shook his head in disbelief when he had heard it all. 'Why did such evil men survive?' he asked. 'All the millions of good people who died and yet... and yet scum like them survived. It shakes your belief in god.'

Carder thought once again about Tom and Trish, the couple he had met just outside London. They had a belief also. They prayed to a god and Carder had been astonished by their intensity and the depth of their trust in their religion.

'Greg, I do not understand the religious bit. It's not something I know much about.'

Greg sighed. 'I don't always understand it either. Why things like this can happen when there is a god looking over us, I just don't know' he paused before adding, 'those poor people in the Village. We thought about joining them but decided to stay put. It's lonely out here but it is also peaceful and it has given us time and space to remember everything.'

Greg stood up and walked over to a side cabinet where he opened a draw. He pulled out a photograph and passed it over to Carder.

'Our two children, Jaime and Maria. All their lives were ahead of them. We... we have to believe that someone is looking after them. David, we have to believe that because they were taken from us so young.'

Carder looked at the two youngsters in the photograph and saw the likeness to their parents. He nodded. 'I think... I think I'm starting to understand, Greg,' he said quietly.

Greg had fallen silent and Carder left him to his thoughts. He had to think about what he, Sarah and Charlie were going to do next. Where they would go.

When the night gave way to the new dawn though, that decision would be made for him.

CHAPTER 40

Bedrossian walked round the camp, waking his team quietly. They were ready in minutes. The sky was just beginning to lighten in the east and the wind had picked up.

Two men were to go to the back of the farmhouse to cut off any retreat, whilst the others would force their way in and capture their quarry. Bedrossian repeated the instruction that Carder must be kept alive. He sent a brief message to Gorman to tell him to expect a present later that day.

The six men set off across the field. Dark figures in a dark landscape. A cockerel stirred in the farmyard, welcoming the coming day.

In the farmhouse, everyone except Carder slept. He had intended to get them all up early but decided they needed the sleep. They had been exhausted, close to dropping, and they had further journeys ahead of them. He lay awake, next to Sarah, listening to the cockerel's calling.

Bedrossian led three of the men to the farmhouse door and the other two circled round to the back. The time had come. All the men had guns and heavy clubs.

Carder heard the faintest of noises. A twig snapping maybe. It was enough though to make him slide out of bed and silently he got into his clothes. He picked up the gun Charlie had taken from the Village.

He went to the back window and peered through a small crack from behind a curtain.

His worst fears were confirmed. He saw two figures with guns standing in the back yard, guns at their side.

He wanted to warn Sarah and the others but the loud bang at the front door beat him to it.

Seconds later, a pane of glass broke and he knew that they were in the house downstairs.

There was shouting and everyone was awake now. Sarah and Charlie had rushed together, and Carder beckoned them to go into the bathroom behind him whilst he slowly approached the top of the stairs. Greg appeared at his side.

'I didn't want this to come to your house, Greg,' Carder whispered.

'Glad to help out,' the farmer replied grimly.

They crouched there at the top of the stairs for a minute and then a shot rang out. Greg cried out and lost his balance, shot in the leg. Instinctively, Carder aimed at where the shot had come from and fired.

Suddenly there was mayhem. More shouts came from downstairs and then there were more shots, and then screams of pain.

Carder ducked but was puzzled that none of the bullets seemed to be coming his way. He slid along to the top of the stairs and tried to peer down into the darkness.

The shots stopped. The screams had stopped also. There was complete silence.

Caris was tending to Greg. Sarah and Charlie were still in the bathroom.

Carder shouted. 'Who's down there? Drop your weapons!'

There was a short pause before a loud voice boomed up.

'You again! Wherever you go there's trouble!'

For a moment Carder was confused and then the realisation hit him.

'Connor! Is that you?' he yelled.

He could now see the familiar figure of the giant at the bottom of the stairs staring back up at him. And he started laughing uncontrollably with relief.

Sarah and Charlie had heard and rushed out.

'You two as well!' Connor roared in delight 'Well, ain't this a grand reunion!'

Sarah and Charlie hugged Connor whilst Carder checked on Greg. He was alright. A grazing wound, nothing deep, and Carder smiled as he looked down at the farmer.

'We're safe for now, Greg.'

Caris hugged Greg, sobbing quietly, and Carder left them to go downstairs and meet his old friend.

CHAPTER 41

Sarah looked up at the giant who had come to their rescue.

'We thought you were dead, Connor. You were in a very bad way at the hospital and then when those thugs came...'

'They thought I was dead too, Sarah,' Connor said, 'so they left me alone. I managed to get out with a few others before everything was burned down.'

'There are others?' Sarah asked. 'Mary... did Mary?'

'Yes,' Connor said smiling, 'Mary's fine. Tough as nails that one'

Sarah hugged Connor again.

'Marlon is here with me. He and I saw this little gang a few hours ago and followed them.' Connor continued. 'He's out the back somewhere. You'll see all the folk soon enough, but let's see what we've got here first.'

Marlon had dealt with the two men Carder had seen at the back. Carder had killed one in the house and Connor had taken care of the rest.

'I've seen this one before,' Carder said grimly looking down at Bedrossian. 'Not a face you'd easily forget. In London... he's one of the Council's top men, I think.'

'They'll not let us get away with this easily,' Connor grunted. 'We've wiped out a complete team here.'

Greg limped down the stairs, leaning on Caris. The introductions were done all round. Caris looked bewildered by it all as she made hot drinks and breakfast for everyone. Sarah went to help her and gave her what comfort she could.

'We can't stay here anymore,' Greg said.

'I know, Greg, and I'm really sorry,' Sarah replied. 'Those people will come again.'

'Maybe not,' Charlie said.

Everyone swung round to look at the boy. He had been standing quietly in the corner.

'Those ships we saw, Mister Carder, they might stop the Council doing any more bad things.'

'Ships?' Greg said.

'The ships that came in the night,' Charlie said.

'Is that what they were? I saw them too,' Connor said. 'Loads of them, all going the same way. Where were they from?'

'They came from the moonbase, Connor,' Carder spoke. He had to tell them all now.

Connor and Greg looked at Carder in amazement.

'Did you say moonbase?' Greg asked. 'As in the moon?'

'Yes. You'd better sit down... both of you, please.'

But they both carried on standing, rooted to the spot as they listened to Carder. They let their food and drink go cold as they let him finish.

Connor had a look in his eye that Carder had seen before. He walked slowly towards Carder.

'Come outside,' he said quietly but with considerable menace.

No, Connor,' Sarah said. 'No. I've told you before. David is here to help us.'

'Help us?' Connor roared. 'He ain't even one of us!'

'Connor...' Carder began before he was interrupted.

'When this is all over I'm going to sort you out once and for all. You're nothing but trouble. You have brought us death and misery. You are nothing but walking, living, breathing trouble,' Connor growled.

'Connor, stop it now, please.' Sarah walked up to the giant. 'David knows the people on those ships. He can help them and he can help us. This is the opportunity to destroy the Council and then maybe we can all go back in peace to the Village.'

After a moment, Carder spoke. 'We have a choice. We can go on the run again or stay here and hope that the Council will be squashed by the moonbase settlers. At the very least the Council will have a new force to deal with and they will have less time to hunt us down.'

'My folk are about a mile away, holed up in a barn. There's more space here.' Connor said, calming down a bit but still eyeing Carder coldly.

'Then we will stay,' Caris said. 'You bring your people here Connor, and we will all be in this together.'

Greg looked across at Caris admiringly. She was so strong and resilient. Minutes ago she was shaking and scared, but she had quickly pulled herself together and found a new determination. She was a survivor and she was also his rock.

'Yes, and we will work together to get ourselves enough food and water supplies and put up some good defences,' he added.

'We'll need round the clock guards, posted outside and in the woods,' Carder added. 'There'll be no more surprise attacks.'

And the mood lifted a little.

Connor left to call in the rest of his folk and Carder went with him. He had some bridges to mend with the giant. They could not afford to be enemies.

Halfway to the barn, Connor stopped suddenly and Carder turned to ask him what the matter was.

'This,' and Connor swung a huge fist into Carder's face and knocked him backwards, blood pouring from the recently healed wounds on Carder's face. He picked himself up, only to take another punch in the stomach.

'That is for not telling me who you were. For taking me for a fool.' Connor said and walked off.

Carder gingerly picked himself up and swore. 'You lumbering ogre!' he called. 'Come back here and try that again!'

But Connor just laughed loudly, and Carder then realised the animosity from Connor was over.

'Now that, Mister Carder,' Connor laughed, 'really did make me feel better!'

CHAPTER 42

Carla's unit had been sent towards the northwest of the City. There were six of them in the unit and all of them were moonbasers.

Carla Maldini and her great friend Joe Tennison were joint leaders of the unit and they were both looking puzzled.

'We've seen no-one at all yet. No-one, and that's after an hour's walking through the streets,' Tennison said.

'The place is deserted,' Carla agreed, 'and creepy.'

They were talking through the headsets built into their helmets. Pirrin had insisted that all units must wear the protective suits because he said there was evidence that the virus was still lingering. He also said that the locals were likely to be hostile and so he was sending out the units fully armed.

As she walked on through the empty streets, Carla's mind was working furiously. How could David still be alive? Did he survive the ship's blast and is he somehow immune to the virus? Maybe Pirrin is wrong. Maybe the virus has completely gone now. It may well still be around in some parts but not here. And what about her father's message? Find David before they do? Nothing added up to

Carla except the growing feeling that something was badly wrong and she didn't know who to trust.

She hadn't told Peter Straker about the message yet. She and Straker had been sleeping together for the last two months on the moonbase. There had been a physical attraction between them for a long time and Carla had needed comfort. She had accepted that Carder had gone and had turned to Straker for that comfort. But now, having received the message, she had to work out in her own mind what the next step was. And somehow, if he was alive, she had to find Carder.

Her thoughts were interrupted by Tennison tugging her arm and pointing.

There was a small huddle of people out on a street corner ahead. They were just talking to each other but they all looked up in wide-eyed amazement at the six white-suited figures walking towards them down the centre of the wide road.

They looked curiously at the moonbasers but there was no hostility in their look.

One of the group, an old man hobbling with a walking stick, came out to meet the unit.

Carla told the others to stay where they were and she walked on alone to meet the old man.

'What are you doing here? And who are you?' asked the old man in a deep rumbling voice from behind his white beard.

Carla thought for a moment and then slowly took off her helmet.

The old man's eyes widened when he saw the long wavy red hair come tumbling out over her shoulders.

'If I've just gone up to heaven then I like it very much,' he said in astonishment.

Carla smiled. 'We are here to help you. We have just arrived in the City and are finding our way around. Seeing if we can do anything to help.'

A couple of others had joined the old man. One of them, an Asian woman, asked, 'So where do you come from?'

'It's a long story,' Carla said. 'Let me introduce you to my friends and then I will tell you.'

The two groups spent an hour together. All of the moonbasers took off their helmets, following Carla and Tennison's leads.

The moonbasers gave the people some bottles of water and some biscuits, and then they moved on saying their farewells.

'So where's all this hostility Pirrin talks about?' Tennison asked Carla.

'I don't know, Joe. And these people haven't seen a virus case for over three years. We'll report it all back this evening.'

CHAPTER 43

The following day another unit was out on patrol in the eastern part of the City. There were four moonbasers in this unit and it was led by two of Gorman's men, Carlucci and Osman, both of whom had a great deal of blood on their hands from their work with the Council.

As the afternoon sun was beating down on the old City, the unit was making its way down one of the one-time busy major routes out of the old financial district.

Shiny glass skyscrapers gave way to low level untidy shops and cafes, all of which seemed to have been emptied and burnt out long ago.

Ahead of them at what must once have been a frenetically busy traffic crossroads, they could see a group of people sitting around a long table having a meal.

'Twelve of them.' Carlucci spoke to Osman through the private channel on his headset.

Osman nodded. 'I'll stand back behind the unit,' he replied.

The group at the table looked up in astonishment at the white figures coming down the road towards them, but none of them got up. They continued to eat their food.

'Who are you?' called out a young man from the far side of the table as the unit came closer.

Carlucci switched on his speaker.

'We are from the New Council. We are carrying out patrols throughout the City.'

At the mention of the Council the group around the table looked at each other and became more wary.

'Would you like some food?' the young man asked.

'No, but we would like to ask you some questions,' Carlucci replied harshly.

Two of the moonbasers exchanged glances. This was not the approach they were expecting.

Carlucci asked them where they lived, where they got their food from and if they had seen any people with the virus.

The young man would not say where the food came from.

'You stole it then?' Carlucci said.

All four of the moonbasers were now looking uneasy. Carlucci was provoking a confrontation.

'No, it's ours,' the young man replied swiftly, 'but you can have some of it if you like.'

Carlucci snapped back. 'You must have stolen it. If you won't tell me where it came from then you must have stolen it. This sort of crime is not tolerated by the New Council.'

The young man shrugged and went back to his meal. The others around the table did the same.

Carlucci turned on his private channel again to Osman and spoke one word.

'Ready?'

Osman nodded.

The next fifteen seconds brought a mayhem to that quiet hot summer afternoon.

Osman opened fire and ruthlessly cut down all the moonbasers from behind. They didn't stand a chance. At the same time Carlucci was firing. Sweeping his gun across the table and cutting down everyone who had been enjoying their meal a few minutes earlier.

Where some of them survived the first volley of bullets Carlucci ran round the table and fired more bullets into them until he was sure that there was no-one left breathing.

The screams and yells died down and the explosive sound of the guns stopped abruptly.

The afternoon was quiet again.

Carlucci and Osman stood there surveying the carnage before eventually turning away and walking on. As they did so, Carlucci spoke into his communicator.

Back in his office in the centre of the City, Gorman listened to his communicator and smiled grimly.

He then picked up his internal phone and punched one number in.

'Yes?' Pirrin answered the phone in his office.

'It has begun.' Gorman said simply and he put the phone back down.

CHAPTER 44

The morning briefing had a sombre mood.

Pirrin was telling the audience about the incident the previous day in east London.

'These people are hostile,' he said. 'Armed and dangerous. We lost four good men and women in the battle before the hostiles had been subdued.'

Carla glanced at Tennison and whispered. 'It must be far worse in the east of the city then. We only met people who were warm and friendly. It's all very strange.'

Pirrin was continuing. 'We will keep the same units for the rest of this week. But be warned that it is very dangerous out there. You need to be armed and prepared to use your weapons.'

Pirrin was convincing, Gorman had to admit to himself, but he was increasingly resenting Pirrin commanding the centre stage. He was beginning to feel sidelined.

Gorman was also dreading the meeting later that morning with Pirrin when he would have to report the failure of Bedrossian's mission to capture Carder.

Carla sighed. 'I will have to go and see Pirrin,' she said to Tennison. 'That was not a balanced briefing he gave this morning. I'm going to see him and try and find out what's really going on.'

But Carla didn't have the chance to arrange the meeting. Pirrin summoned Carla first.

She received the message to see Pirrin later that morning. Pirrin wanted to talk to her. Something to do with her father.

As Carla approached Pirrin's office, she told herself to be calm and not to reveal the message her father had sent her. Trust no-one, not yet she told herself.

She knocked on the polished oak door and walked in to Pirrin's opulent office suite.

'Carla, please take a seat.' Pirrin pointed to the deep leather chair in front of the desk.

She walked forward and sat back in the comfortable chair, feeling tiny in the deep folds of the leather as she faced Pirrin across his large desk.

Pirrin then dropped his bombshell. 'Carla... I'm afraid I have some bad news for you.' He spoke softly.

A slow chill spread over Carla's body.

'I'm sorry... but it concerns your father.'

'My father?' Carla blurted out. She was fearing the worst as Pirrin stood up and paced slowly in front of his window,

'What about my father?' Carla asked and she could feel the moisture in her eyes.

'I'm sorry; Carla but there was an explosion on your father's ship. We... we don't know what... some sort of explosion.'

Carla's heart was thumping in her ears.

'And your father... and all the others on board have perished in the explosion. I'm really sorry... your father was such a fine man.'

Carla just sat there frozen and dumbstruck.

After a minute she couldn't stop herself. She broke down and the tears came. In between her sobs, she asked, 'How? The ships were safe... what sort of explosion?'

'We just don't know, Carla.' Pirrin replied. 'We will probably never know.'

Pirrin walked round his desk and placed a hand on Carla's shoulder.

'Your father was very proud of you, Carla. He would want you to carry on the good work you are doing here.'

Carla wiped her eyes and slowly stood up.

'I think I'll go now,' she said and with that, she turned and walked through the door feeling as though everything in her life had fallen apart. She didn't notice Gorman walking past her towards Pirrin's office.

CHAPTER 45

Carla walked out onto the street and gulped the fresh air. Across the road from her a stray dog took a look at her but then grumpily sloped off down a dark alleyway. Nothing else moved in the deserted street.

The words in her father's message kept ringing around her head. Who was after David? Who was her father warning her about? And now... her father was dead. In an accident on the ship... out in the vast lonely blackness of space.

The tears came to her again as she sat down on one of the pavement benches.

After a few minutes, she realised that she had wanted to see Pirrin anyway to talk about her unit's experience with the locals. She had heard about other units having friendly encounters too. It would be very rash she thought to go on the offensive like Pirrin was suggesting.

She turned back towards Pirrin's headquarters and hurried along the corridors towards his office. She stopped short of the office though because the door was open and she could hear raised voices inside.

'I will send a ship and a unit, Gorman' Pirrin was shouting. 'Your people have failed! You have failed! I will send unit fifteen out there to kill him and the others that are with him. I don't need him captured now. I want him finished!'

Gorman muttered something which Carla couldn't hear and then Pirrin was shouting again.

'And, Gorman, don't fail me again! You have had your one chance!'

Carla turned round in shock and hurried away, back down the corridor and out onto the street.

She made her way over to the vehicle where Tennison was waiting to drive her back to the base near Heathrow. She burst into tears as she got into the car saying 'just drive please, Joe' to the anxious Tennison.

As Tennison drove, Carla tried to get her mind working on the new information.

Pirrin must be behind it all she thought. Her father is dead. Pirrin is sending a unit out to get someone he wants dead. It must be David. Unit fifteen. She must find out where that unit is being sent to.

She told Tennison about her father but kept the other things she had heard to herself. She trusted Joe but did not want to endanger him.

That night Peter Straker tried to comfort her but she spent the night alone on the sofa, grieving for her father.

CHAPTER 46

At the following morning's briefing, Pirrin repeated the need for units to be on alert. He said that units one to twelve would continue with their patrols in their allocated areas of London, continuing to radiate out from the centre, but then he went on to say that three units, thirteen, fourteen and fifteen, would be assigned special duties in areas outside the City where there were known trouble spots and where hostile groups had gathered together.

'The work will be dangerous,' he summed up, 'and there may well be casualties. But I have stepped up our weaponry and extended the authorisation to fire.'

When Gorman read out who was in each unit, Carla waited for him to get to unit fifteen. She had to find out who was in the unit and where they were heading.

Eventually, Gorman read out all the names and by the time he had come to unit fifteen Carla had realized that she had an opportunity. Peter Straker's name had not been read out yet.

Sure enough, Straker was one of those in unit fifteen and Carla breathed in deeply.

She would ask Peter if he would swap units with her. She now had a chance to get into unit fifteen.

She had a week to work on Straker before his unit went out on assignment, but for the first few days she didn't raise the subject.

During those days she went on her normal patrols with Tennison and the others. The only encounters with locals were again friendly ones but Carla was shocked at how few people there were around. So few people had survived in the vast City.

Each morning's briefing brought fresh news of other violent incidents around the City. There were more casualties announced each day as Pirrin spared no details in relaying news of the hostilities.

On the fourth evening, she decided to tell Straker everything.

They had enjoyed a good meal and Carla had ensured that Straker had more than his share of the wine.

She led him into the bedroom and they made love for the first time in a while.

Afterwards, and as they lay entwined, Carla broached the subject.

'Peter, I have something to tell you. Something to confide in you.'

Straker brushed a lock of her hair away and looked into her eyes smiling. 'You can always confide in me, Carla. Always.'

And so Carla told him. Told him about the message from her father. About her overhearing Pirrin shouting. About how she wanted to join unit fifteen because if it was Carder out there, she wanted to be on hand to protect him from being killed.

Straker listened and said nothing for a few moments but then shook his head.

'No, Carla, it will be much too dangerous. There will be casualties… it is far too risky for you to go.'

They argued for a while but eventually, Straker said firmly 'Carla, I will be in that unit. If Carder is out there, which seems highly unlikely, I will personally ensure that he is not killed. Please accept that and I will take the risk, not you.'

Reluctantly, Carla accepted what Straker said. It would be difficult for them to swap units without arousing suspicion. Peter was right. She had to trust him to protect David.

As she took a shower in the morning, she felt some relief that she had been able to share her information with Straker. She knew the information was dangerous but she was glad to have someone she could trust.

CHAPTER 47

The reunion at Greg and Caris's farmhouse was an emotional one. There was joy at seeing old friends but also deep sorrow with all the exchanged stories of how lives had been lost. The loss of the Village hurt everyone.

Carder noticed though the determined sense of purpose which permeated through the group. These people were hardened survivors. All of them. There were nearly forty men, women and children crowded into the farmhouse and small outbuildings. They all seemed to be busily at work and it was a natural thing for them to pull together for the common good. Carder thought how proud Benjamin would have been of them all.

Some small huts were already taking shape, as was some new wooden fencing.

Carder and Connor surveyed all the activity with satisfaction, as they walked out with six of the men to set up some defensive positions out in the woods.

Sarah now had a much smaller class. There were just six children now, and she flinched each time she thought about the horrors these six had been through.

She hoped and prayed that Connor was right in thinking that most of the other children would have escaped unharmed when they ran away with those men and women who had deserted the Village after the first round of the fighting.

Charlie was the natural leader of the children. He wasn't quite the eldest but the others looked up to him. He was so capable, Sarah realised. He could help the men with the building work, he could help with the cooking, he helped Sarah with some of the teaching, and to the astonishment of everyone, he had a wonderful way with all the animals on the farm. Carder had told Sarah about his abilities, but she still marvelled at the way he seemed able to effortlessly communicate and control the animals.

Sarah was beginning to recover her strength after the arduous escape from the Village and all the horrors she had witnessed, but she became anxious again when Carder said that they might need to steel themselves for more trouble.

'But surely your people will overwhelm those thugs on the Council?' she asked.

'Maybe, Sarah. Maybe,' Carder replied, 'but we need to be ready just in case. No more surprises.'

What Carder didn't realise though was how fast time was running out.

CHAPTER 48

Pirrin paced around his office looking thoughtful.

Gorman stood silently by his desk looking grim-faced, whilst Straker sat in the leather chair looking relaxed. Gorman felt like the outsider he had become. Not only was Pirrin taking control and power away from him, but now there was a blond-haired creep called Straker who seemed to have Pirrin's ear and confidence.

'You have done well, Straker,' Pirrin said. 'Very well indeed. We can now kill two birds with one stone. I will assign Tariq and Carlucci to unit fifteen. You... you know what you must do next?'

'Of course,' Straker smiled, 'consider it done...'

Later that day, Carla took the call as she was just finishing another uneventful daily patrol.

'Peter, how are you?'

'I'm fine, Carla. And I have some news for you.' Straker's smooth voice purred over the channel to her communicator. 'I have to stay in London tomorrow. I have a lot of reports and analysis work to do on all the units' feedbacks. In short, Carla, I can't go out tomorrow with unit fifteen.'

'But Peter...' Carla began.

'I know, I said that it will be risky, Carla,' Straker interrupted, 'but do you still want to go in my place?'

'I... I... yes! Peter, yes I will,' Carla replied, 'but what about Pirrin and Gorman, won't they...'

'They won't know,' Straker interrupted her again, 'they don't need to know. And if they do ever find out, I'll square it with them.'

'Thank you, Peter. Thank you.' Carla replied and switched off her communicator.

Later that evening Straker called again, asking Carla if she wanted to come round for the night.

'If you don't mind, Peter, I'll stay here tonight. I have to now get rest before going out with unit fifteen tomorrow. We'll make a date for tomorrow night and I can then tell you all about the mission.'

'That's okay, Carla. You rest up. Good luck tomorrow and take care.' Straker said as he put the phone down.

Smiling, he said quietly to himself, 'and goodbye, Carla Maldini.'

CHAPTER 49

The drizzle had developed into a steady beating rain as the white-suited unit made their way along the old grass path with dense woodland on either side of them. It was late afternoon but the thick low cloud had cast a gloom over the countryside, and it seemed as though the night was only minutes away.

Carla's vision was limited through the drenched face visor as she walked behind the leader of the unit, a man introduced to her as Carlucci. There were three other moonbasers in the unit and the sixth person was the quiet, dark-eyed Tariq, a man Carla had met once before and taken an instant dislike to.

The ship had brought them to within a mile of the location where Bedrossian's team had been wiped out, and they were walking the final stretch.

Carlucci motioned to them to all get off the path and into the woods. They were getting very near, but the last part would be very difficult going through the dark tangle of branches and bushes.

Under the cover of the trees canopy, the rain didn't seem so bad but the going underfoot was treacherous.

Carlucci's hand went up telling them all to stop moving and crouch down. Carla could see Tariq switch on his thermal sensor built into his helmet and start to scan the area around them for any signs of life.

After a few minutes, Tariq pointed. He had spotted something and his voice came over the headset.

'One hundred yards to our right. Something moving.'

Carlucci and Tariq exchanged a few words and then Tariq broke off to the right and disappeared into the woods, whilst Carlucci signalled for everyone else to follow him.

Carla's adrenalin was racing. They were near. Very near.

Everyone had gone inside at the farm to shelter from the rain. A delicious smell of some meat cooking was coming from the newly built hall, which had just been joined on to the side of the main house.

Caris and Mary had taken on the cooking responsibilities and had been coming up with some fine meals for the small community, despite the scarce resources they had to draw on.

Charlie would often watch the two women as they set about their food preparations and as they did the cooking. He would sometimes ask if he could help out and Carder and Sarah would chuckle at his ability to learn so quickly. They knew that he was an exceptional boy and he seemed to be growing with stature each day. Even Connor would pay him compliments and recognised that he was a valuable person to have around.

'He puts some of my lads to shame,' he once confided in Carder. 'He can lift as much as them and he works twice as hard. Tell me where you found him and I'll go back there and find a couple more like him.'

Carder had been looking out of the front window at the rain lashing down when Sarah came to join him and slipped her hand in his. For a long moment the two of them were silent before Sarah spoke quietly.

'You don't get this sort of weather where you come from then?' she asked smiling.

'No. There's no weather at all,' Carder replied, looking into her beautiful eyes upturned to meet his. 'You wouldn't like it up there. Trust me.'

Behind them there was a call for the early evening meal and they turned to join the others.

CHAPTER 50

Carlucci spoke quietly through the headset channel.

'There it is. Over there.'

Carla peered through the gloom in the direction he was pointing. She could just make out a dim flickering light coming from some sort of building on the other side of a field.

Carlucci had brought the team to the edge of the wood and it was open ground between them and the building.

A branch snapped behind them and then another.

The team whirled round with their guns raised.

Tariq called out to them not to fire and he came noisily through the branches, pushing ahead of him a terrified and drenched man. Tariq's gun was in the small of his back.

'Found this one out in the woods. He had a gun.' Tariq said, pushing the man into the middle of the circle.

Carlucci walked forward menacingly and switched his speaker on. 'How many of you are there in the farmhouse?' he demanded.

'What farmhouse?' The man replied.

Tariq cracked the butt of is gun across the man's head and then pushed him to the ground.

'Hey! Slow down.' One of the moonbasers called out. 'Take it easy, he'll talk to us.'

'Shut up' Carlucci snapped. 'These people are dangerous.' Then he turned to the stricken man and asked again how many there were in the farmhouse.

'About ten,' the man said, groaning and rubbing the back of his head. 'Just ten... and women and children.'

'I don't believe you,' Carlucci said and gave the man a powerful kick in the side.

'Carlucci, take it easy,' Carla said, 'you'll kill him. Let me talk to him.'

'Stay where you are,' Carlucci ordered, 'and that goes for you there too,' he added, looking at the other moonbasers.

Carlucci lifted the man half off the ground and then punched him hard in the face. This time the man fell back onto the ground with blood pouring from his mouth and nose.

'Enough!' shouted Aaron Baker, one of the youngest moonbasers of them all and he moved forward to stop Carlucci. It was the last thing he ever did.

Tariq opened fire from close range with a short but lethal burst. Baker fell face forward into the mud.

Carla cried out in shock and rushed forward to push Carlucci. As he stumbled towards Tariq he was thrown momentarily off balance.

Carla cried, 'Get away! Run!' to the other moonbasers.

The three of them burst out of the woods and into the open field, but Carla knew that they didn't have enough time. They couldn't move fast in their suits and although it was very dark, Tariq had time to pick them out. He moved to the edge of the woods and started firing as he swept his gun back and forth.

All three of the white suited figures crashed to the ground in the muddy field. After a few moments the firing stopped and the only sound then was the incessant beating of the rain.

CHAPTER 51

At the sound of the first shot, Charlie turned towards the window.

'What was that?' he asked but no-one else had heard anything other than the rain beating on the window.

Seconds later though there were more shots and everyone in the dining hall jumped to their feet.

'Women and children upstairs!' Carder shouted. 'All the men to their positions.'

The dogs were barking and there was mayhem for a few minutes as everyone rushed around.

Then it went quiet again.

Apart from the rain outside and the occasional bark from one of the dogs there was no noise.

'Can't see anything,' Connor said.

'No, nor me,' Carder replied. 'The shots may have been from Dexter. He's out there tonight.'

They peered through the windows for a few minutes but saw nothing. Then Charlie shouted.

'Look, someone's coming!'

Carder and Connor moved towards the door with their guns held ready.

'Just one person. Limping badly. They're hurt,' Charlie said.

They opened the front door and looked out into the terrible night.

At first Carder and Connor couldn't see anything, but then their eyes focused on something out there that was moving very slowly towards the farmhouse.

'That's a moonbaser's suit, Connor' Carder whispered. 'It's a moonbaser out there!'

At that moment, the figure outside fell to the ground just outside the farm gate.

'Could be a trap,' Connor said.

'Maybe, but we have to find out, one way or another,' Carder replied and they both walked forward looking all around warily.

The figure on the ground had not moved and was lying face down.

Carder and Connor stooped down and they could see the bullet holes in the white suit, with the red patches being washed by the rain.

'Must be a goner,' Connor said.

Slowly and carefully they turned the body round so that it was lying face up.

There was no sign of life but they couldn't see the face clearly because of the rain on the face visor.

Very carefully, Carder unbuckled the helmet and gently slid it off.

As he did so his heart lurched and he could feel his head swimming.

The red hair that tumbled out of the helmet was hair that he knew so well.

As the helmet came off, Carder gazed down upon Carla's lovely face.

'No... oh please, no...' he said.

'You know her?' Connor asked.

Carder moved his ear close to Carla's lips and felt the slightest of breaths.

'She's still alive... she's still...' his voice trailed off as Carla opened her eyes gradually and focused on his. She managed a weak smile.

'It's true... David... thought you were dead... how...?'

'Let's get you inside, Carla, lets...'

'No... can't... David. Get out of here... go... they've got the ship near.' Carla was making a huge effort to speak but her voice was getting weaker.

'No chance... go... everyone will be killed... go...'

Carla's eyes fluttered slightly and she tried to say something else, but no words would come. She looked into Carder's eyes but as she did so, the life left her. She had gone.

'No... Carla... no.' Carder sank to his knees in the mud and held Carla close to him.

He stared at her lifeless face and held her close to him, asking himself aloud, 'Why? Why you, Carla?'

After a long moment, Connor touched him on the shoulder.

'We'll get her inside. Come on, you too,' he said, as he helped Carder up to his feet.

CHAPTER 52

Carlucci was satisfied.

'Good work, Tariq. We'll finish the job in the morning.'

'Do you want me to get the bodies?' Tariq asked.

'No, leave them in the field. We'll get back to the ship and return at first light. It's too dark to see anything.'

They couldn't see that one of the bodies in the field had moved. Carlucci was convinced that all three moonbasers had died in Tariq's hail of bullets as he relayed the news into his communicator.

'Very good.' Pirrin's voice crackled into his earpiece. 'In the morning, leave no trace. I don't want anything to be moving after you have finished.'

Carlucci switched his communicator off and turned to Tariq.

'Come on, back to the ship.'

'What about this one?' Tariq asked, pointing at Dexter who was tied to a tree, blindfolded and gagged.

'He's yours,' Carlucci said simply and took the blindfold off Dexter whose eyes then widened in terror as he saw Tariq, grinning from ear to ear, as he pulled out a long narrow blade and then started to come towards him.

Back in the farmhouse, the mood was sombre. The rain was still rattling against the windows and Greg was peering out to make sure that there were no other visitors.

Carla's body had been carried in and placed on the table. Carder could see that she had taken several bullets in the back and it was a miracle that she had survived even a few minutes. Survived long enough to warn him. But why? What had gone wrong? How had Carla ended up here?

Carder's thoughts were interrupted by Sarah's touch on his arm.

He turned to look at her. 'Sarah... she came to warn us. She... came to tell us to get out of here.' His words came slowly as he was still in a daze.

'This... this is Carla?' Sarah asked.

Carder nodded.

'I'm sorry, David. I'm so sorry,' and she squeezed his arm.

'Who shot her?' Connor asked. 'Who has done this to her and where is Dexter?'

Carder shook his head. 'None of this makes sense. Carla said they had a ship but... they had come to kill us.'

'They must have Dexter,' Greg said. 'He would have turned up by now.'

Carder tore himself away from looking at Carla and turned to face everyone in the room.

'They have a ship. We cannot fight that. They will come in the morning, when it is light. We must leave. Tonight.'

There was silence in the room, before Mary eventually spoke.

'We can't keep running. We have to have a home. We are all tired of running.'

There were murmurs of agreement, but Carder put his arm up and then spoke again.

'The ship has weapons. Terrible weapons. We must leave quietly and let them think that they have destroyed us. It is our only chance.'

'I think he's right,' Greg sighed, looking across at Caris. 'I think our time is up here.'

Connor nodded. 'I agree. Although I don't understand what is happening or who we are fighting, I know we must go. This woman died trying to warn us.'

Everyone stared at Carla lying on the table. There was silence for a moment and then Mary said, 'Come on then, get the basics together. Not too much though...' and they hurried out of the room leaving Carder and Sarah alone.

'Your people wouldn't do this, would they?' Sarah asked.

'I don't know, Sarah,' Carder replied, 'but I will find out who is behind this.'

That night, they all huddled together under the shelter of trees. The rain eased off slightly but they were all wet and cold. They were a forlorn group crouching down, looking back across the fields at Greg and Caris's farm in the distance as the first grey smudges of dawn started to appear.

They didn't have long to wait.

The rain had stopped, but the clouds were still heavy in the sky when they first heard a low droning sound coming from beyond the woods to the south.

The noise grew louder and all eyes were on the woods as the silver ship slowly appeared above the tops of the trees. There were some gasps, but Connor told everyone to be still and silent and to stay out of sight.

The ship hovered across the field until it was directly above the cluster of buildings.

Carder knew what was going to happen next.

'Shield your eyes,' he said urgently. 'Now!'

A blinding flash of light illuminated the field and woods, and this was accompanied by a loud roar. Someone screamed but after a few seconds, it went quiet again and the light had gone.

The group huddled in the trees opened their eyes again and looked back at the farm buildings. There was nothing to see. Nothing at all. No buildings had survived the blast.

There were just a couple of wisps of smoke lingering close to the ground, but it was as if nothing had ever been there. Just an empty field.

There were some sobs from behind him but Carder's eyes remained fixed, like steel, on the ship as it hovered for a moment before sliding off back over the top of the trees, and eventually disappeared from view.

CHAPTER 53

Connor and Carder insisted that the group stayed hidden in the woods all that day.

There were some arguments about where they should head to next. Some people wanted to stay put, but others wanted to head north and as far away from London as possible.

In the afternoon, Carder sat alone with Charlie and broke the news to him that he was leaving.

He had come to the conclusion that he had to confront the problem head on. Hiding and running were no longer options.

'I need you to look after Sarah for me. Protect her,' he began. 'I need to go to London and find out what is happening, and then do what I can to stop all this evil.'

'But, Mister Carder, we need you here,' Charlie protested.

'I will return, Charlie. I will find you because I know that you will help them choose the best place to make a new settlement. I will come back, Charlie, but first I have to stop the evil.'

Sarah had guessed already. She had seen it in his eyes as soon as Carla's lifeless body had been taken out of the farmhouse for burial.

She walked through the trees with Carder and she cried and she hugged him, but deep within she knew that he had to go.

'You can't do it all alone, David,' she pleaded. 'You can't stop them. Whoever they are.'

'I have to try, Sarah. I have to try,' Carder replied, as he bundled a few provisions into a rucksack.

He said his goodbyes to everyone in the group and then came back to Sarah.

He held her hands. She was bravely holding her chin up and the tears back.

'Come back... please,' was all she could say.

Carder nodded. 'I will, Sarah. I will come back and find you.' And he let go of her hands and turned towards the east.

Sarah buried her face in her hands.

'Don't worry, Miss Sarah,' Charlie said, 'he will come back.'

'Yes, he will,' Connor chipped in. 'He's indestructible, that one. He'll be back.'

CHAPTER 54

Six months later.

Gorman was feeling uneasy. He was in Pirrin's office and had just reported back on the recent patrols.

'Good,' Pirrin said, 'so there is no hostile activity left in the city. We need to start stretching out further now, across the country.'

'Surely we should just consolidate the city now,' Gorman replied. 'Harness the resources and make good our base.'

'No!' Pirrin snapped. 'There are still plenty of hostiles out there. They can re-group at any time and come back to the city.' His voice had started to rise slightly. 'We must wipe them all out. All of them!'

Gorman said nothing. He just stared at Pirrin, realising how fanatical the man was.

'What of the moonbasers?' Pirrin asked, turning to Straker.

'Only about fifty left now, sir,' Straker replied.

'Are they all loyal?' Pirrin asked.

Gorman raised an eyebrow but said nothing.

'I can't be sure, sir,' Straker replied and then smiled, 'but we'll flush out any that are not.'

Not for the first time, Gorman had a chilling feeling.

These two men were not content with just controlling London and wiping out hundreds if not thousands of lives. They were power crazed. The killings would continue. Gorman's Council had been a small scale operation by comparison, and he had always believed that his tough regime was justified to ensure survival. But this was different. This was taking things much further. These people would never stop. And sooner or later Gorman thought, he would not be a part of it.

CHAPTER 55

The winter had been a hard one for Sarah and the small community around her.

For the second year running, snow had fallen and this time the deep frosts had lasted for much longer. Two of the elder women had died from the cold, and the spirits of the group had been forced to a low ebb during the dark days and long nights.

The first signs of spring though brought some small, much needed encouragement.

They had eventually decided to return to the original Village near to the old ring of stones. They had all agreed, after much debate, that they didn't want to run to the north.

Charlie had been the one to suggest going back. He had said that it was the right place to start all over again.

At first, they thought the boy was mad but the idea caught on after they considered all the options, and they returned there with some renewed hope and purpose.

A few more people had joined the group. Small families mainly, clinging to their last hopes of survival, had come walking in bedraggled, cold and starving across the fields. All of them brought tales of terrible hardship and suffering.

The men were busy as Sarah watched from the front of her makeshift schoolroom, which was little more than a fenced-off area. Connor had promised to put a roof on as soon as his men had finished the boundary fences.

'It won't be long now,' Charlie said, running over. 'You'll have your roof next week, Miss Sarah.'

Sarah smiled at the youngster. He seemed to be thriving. He had been a comfort to her in her darkest moments, and she had developed a great warmth and affection towards the boy.

'Charlie, you keep nagging them,' she said. 'I want that roof on as soon as possible.'

She paused for a moment, before continuing, 'I just wish... I just wish that David was here to see this. It's been six months Charlie, six months...'

'He'll be back, miss. Just wait, he'll be back.'

'I do hope you're right, Charlie,' Sarah said wistfully, although in her heart she was beginning to fear the worst. She had warned David that he could not take them all on alone.

She turned and walked slowly back into the open schoolroom, with both her hands held gently over her large swelling belly.

CHAPTER 56

The drizzle and the mist had reduced visibility to a few yards as Gorman made his way along the river embankment. It was early evening and no-one else was around.

Gorman was in deep despair. He had nowhere to turn to.

Pirrin and Straker were running the City and Gorman knew that they were both monsters, although in different ways. Pirrin was overtly fanatical and cruel. Straker was much more subtle and that made him even more dangerous.

Gorman was trapped. He had run the Council and had blood on his hands. Many of his trusted people were now either dead or had switched their loyalty over to Pirrin and the new order.

He knew that he had no friends and no hiding place. And despite the crimes that he had committed in the past, he could not now fall in line with Pirrin and be part of his murderous plans to wipe out all resistance across the whole country.

Pirrin would not stop there either. Gorman had realised now that Pirrin intended to set up his bases on the continent and take control of people and resources on a much grander scale.

And all the time at his side was Straker. Cold, calculating Straker. Always smooth. Always there with a charming smile. The smile of death.

Gorman turned onto Waterloo Bridge and looked down to the river. The black, swirling waters continued their daily ebb and flow but to Gorman, it almost seemed that the river itself ran with blood.

These were dark days for London in every sense.

Gorman looked around him and up and down the river but there were no lights to see through the gloom. No lights anywhere among the thousands of buildings that crouched either side of the old river. It was a forbidding place. Pirrin had seen to that. His patrols had wiped the people out. Those who had resisted had been killed. Those that had survived had fled to the countryside believing that they would be safe. Soon, they would find out that they were not safe.

Gorman hunched down into his thick coat as the drizzle ran down his bald head and down his cheeks. He didn't notice the wet as he trudged on to the centre of the bridge and once more looked over the side.

It was a long way down to the swirling river. A long jump, Gorman thought as he climbed over the bridge railings and stood there. Nothing but air between him and the water. He couldn't swim and he was glad of it. His time had come.

He stood there as the drizzle continued to soak him and he prepared himself.

'Stop! Don't do it!' A voice cried out from the murk behind him.

Gorman froze there. Confused. He hadn't expected anyone else out on this dreadful night.

He looked back over his shoulder and could just make out a tall, untidy figure standing there in the gloom.

'Don't jump, stay alive!' came the voice again.

'Why should you care, stranger?' Gorman asked.

'I've seen too many die. Don't add to it.'

The figure came a little closer. Gorman could see that the man had long, straggly hair and a bushy beard that was drenched by the rain. His threadbare coat was giving him no protection from the elements. He looked wild, almost like an animal.

'Nothing to live for,' Gorman replied and turned back to the river.

'I know you.' The voice came again, this time with a change in the tone. 'I know you.'

Gorman could sense some anger in the man's tone.

'I doubt it, now get lost!' he shouted back.

'I have seen you once before, Councillor Gorman,' came the reply.

Gorman whirled round. 'How do you know... who are you?'

'Someone you wanted dead. Someone who didn't want to die. Not like you. I didn't want to die. My name is Carder.'

CHAPTER 57

The journey to London had been arduous.

Carder did not want to be seen on the open routes so he walked across country for the most part. At one point, he came across an old railway track and followed that for a while. It wasn't long before he ran into trouble. He was ambushed by three men and robbed of all his food and water supplies, before being beaten and left for dead by the side of the track.

He might still have been lying there except for some good fortune. He was found by a man who dragged him into the shelter of a rundown cottage, and gave him a chance to live.

A diet of mouldy fruit and sour goat's milk kept him alive and slowly Carder regained some strength. It was only then that he found out who his rescuer was. He looked strangely familiar but Carder couldn't at first remember.

'Some time ago, you gave me a chance,' the stranger said, 'you and the boy. You gave me a chance.'

Carder remembered him then. It was the drunk that he and Charlie had found at the side of the road on their way to the Village. He still looked ill but he was sober now.

The man was called Slater, and Carder heard how he had somehow survived in the wild all this time. He had thrown away his drink the day he met Carder and Charlie.

'You gave me a reason,' Slater said simply. 'At least... you showed me that there was still some humanity left... some good left in the world.'

Slater's story was a sad one. Like so many others who had survived. He had lost everything. His family. His livelihood, his reason for living. The only comfort he could find was from the bottle, and that would have killed him by now if he hadn't stopped.

'Come with me,' Carder said. 'Come to London with me. I could use some help.'

After a while, Slater agreed and the two men set off together towards the city.

They did not get far though before they were stopped in their tracks by a new hazard. The cold. A deep penetrating cold. The harsh winter started early that year and snow and sharp frosts showed no mercy to those who were clinging to survival.

The old and the weak were vulnerable, and Slater's life was one of many claimed during those winter days.

Carder did what he could for him. They sheltered for a month in a church, but Carder could do nothing to keep his new friend alive. He watched him die in the church. Although Carder didn't realise, it was the last day of the year when Slater finally slipped away.

The New Year brought no respite from the cold but Carder had to move on. He had to get to the city where he might have a chance of getting food and water.

Eventually, he reached the edge of London and broke into a house to find shelter. For three months he used the house as his base whilst he went out foraging for supplies.

It was a desperate time. Very few people were out on the streets and Carder would go for days without seeing anyone.

London was empty and although he had come through the worst of the winter, Carder was losing his strength and his will-power as he stumbled onto Waterloo bridge that murky evening.

CHAPTER 58

Gorman's eyes widened as he heard the name.

'Carder? How... you were killed... you were...'

'No.' Carder interrupted. 'You failed Gorman. The ship vaporised the buildings but I got out.'

Suddenly Carder's mind had cleared for the first time in months. He had found his purpose again.

'The ship... no, I didn't send the ship. Pirrin... Pirrin sent it.'

Carder stared at him. Commander Pirrin. A name from the past.

'Pirrin? Is that who is behind all this,' Carder replied. 'Pirrin... I want to see Pirrin. You can take me to him.'

Slowly Gorman climbed back over the railing. Everything had changed now, he thought.

Pirrin and Straker had failed. He could now redeem himself and take Carder in. He was thinking furiously as his hand slipped inside his coat pocket and felt the cold metal of the gun. One swift movement and he would finish Carder once and for all.

The two men faced each other on the bridge.

There were no sounds or lights from the City around them. Even the river below seemed very still at that moment.

'So where is Pirrin?' Carder asked 'Close by?'

Something in Gorman's eyes put Carder on alert. They no longer had a look of despair and defeat. He now had a hungry look. A greedy look.

Carder saw the movement just in time.

Gorman started to bring his gun out but Carder was quicker.

The old rifle he had taken from Slater was lethal at such short range, and made a huge noise as he fired it at the astonished Gorman.

Gorman stared at Carder for a long moment, before he slowly toppled forward and crashed to the ground.

Carder stepped forward and started to search Gorman's pockets, but was stopped by a voice behind him.

'Freeze! Don't move!'

Carder heard footsteps running towards him.

'Throw your gun on the ground. Away from you and out of reach!' The voice came through the murk again.

'Now stand up slowly.' A different voice this time.

Carder stood up and then felt hands searching through his pockets. He also felt the cold metal of a gun pressed against the back of his neck.

'Now, turn around... slowly.'

Carder looked down at Gorman and looked at his gun on the ground. Too far. He wouldn't make it. He had no choice.

Slowly he turned round to face the men.

There were two of them. White suited but not wearing helmets. They both looked at him warily and in some disgust at his dreadful and dirty appearance.

On Carder's face though a smile started to appear from underneath the thick moustache and beard.

'Joe… Joe Tennison,' he said, chuckling softly.

Tennison was startled and aimed his gun.

'How do you know... how?' And then his expression changed.

'Carder? Is that you?'

Carder nodded.

'Yes, Joe, it's me.'

Tennison turned to his colleague. 'Parentes, it is him, isn't it? I'm not going mad, am I?'

Parentes nodded and smiled. 'It is him… and he's just killed Councillor Gorman.'

'You took your time getting here,' Carder laughed, and the three of them embraced and slapped each other's backs.

'I don't believe it,' Tennison said. 'How did you... we thought you were dead…'

'Let's talk later,' Parentes interrupted urgently. 'That shot would have been heard. We should tip Gorman into the river and then get back to the safe house.'

Gorman's lifeless body was sent into the Thames and the three men hurried off into the dark night.

CHAPTER 59

Carder ate hungrily as Tennison talked.

There were two others in the room. Parentes and Mai, the quiet woman who Maldini had trusted with his most confidential information.

Carder didn't know Mai well but he liked her. She was always calm and always logical.

At times on the moonbase he had been envious of her close relationship with Maldini, but he had always trusted her.

Carder listened with increasing horror to what Tennison was telling him.

He heard about Pirrin's patrols in London. The killings and the stealing of food and property. He then heard about Maldini and his anger boiled over.

'Murderer! He killed Maldini? He owed his existence to Maldini! Maldini kept us all going…'

Tennison nodded. 'He killed the father and then… he sent his daughter to her death.'

'I know,' Carder said, looking sadly at Tennison.

'What?' Tennison stared back in astonishment.

'I saw Carla,' Carder replied.

'You saw her? How… we heard she was killed in an ambush in some woods somewhere.' Parentes said.

'She found me,' Carder said. 'She came out with a patrol and with a ship.' Carder paused and took a deep breath. 'The unit turned on Carla and on the other moonbasers. They were all killed. Shot dead. All of them… but Carla somehow managed to find the strength and stumbled across a field to come and warn me.' Carder paused again and looked around at the three stricken faces looking at him.

Mai's eyes were huge, dark ovals and she was slowly shaking her head.

'She warned me,' Carder continued. 'She knew they had come to kill me. Pirrin wanted me dead.'

There was silence in the room for a long time before Mai spoke.

'She was so brave. She told none of us what had happened to her father until it was too late. She sent a message to Joe but by then it was too late. And she didn't mention you, David. She wanted to protect us. And save you.'

'We owe it to Carla to get rid of Pirrin,' Parentes spoke bitterly. 'We have to stop him.'

Carder nodded. 'That is why I am here.'

Tennison stood up and paced around. 'We don't have long. Gorman's body will turn up before long. Pirrin is getting stronger by the day. And there are less and less moonbasers. He is wiping us out.'

'How many moonbasers can you count on?' Carder asked.

Tennison thought for a moment before replying.

'In total there are only about fifty left.'

Carder was horrified. 'Only fifty?'

Tennison nodded. 'And we can't be sure of them. Pirrin has his allies. His spies. His followers. There are maybe only four others that we could totally trust with this.'

Mai nodded. 'I agree. There's Anya Letowski, Lenton, Holloway and Jonah.'

'Yes,' Tennison concurred. 'They are all one hundred percent trustworthy and can do this with us.'

'Eight of us,' Carder said grimly. 'Eight of us to take them on. It's not great odds.'

'It is the reality,' Mai said. 'The other reality is the timescale. Maximum one week from now. We have kept our heads down so far, but as soon as Pirrin finds out about Gorman then we are all in danger. And Straker, let's not forget Straker.'

'Straker?' Carder asked.

'Yes, Straker is close to Pirrin. He is dangerous,' Mai replied.

Carder was exhausted. He had so many questions to ask them but it was his turn to tell them his story.

He told them about meeting Hugh Hanson and the escape from the Council. Then he told them of the terrible scene in the field where the ship vaporised Scott along with their pursuers.

'That's not the version we heard,' Mai said, looking thoughtful.

Carder told them about his travels across the countryside and about Charlie and the Village. And Sarah.

Mai was very interested in the Village and wanted to know more about the people there, but was quiet as Carder told them about Stein's horrific attack on the Village and all the killings.

When he had finished the others were silent for several minutes. Carder wondered what was going on in

Mai's mind. The other two looked shocked but Mai looked thoughtful. She knew things. Carder was sure that she knew more than anyone else in the room, but he was too exhausted to find out. It would have to wait. They all had to focus on Pirrin now. The time for questions would come later.

CHAPTER 60

The other four came to the safe house in the morning and the introductions were done.

Carder had washed and shaved and looked more recognisable to them. He had met them all before but didn't know them well. Except for Jonah. The huge African had been well known on the moonbase for being the strongest one there. His enormous strength had been invaluable in moving some of the heavy machinery around the moonbase, but he was best known for being the undefeated arm-wrestling champion. Carder was glad to have him on his side and he shuddered to think what Jonah and Connor would be like together.

Mai outlined the timetable. Six days was all she was giving the team to achieve their goal. The elimination of Pirrin.

Carder watched Mai in admiration. She hadn't shouted and insisted that she should be the leader. Instead, all the others had respected her quiet authority. She had assumed command and no-one had thought for even a moment about challenging it.

Carder and Tennison were charged with coming back in forty-eight hours with the plan and who would do what.

Letowski, Jonah, Lenton and Holloway had to gather as much weaponry and ammunition as possible without being detected.

Parentes would work with Mai on the detailed layout plans of the Heathrow briefing hall, which Mai had chosen as the likely location for their attack.

Carder smiled ruefully. This was a good team. But was it too little, too late?

CHAPTER 61

Two days later.

Pirrin stared out of his office window at the grey sky with the heavy rain-laden clouds.

'Tell me again, where was the body found?'

'Just here, sir,' Carlucci replied, pointing to the City map on the wall. 'Just off Waterloo Bridge. One of my team found it on the north bank this morning.'

'And no-one heard anything?' Pirrin asked incredulously. 'No-one heard a shot?'

There was silence in the room.

'It could have been a random killing, sir, but I don't think so,' Straker said.

'Go on.' Pirrin turned his dark eyes on Straker.

'If it had been just an opportunist robbery then why not just leave the body. Why take the trouble to ditch it over the bridge. As it is, it didn't take long for the body to be found. It was a fresh killing. But my guess is that the killer wanted the body to remain undiscovered for a long time.'

Pirrin paced thoughtfully around his office. 'It is probable then that we have some traitors amongst us,' he said before turning to Straker. 'You told me that you would flush these out.'

'Yes, sir,' Straker replied coolly.

'Then do it.'

Straker and Carlucci left the office and then went their separate ways.

As he walked down the empty street, Straker smiled to himself. He had already narrowed his suspects down to a small number. He was ahead of Pirrin. One step ahead and that was where he wanted to be. He would call Tennison over for a drink that evening.

CHAPTER 62

'What was this place?' Carder asked as he looked around at the strange furnishings in the safe house.

'It was a drinking place,' Tennison replied, 'and for eating too. The people from the City would come in here to relax. This bit over here,' Tennison pointed, 'was where all the drinks were served.'

'There are many of these places all over the City,' Mai said. 'Nearly all of them have been burnt out or damaged badly, but somehow this one has survived nearly intact.'

'It was in our patrol area,' Tennison added, 'so Parentes and I took it over and told no-one. Call it a contingency plan.'

'Contingency for a time like this' Carder said grimly. 'It was good thinking. To have a place not on Pirrin's radar.'

Tennison left to pick up some water supplies and Mai came over to sit opposite Carder.

'David, there is something I have to tell you.'

'What's that, Mai?' Carder replied.

Mai looked uncomfortable. 'It was Carla... she thought you were dead. We all did. She thought there was no chance that you had survived.'

'That's understandable,' Carder said, not sure where this was leading.

Mai took a deep breath. 'After a while... she... took up with Straker.'

Carder felt a stab of jealousy but he knew he had no right to. He looked at Mai and nodded.

'I'm not surprised, Mai. She thought I had gone. She would have needed someone. Still... Straker... that slime ball.'

'Yes, and a dangerous slime ball. I don't know where Straker fits in here. Or... if he had anything to do with Carla's death.'

'What? Why would he...?' Carder was astonished.

'Ambition,' Mai replied. 'Greed.' She stood up and walked round the old room, running her hand over the smooth wood at the bar.

'Maldini,' she continued. 'He saw it in Straker. He told me that he feared Straker. He said that Straker was the person he had most difficulty in reading. Always holding something back. Always restrained. And always calculating.'

'He was always too polite and charming for me to like him.' Carder shrugged but then changed his tone. 'If he did betray Carla... if he did, then I will kill him.'

'First, we must focus on Pirrin,' Mai said, 'but we must watch carefully what Straker does.'

Carder sat quietly for a moment before looking at Mai.

'Mai, when this is all over I have a lot of questions for you, but for now I have just one. Who ordered Silves to fire the vaporiser gun and kill Scott along with all those others?'

'I've been thinking about that,' Mai replied slowly. 'The version of events back at the moonbase was very different to yours. Pirrin said the locals were hostile and threatening the ship. He was lying. He was behind it, David. He gave the order and he thought that there were no surviving witnesses. So when he found out that you were alive, he had to find you and finish you.'

Carder nodded. Pirrin must have been visualizing all of this long ago. Planning for his opportunity to seize power and rule by terror. Maldini had a monster in his own backyard.

Mai interrupted his thoughts.

'The Village, David. When this is over, I would very much like to go there to meet these people.'

'I'll take you there, Mai,' Carder replied, knowing that some sort of plan was developing in Mai's mind.

She was looking at him thoughtfully.

'They have shown a real spirit and strength. And they know the value of working together for something. In a strange way, they are a mirror to what Maldini was doing at the moonbase. Maldini would have wanted to meet them too,' Mai paused for a moment before continuing.

'I have a question for you now.' She was half-smiling. 'This Sarah. Is it serious then?'

Carder looked at Mai and didn't quite know what to say.

Eventually he managed, 'She's important to me… Yes, she's important to me.'

Mai chuckled. 'That sounds pretty serious to me, David Carder.'

CHAPTER 63

Everyone was alarmed when they heard that Tennison had been invited over for a drink with Straker that evening.

He had to go through with it or else Straker might think it odd. Carder thought it could be a chance for Tennison to find out about Pirrin's movements and plans, but they were all anxious as Tennison walked out of the safe house and made his way to Straker's accommodation up high in one of the old hotels in the City centre.

As ever, Straker was the charming host.

He talked of the days back on the moonbase and for a while, Tennison was almost lulled into thinking that they had all read Straker wrong. But then Straker turned his silver tongue onto the subject at the front of his mind.

'Strange business about Gorman,' he said casually. Tennison tried not to show any tension but Straker had noticed it.

'No-one saw anything. No-one heard anything.' Straker continued. 'I find it very puzzling.'

'He was probably just in the wrong place at the wrong time,' Tennison said. 'Maybe some desperado saw him as an easy target and just took him out.'

'Yes, maybe you're right.' Straker shrugged but he was watching Tennison carefully. He changed the subject again. There were a couple more drinks before Tennison thanked his host and got up to leave.

'I just wanted to say,' Straker said. 'I'm sorry about Carla. I know you two were old friends.'

Tennison just controlled his anger but again Straker saw the change in his eyes. He knew that Tennison envied him for taking Carla as a lover. Tennison had resigned himself to just staying on a basis of friendship only with Carla, but he was deeply unhappy when she had sought physical comfort and started sleeping with Straker. And he knew that Straker had swapped units with Carla for that fateful mission of unit fifteen.

Tennison just nodded. He couldn't find any words to reply to Straker. He turned and walked through the doorway, not seeing Straker's cold smile behind him. When the door had shut, Straker punched a number on his internal phone pad and spoke quietly.

'Get me the communicator messages for Tennison, inbound and outbound.'

An hour later, Straker was smiling with grim satisfaction at the printouts lying on the table in front of him. He had circled one of the messages which was from Carla Maldini and read:

JOE.

SWAPPED WITH PETER TO GO ON UNIT FIFTEEN.

WATCH PETER AND WATCH PIRRIN. SOMETHING BADLY WRONG.

DON'T TRUST THEM.

CARLA

Of course, Straker thought. Why hadn't he thought of it before. Carla had warned Tennison.

He went back to his desk and punched the familiar number on his phone. He was sure now.

'Tennison is involved. Do you want me to bring him in?'

There was a pause at the other end.

'No. Follow him. Find out who is with him and then bring them all in.' Pirrin replied and then sat back in his office chair watching his cigar smoke slowly drift up to the ceiling.

CHAPTER 64

The plans had taken shape. As they poured over the detailed site layout of the Heathrow briefing hall, Carder began to feel that they just might defy the odds and pull it off. They would need luck and timing though.

Lenton ran through the list of weapons and ammunition. Carder was impressed. They had gathered what was needed without being detected.

Letowski had also compiled a list of all the remaining moonbasers.

'Forty-eight, including us,' she said. 'Take away Pirrin and Straker and that leaves forty-six. Of those, we can expect most to back us once they see what is happening in the briefing hall. But there will be some who stick with Pirrin. Identifying who these will be is one of our biggest problems.'

'Let's go through that list, Anya,' Mai said. 'We're going to have to come up with a best guess and seek out those who we're worried about.'

'And then there are the others,' Holloway said and he produced a list names. Twelve names. 'These are people who used to be on Gorman's Council. We can expect them all to be armed and they are extremely dangerous.'

Carder glanced at the list of names but they didn't mean anything to him.

Tennison pointed to the first name on the list. 'Carlucci. He's their leader. We need to take him out first.'

'That's you, Jonah,' Mai said, turning to the giant who stood arms folded across his barrel chest. 'You will need to deal with Carlucci.'

There was a nervous tension in the air. The attack would take place at the start of Pirrin's briefing the following morning.

Carder would stay in the safe house that night. All the others would return to their accommodation and then in the morning, make their own way out to Heathrow in the shuttle cars.

Everyone was quieter than usual during the evening meal. At the end of it, Mai stood up and briefly addressed the team.

'Tomorrow we take on a huge risk. But we are doing it because it is the right thing to do. If Maldini can see us, he will be proud. And his vision of a peaceful world must prevail. We will stop this evil. Thank you. Thank you, all.'

They wished each other good luck as they departed.

Finally, Carder was alone.

He sat on one of the barstools and looked at his reflection in the mirror underneath the old drinks optics.

'Sarah,' he said aloud to himself. 'I will be with you again soon,' and he sat there hoping, as he had hoped every day since he had left her, that she was safe and well.

CHAPTER 65

'Seven of them, sir,' Straker said as he looked triumphantly across at Pirrin.

'Seven came out of the place. We know them all. That woman, Mai, is probably the ring leader. I have never trusted her. Too close to Maldini. Shall I get them in?'

Pirrin thought for a moment, stroking his chin.

'No. Just get Tennison. Find out from him what is going on and then after the briefing tomorrow, we can deal with the rest of them.'

Straker was disappointed but he didn't let it show. He desperately wanted to see them all killed immediately. His way would then be clear. Still, he consoled himself with the thought that he could have some fun interrogating Tennison first.

'Very well, sir,' he replied.

'You have done well, Straker.' Pirrin said. 'All the plans are starting to come together and the resistance is being wiped out. Very soon, Straker... very soon there will be nothing to stop us. Nothing at all.'

Straker turned to go but Pirrin stopped him.

'This place, Straker. Where they all met... why didn't we know about it?'

'It looks like an empty shell from the outside,' Straker said. 'Do you want me to get someone to go and check it out?'

'No need. Tennison will tell us all we need to know.'

Pirrin looked thoughtfully at Straker for a moment. Something deep inside was troubling him about Straker. Always smooth, always efficient. But Pirrin knew that there was more to Straker. There was something there that he could not yet work out. He would keep an eye on Straker.

The bright red orb of the new day's sun had just showed its uppermost edge above the eastern horizon when Tennison heard a loud bang on his door.

He was alert instantly but the loud bang was swiftly followed by another one, and then came the sound of the door cracking and breaking.

He had no time to react. One after another the men burst into his room. All of them with guns.

He was hit several times before being tied up and then carried out. He was barely conscious as he was tipped roughly into the back of a vehicle. As he fell to the floor of the vehicle, two guns were pressed against his neck and chest and he heard Carlucci say, 'Good morning, Tennison. We thought you might like to come for a ride with us and answer a few questions.'

When the vehicle stopped, Tennison was bundled out and pushed roughly along the street.

He recognised the building. Pirrin's headquarters.

'Take him to the Chambers.' Carlucci ordered and Tennison found himself being pushed down some steps, and then along a dimly lit corridor.

At the end of the corridor he saw the metal door slowly open and then his heart sank.

Straker stepped out. The cold smile was there to greet him.

'Tennison. Good of you to join us. Come on in.'

Tennison was shoved into the room and fell onto the centre of the hard concrete floor.

He sat up and looked at the evil face of Tariq, who was gleefully looking at him as he sorted out his knives on the table.

CHAPTER 66

Carder was picked up by Holloway and Lenton in their car and they set off for Heathrow with the early morning sun blazing through the rear window.

The others were all travelling individually and would take their assigned places in the briefing hall, half an hour before Pirrin was due to arrive.

They travelled alongside the river for a short while before cutting in to the deserted labyrinth of streets, and then picking up the road signs to Heathrow.

'No-one around,' Holloway commented. 'When we first arrived, we would have normally seen some people by now. What have we done to this place?'

'After today, maybe we can start to put it right,' Lenton replied.

'It will be a big job,' Carder said. 'I'm sure that Mai has some sort of plan forming in her mind, but it will be a big job and take a lot of time.'

The car sped along the roads unimpeded by the long redundant traffic lights. The only hazard was the occasional abandoned vehicle which had been left on the road, but it was not long before Holloway turned off the main route and then towards the huge hangar where Pirrin held his briefings.

The site was fenced off but the guard at the gate was relaxed and waved them through without a second glance.

Ahead of them they could see Mai walking from her car towards the main hall.

Holloway and Lenton were wearing long jackets and could easily conceal their guns and explosives in their pockets.

Carder watched them follow Mai into the hall whilst he parked the car a hundred yards away from the entrance. He had a clear view of anyone entering the building and could see the airstrip behind.

His eyes took in the site layout. It was exactly as described in the plans he had looked over back in the safe house. In the distance he could see the ships. Crouching low on the airstrip, the rays of the sun were basking them in a strange red glow as Carder moved his eyes across them.

Mai had told him the location of her ship and he reached into his pocket and pulled out the key she had given him, and then placed it on the seat next to him.

He saw Jonah arrive and Letowski. They both glanced quickly in his direction and then walked into the building.

Carder was parked up next to the other vehicles so as to not attract any unwelcome attention from the solitary guard, who was walking lazily round the hall.

Another ten minutes went by before Parentes arrived. His body language was different to the others when he climbed out of the car and that puzzled Carder.

Parentes looked agitated. He looked around at the parked cars and then paced around the cars taking a closer look, before turning round to look back at the entrance.

He stood there for a moment before taking one more look back at Carder. It seemed to Carder that he was trying to communicate something to him.

Carder realised then. Tennison. Parentes was looking for Tennison.

The two of them would normally be in close communication with each other and Parentes had expected him to be here.

Behind Parentes, two other cars turned into the entrance but Tennison was not in either of them.

Parentes walked slowly over to the main hall and went in. Carder slid down a little lower in his seat.

It was nearly time but where was Tennison?

There was now a steady stream of cars arriving at the hall and Carder hoped that Tennison was amongst the groups of people he could see moving in to take their seats for the briefing.

Tennison's task was to cover Straker, and Carder imagined him taking his seat on the right hand side on the front row with Mai on the front left end seat.

Carder then saw Straker arrive.

His tall frame and blond hair were very distinctive and he walked confidently across to the entrance.

A few others arrived and then finally Pirrin's car turned into the entrance. A long, black limousine nosed its way round to the front of the hall, and a man jumped out from the driver's seat and ran round to open the rear door.

Pirrin's short, stocky figure was instantly familiar to Carder and he felt his anger rising within him. He had been involved in many arguments with the man back on the moonbase, but he would never have imagined him to be capable of the atrocities he had committed. Pirrin had betrayed Maldini's vision and he had let his personal greed and ambition take over.

Carder watched as Pirrin walked into the hall and then checked the position of the guard.

He had to wait a few seconds until the guard had disappeared behind the back of the hall, and then he sprang into action.

He jumped out of the car and started running towards the airstrip.

He was heading straight towards where Mai had said her ship was located. It was at least eight hundred yards to the airstrip and Carder's heart was pounding in his ears as he kept running across the open field.

CHAPTER 67

Inside the hall everyone was taking their seats.

Only the first six rows were occupied now. When the moonbasers had first arrived and had been addressed in the same hall by Maldini, the hall had been full.

Over four hundred empty seats were arranged in neat rows behind the audience that morning.

And Mai was worried. Very worried.

Parentes had come straight to her and said that he hadn't been able to call up Tennison on the communicator.

The seat that Tennison should have been in had been taken over by one of Gorman's old team.

Mai feared the worst. Has Tennison been captured? Has he been forced to tell Pirrin about their plans? The advantage of surprise may have been lost.

As Pirrin walked onto the stage at the front, Mai searched his face for any expression that may have given away something. Did he know? She couldn't see anything though, and then looked across at Straker. There was nothing unusual there either. He was chatting casually and laughing with one of the women. He did not look at all agitated.

Mai looked back at Parentes and gave him the slightest of nods. They had to go through with this. Wherever Tennison was, it did not look as though he had let anyone know about the attack. If he had, then Mai and the others would not have got this far.

Apart from Tennison, they were all in position. The weakness was that they didn't have Straker covered, but Mai thought that as long as they ensured that Pirrin was taken care of then they could deal with Straker later.

As Pirrin started his briefing, Mai settled back into her seat waiting for the sound that would trigger her next move.

CHAPTER 68

Carder was closing in on the nearest ship when he heard the shout from behind him. He turned and saw the guard, a tiny figure in the distance standing next to the huge hangar.

The guard shouted again and started running towards him.

Carder turned and ran on. Number thirty was blazoned in red across the nearest ship. He was looking for number forty-one.

He kept running as he heard another shout and passed two more ships. And then he saw it. Exactly where Mai had said. Number forty-one was directly ahead and Carder sprinted up to it and leapt onto the small platform below the door.

He slotted in Mai's key and the door slid open.

There were more shouts behind him now and out of the corner of his eye he could see two vans travelling fast across the fields towards him. He didn't have much time.

He jumped into the pilot's seat and felt the relief wash over him as it all came back to him. Familiar dials, levers and controls.

He pushed in Mai's key again and the cockpit came to life.

Pressing buttons in rapid succession, he felt the enormous power of the ship starting up.

A large bang on the cockpit window made him look up. They were firing at him. The glass had cracked but not shattered. Half a dozen men were now firing at him.

He smiled, 'No chance!' he said aloud as the ship slowly lifted off the ground and he hovered above the men.

'This is for you Maldini,' he shouted as he hit the vaporiser gun button.

The blinding flash came and went and then Carder looked down at where the six men had been a few seconds before. There was nothing there except black scorched earth.

Carder lifted the ship higher and moved across to the first group of ships.

He shouted, 'You're finished, Pirrin! Never again will these be used to kill here!' as he fired the lethal gun again.

A series of blinding flashes and huge blasts ripped through the air as Carder wreaked havoc across the airstrip, and set about destroying Pirrin's entire fleet of ships.

CHAPTER 69

Pirrin broke off mid-sentence as the shot rang out from somewhere outside.

'What was that?' he asked.

Mai waited. It seemed like long minutes but it was only seconds. And then it came. The blinding flash lit up the briefing hall and Pirrin was grotesquely illuminated as he stood on the stage.

Mai stood up and moved forward, her gun trained on Pirrin.

'That, Pirrin, was the end of your dreams. You have committed horrendous crimes. You have brought evil to this place. You have betrayed us all!'

'Who do you think you are speaking like that?' Pirrin roared back. 'You were always Maldini's puppet. You had no vision. No concept of what could be achieved.'

'Maldini wanted peace.' Mai continued calmly. 'He always wanted us to return and re-build in peace. Together with those brave people who had survived here. The noise you have just heard, Pirrin, was David Carder. The man you thought you had killed is out there on your airstrip destroying the ships and your weapons. You have turned our ships into killing machines and now they have all been destroyed.'

'Carder!' Pirrin exploded. 'Impossible! He died months ago!' He glanced across at Straker.

'No, Pirrin. He did not die. He lived and he came to hunt you down.' Mai replied.

Pirrin's face went purple with rage as he went for his gun, but Mai was much quicker. She gave him no chance, firing repeatedly at him as Pirrin slumped to the floor in a stream of blood which started to flow off the end of the stage. Mayhem broke out in the hall.

Mai was hit in the leg by a bullet and cried out in pain as she crashed to the floor next to Pirrin. His lifeless body gave her some cover though and saved her from the hail of bullets coming from Carlucci's gun.

There were further shots and screams from elsewhere in the hall but Carlucci's gun had fallen silent.

Mai peered over Pirrin's body to see Carlucci's eyes bulging as he stared in her direction.

Jonah was behind Carlucci, one of his giant hands had twisted the gun away from him whilst the other had done its work with the knife.

The red line right across Carlucci's throat grew deeper and wider as Jonah was quietly saying something in his ear. As he brought the blade away Jonah let go of Carlucci and pushed him forward.

Carlucci tumbled head first onto the stage, his blood starting to mix with Pirrin's.

Parentes was on the floor motionless and there was another sporadic gunfight breaking out in the far corner of the hall.

Curtis, one of Gorman's thugs, was firing from behind a woman he was using as cover. It was Letowski, Mai realized with alarm. He had grabbed Letowski and was using her as a shield.

Lenton and Holloway had cornered Curtis but couldn't get at him with Letowski there. It was a stalemate and Letowski knew it. She kicked backwards at Curtis and smashed her elbow into his stomach. It surprised him but not enough. As Letowski struggled free she took a bullet in the back of her head and fell to the floor.

Lenton roared at Curtis, firing non-stop in uncontrolled anger.

Holloway hauled him back.

'Leave him. He's dead. We have other battles to fight!' he yelled.

Mai was trying to take it all in but then she remembered with a jolt. Straker! Despite the pain in her leg she whirled round with her gun but only to see that his seat was empty. Straker had gone.

There was no time for her to dwell on it though as she limped back through the hall to help the others.

She shouted at all those sheltering on the floor to stay down.

CHAPTER 70

Carder looked down with grim satisfaction at the empty airfield.

Patches of scorched earth were all that was left where the ships once stood.

He had completed his task but now he had to get into the briefing hall to help the others.

He brought the ship down gently and looked over at the hall. 'Okay, Mai, I'm on my way,' he shouted as he got out of the pilot's seat and then jumped down from the ship.

He hit the ground running and charged over to the entrance. He could hear the shots ringing out and pulled his gun out.

The scene that greeted Carder was horrific.

Bodies were on the floor. Bloodstains on the walls and floor, and shouts and screams everywhere.

He could see that Mai was hurt and ran over to her.

'I'm alright, David...' she gasped. 'Pirrin's dead... but Straker's gone... he got away.'

Carder looked around. The shots had stopped. He could see Holloway, Lenton and Jonah and they seemed to be in control.

'Go David... go and get him. We'll be okay in here,' Mai said, grimacing in pain as she held her leg.

Carder ran back out of the briefing hall.

Straker must have headed back to his car but Carder couldn't see any cars on the move as he ran out.

He looked towards the site entrance but there was no one there. The guard must have been one of those that he had wiped out from the ship.

The gate barrier was down and there was no sign of any car speeding away.

Carder turned back in frustration and then he saw him. In the distance. His blond hair was unmistakeable. Straker was out there on the airstrip and Carder groaned.

Although he had Mai's key in his pocket, Straker probably had the master key for the ships.

And he was running straight towards Mai's ship.

Carder set off at a sprint but he knew that he was too late. Straker would get to the strip and get airborne. He could then turn the vaporiser gun onto the briefing hall.

Carder saw Straker leap up onto the ship's platform and then the door slide open. He took aim and fired, although he knew that he was still way out of range.

Straker turned round briefly before disappearing inside the ship, and the door slid shut behind him.

Carder continued sprinting and firing but he knew that Straker was safe. The reinforced glass of the cockpit would resist the bullets.

Carder could see Straker climbing into the pilot's seat and hitting the buttons to fire up the ship.

And then slowly the ship started to rise from the ground.

Carder had stopped running and he had sickeningly realised that he was in great peril. He was totally exposed out there on the airstrip, as Straker turned the ship round so that it was hovering above Carder with the lethal shaft of the vaporiser gun pointing directly at him.

Carder could see the utter astonishment on Straker's face when he recognised Carder. He could not believe what he was seeing. Carder was supposed to have perished months ago.

Carder took careful aim at the cockpit and fired repeatedly. He was aiming at one spot on the glass and hoping that the barrage of bullets would break through.

The gun dried up though. Carder had exhausted his bullets. He looked up at the cockpit and saw the glass still intact. And he could see Straker's piercing blue eyes staring down at Carder in fury. But then a slow smile spread across Straker's face. He had Carder at his mercy.

Carder prepared for the end. He could see Straker's right hand move towards the vaporiser button and he shut his eyes.

But there was nothing. Carder waited but still there was no blinding light and huge blast.

He opened his eyes again to see Straker frantically pressing the button repeatedly, and then looking out in frustration at Carder.

The vaporiser gun was empty. Carder had used it all in destroying the other ships.

Straker looked furious but then he regained his normal poise and self control and he smiled out at Carder.

He raised his arm and waved, and then slowly the ship rose higher in the sky.

Carder watched as the ship moved away to the east, slowly at first and then its speed accelerated dramatically as it became smaller and smaller in the sky.

Carder stood there until the tiny silver speck had finally disappeared.

'I will find you, Straker! Somehow I will hunt you down. Be sure of it,' he said to himself as he gazed up at the morning sky.

CHAPTER 71

When Carder returned to the briefing hall, he found that some order had been restored and it looked like some of the moonbasers, who had been lying on the floor sheltering from the bullets, had now engaged with Mai and were helping tend to the wounded.

Carder walked over to Mai and grimly shook his head.

'He got away. In your ship.'

Mai said nothing for a moment. She looked at Carder thoughtfully and then spoke. 'We will talk about Straker later. First we must ensure that this place is secure and the next parts of the plan are in place.'

'Mai, Carder, over here!' It was Jonah calling them over. He was standing over a man who was groaning in pain on the floor.

As they got nearer, Carder could see that the man was dying. He was a small, dark-skinned man, hunched up in a ball on the floor holding his stomach and Carder could see that there was blood seeping through his fingers.

'I think this man knows something about Tennison,' Jonah said. 'He just mentioned his name although he's not making much sense.'

Carder walked over and stooped down close to the stricken man.

'That's Tariq,' one of the men behind Carder shouted. 'He's one of Carlucci's men. One of the worst.'

Carder looked at the man who was staring defiantly back up at him even though he was doubled up in pain.

'Is that your name?' he asked the man.

There was no answer. Just the same defiant glare.

'What do you know about Tennison?' Carder asked. 'Where is he?'

The man opened his mouth to speak and a small trickle of blood slipped out of one corner.

'Tennison…' His voice was faint and rasping. 'Strong... strong man…'

'Where is he?' Carder repeated the question.

Again the man opened his mouth, but this time the words would not come and his head just lolled forward. Tariq was gone.

Carder stared down at the dead man, frustrated that he hadn't got his answers.

'Why did he say that?' Carder asked. 'He called Tennison a strong man.'

'I think,' Mai said slowly, 'I think Tariq tried to break Tennison. Tried to get him to tell them about our plans.' She paused, 'I think… Tennison must have held strong and not told them anything.'

Carder was silent for a moment. He was fearing what Tennison had been put through.

'Where would Tariq have done this? Where would he have been taken?'

'Pirrin's place most likely,' Lenton said.

Carder looked around and then at Mai. 'Parentes? Letowski?' he asked.

Mai shook her head, 'They didn't make it.'

Carder looked around the hall at all the bodies. He stared at Pirrin and Carlucci's bodies up on the stage.

'Are you okay here if Lenton and I go to find Tennison?' he asked Mai.

Mai nodded. 'Yes. Be quick though and please... please bring him back alive.'

Carder nodded 'We're on our way.'

CHAPTER 72

Lenton drove fast towards the centre of the City.

Carder's mind was on Straker as they swept through the empty roads. At one point, Lenton had to swerve violently to avoid a crazed old woman who had ventured into the middle of the road and shouted at the car as it sped past. She was the only human they saw in the entire fifteen miles to Pirrin's office.

'Are all the cities around the world like this?' Lenton asked.

'Maybe,' Carder replied, 'although this was the unlucky one that got Pirrin as a visitor.'

He remembered again something that had been stored at the back of his mind.

'Seville may be worse though. Maldini pulled the Seville landing. He said it might be tricky there, whatever that meant.'

Lenton shrugged. 'I don't know. Silves was hacked off when that mission was pulled but I never heard any good reason why it was.'

The matter went to the back of Carder's mind again as they pulled up outside Pirrin's office block and the men jumped out.

The front door was locked but Lenton blasted it open.

Carder had a growing respect for Lenton. He was a strange looking man. Small and wiry with short, stubbly hair but he was very tough and fearless, and he had a no-nonsense approach which Carder liked. A good man to have on your side, Carder thought.

They walked into the reception area and looked at all the corridors leading off.

'This way,' Lenton said. 'I think there's an area down here that they call The Chambers. That's where I heard Tariq did his work.'

Carder followed Lenton down some steps and into a long dark corridor.

There were two metal doors along each side of the corridor and one further one at the far end.

They came to the first door. Like the other two it was a grey metal door with no glass or viewing window.

Lenton pulled the handle and the door opened. He stepped in.

Immediately there was a soft padding sound and then a spine-chilling low growl.

Lenton leapt back as two Dobermans launched themselves at him. He just managed to shut the door in time as the frustrated dogs hurled themselves against the metal, snarling and barking.

'That was a close call,' Carder said. 'I'll take the next door.'

He pushed ahead of Lenton and came to the second door.

He opened it a fraction. There was no noise so he pushed it open a couple of inches more.

After a few seconds waiting, Carder slammed the door fully open and jumped into the room with his gun ready.

The room was empty. There were some chains and metal bars on the wall, and a solitary chair in the middle of the floor. The floor was stained a rusty red near to the chair. There was nothing else in the room.

'Tariq worked here, eh?' Carder said looking at the red stain. 'Not a very pleasant man, our Tariq.'

They both moved along the corridor to the third door. As they got nearer Carder could see that the door was very slightly ajar. He gently pushed it open further.

As the door swung open Carder's eyes took in the room.

It was similar to the previous one.

A chair in the middle of the room and this time there was a small table at the side.

And this time there was someone in the room.

Tennison.

CHAPTER 73

He was sitting in a corner of the room with his hands tied to a metal post behind his back.

His head was slumped forward in his chest.

'Joe,' Carder said softly. 'Joe... its Carder. I've got Lenton with me'

The head moved a little and then a little more. Very slowly Tennison lifted his head up from his chest.

Carder gasped in horror. 'Joe... Joe... what have they done to you?'

Tennison was facing Carder and Lenton but there were two dark sockets where his eyes should have been. His nose had been smashed and he had blood stains down his chin and on his chest.

His mouth moved and formed a gruesome smile. Carder could see that some teeth were missing.

'Carder', Tennison spoke '... knew you'd come... didn't... didn't tell them.'

Carder rushed forward.

'I know, Joe. I know. You saved us. You saved us all.'

He held Tennison as gently as he could. His friend had been brave and he had stayed silent and stayed alive. But he had paid a terrible price.

'The man who did this to you is dead, Joe,' Carder said. 'He has been killed. Along with Pirrin. Pirrin is dead. It's over now.'

'Straker?' Tennison asked. 'Did you get Straker?'

'No... He got away. For now,' Carder replied.

'Then... then it's not over,' Tennison said and Carder looked down at his stricken friend. Tennison was right. It would never be over until Straker was finished.

Lenton and Carder bandaged Tennison up and treated his wounds as best they could, before carrying him to the car.

'Drive slowly,' Carder said to Lenton. 'Let's get Joe back and get him proper help.'

They drove in silence. Tennison had drifted into unconsciousness and Lenton and Carder were exhausted.

Carder's desolate mood was matched by the empty buildings, overgrown with weeds, that slid by on either side as they drove on. As he stared out at the buildings though, Carder felt a strange flicker of hope and defiance.

Inside some of the buildings, large trees had grown and their branches stretched through what had once been windows. To Carder, it seemed like a new life had taken root and was forcing its way through the old, broken one. A new life that could not be stopped, no matter what devastation surrounded it.

Carder looked across at Tennison and silently vowed to himself that his suffering would not be in vain. Tennison had suffered terrible pain so that the new life could break free from the old.

CHAPTER 74

Connor was feeling pleased with himself. The sun was shining and at last some warmth was coming back to the land.

The new Village was starting to take shape and there was a calm and a purpose about the people around him. For the first time in a long time he felt at ease, and felt that their destiny was back in their own hands.

There was another reason for Connor to be happy that morning.

Mary had told him that she thought she was pregnant. Connor had hugged his wife and roared with delight, probably waking half the Village.

There had been so few babies born anywhere for such a long time. Some of the children in the Village had never seen a baby in their lives. And now there were two on the way.

Sarah could not be far away from having her baby now. Connor didn't know too much about such things, but he couldn't imagine that Sarah could get any bigger than she already was.

Poor Sarah. Connor could see that she was losing hope of ever seeing Carder again. He had caught her more than once looking up at the road that led down from the east. He had seen her walking up to the great stone circle, sometimes on her own and sometimes with the boy Charlie. She would sit there for most of the day and Connor imagined that she went there to pray. She needed Carder to return.

Connor's thoughts turned to Carder. He was sure that he would return one day but he was wary about what his return would bring. Change of some sort. Change yet again.

This Village could thrive as it was, he thought. We should be left alone to build our lives again in peace.

Although he had grown to respect Carder, he would always think of him as someone not from the Village. Not from his community. He was an outsider.

Over the last few days, two more couples had joined the Village. They were both elderly and had come in together to seek shelter.

The long cold winter had taken its toll and they had some sad stories to tell of lives claimed by the snow and the frost.

Charlie had said the weather was changing. He said something odd was happening. No-one really understood him but he spoke of birds that he could no longer find, and other species of bird that had arrived and that were new to him. He said his father had once told him that the birds always knew first. Watch the birds and they will give you warnings.

Connor had teased him relentlessly about this. He liked the boy a lot but he didn't have any patience with this strange side of him.

'You're a dreamer, Charlie,' was his jibe but the boy ignored him and instead went to Sarah to talk about his observations.

Connor could see that Sarah looked both interested and concerned about what the boy was saying, and although he thought Charlie was filling her head with nonsense, he was just glad to see Sarah occupied and not thinking about Carder for once.

As he walked round the Village, Connor took in the scene with pride. The new timber buildings were looking good. The roof was on the schoolhouse now. They had a covered hospital and dining hall also. The dining hall doubled up as the sleeping quarters for the community, but soon the small living rooms dotted around the Village would have roofs and everyone could have a bit more privacy.

The hardships that they had all endured had brought everyone in the Village close together. They had formed a bond and had a strength which came from being together.

'What was that huge roar I heard this morning?' It was Sarah interrupting his thoughts.

'What roar?' Connor feigned surprise.

'Oh, come on, Connor. I know the sound of your voice. You sounded happy about something.'

Connor looked at Sarah and she could see the twinkle in his eye and try as he might the giant couldn't keep the grin off his face.

'Promise to keep a secret?' he asked.

'Of course,' Sarah replied chuckling.

'It's Mary. She's… she's with child. She's going to have a baby. I'm going to be a father.'

'That's wonderful, Connor!' Sarah beamed at him. 'That's wonderful news for you and Mary.' She patted her own belly. 'Our baby will have a playmate now. I'll go and see Mary right away.'

'It is a secret!' Connor protested.

'You can't keep this a secret for too long!' Sarah laughed, looking back over her shoulder as she waddled away.

CHAPTER 75

When they arrived back at the briefing hall, Carder went in first to get some help to come out for Tennison.

After he knew that Tennison was being looked after, he walked back into the hall with Mai who was visibly shaken when she heard what had happened to Tennison.

He could see immediately though that Mai had wasted no time in getting down to work in the hall. There was a sense of purpose and urgency about everyone and the hall was being tidied up and reorganised. Jonah was bellowing out instructions and no-one was arguing with him.

The task facing them all was immense. The scale of the clean up. The need for survival rations and building wells for clean drinking water. The list was endless, and all the time the work would have to be done in a spirit of trust with the surviving population.

Mai had known from her long talks with Maldini that the correct prioritisation of the work was vital. Not everything could be done at once. The timescale would be long and arduous. She also knew that that they had to start from a small, solid nucleus and develop outwards. A big City like London was not where they should start.

The Village that Carder had talked about. That would be their nucleus. She had thought that from the first time Carder had spoken to her about it.

They would spread outwards from the Village. It was the only way that could work.

'We will all be staying here tonight,' Mai said to Carder, 'we need to stay together. In the morning we will have a briefing and discuss the plan for the next few days. After the briefing... you and I should go and find your Village.'

Carder nodded. He was weary and angry that he had let Straker get away but that could wait. He wanted to see Sarah.

'I would like to meet these people you know.' Mai said.

'Yes, Mai,' Carder replied 'I was expecting you to say that.'

And for the first time that day, Mai managed a weak smile.

CHAPTER 76

Mai sat on the stage the following morning and addressed everyone.

There were forty-two people in the hall.

Mai knew that some of them had been involved in the crimes committed in Pirrin's name and she resolved that she would identify anyone involved. For now though, she had to focus on the immediate plans.

Carder watched her in admiration. She was doing what Maldini would have done at this time.

'There will be an initial leadership group of six,' she was saying, 'three chosen from the people inside this hall, and three from the people who have lived through all the horrors on this planet and survived to re-build a new world.' She paused whilst this surprise news sank in.

'We know of a small community out in the countryside that can provide the three people we need,' she continued, glancing across at Carder, 'and we have the opportunity to build a bridge of trust with these people.'

'They will never trust us now,' one of the moonbasers called out. 'We have done them no favours. They will know about what has happened in London.'

Mai stood up and took a deep breath.

'We have no choice. We have to build that trust. David Carder is our bridge to these people. He will not be seen as an outsider. I am telling you now that if we are ever to have a peaceful re-building of this planet, then we will need to re-build the trust. We cannot and must not attempt to do it alone.'

Mai went on to talk about the three leaders.

'Jonah, Holloway and me will sit on the leadership group. In time, this group will develop and widen and then at some point in the future, when we are ready, we will have an elected leadership. But that is for the future. We must focus now on our immediate needs.'

And Mai went on to outline a long list of practical daily tasks covering food, water, transport and communications. There was also a massive cleaning-up operation to be done and Holloway would co-ordinate that across the City.

Her attention-to-detail and her ability to prioritise were outstanding, and the realisation hit Carder that Maldini could not have done this himself. He had groomed Mai to take on this role. Mai's natural ability to lead had pushed her to the fore, but her ability to take control at this difficult time had been a long time in the planning.

When the briefing had finished, Mai came over to Carder.

'Joe wants to come with us,' she said.

Carder was surprised but pleased that Tennison had recovered enough to want to come with them.

'I think it will be a good idea for him to come,' Mai continued. 'They will see the suffering he has been through.'

And Carder could see Mai's thinking. He even quietly suspected that the idea might have come from Mai herself rather than Tennison.

CHAPTER 77

'What makes you so sure that they'll be at this place you've talked of?' Mai asked as she drove along the old empty motorway.

'They would have thought about moving north,' Carder replied, 'but I think they would have decided against it. There would be no guarantees of safety anywhere and they were all tired of running.'

He paused for a moment before continuing.

'The place by the stones would have drawn them in. Although the buildings were destroyed, they would still have the water wells and they would know where the crops could be grown. They would know the geography of land and…' he trailed off.

'And what?' Tennison asked.

'And I think…' Carder was hesitant, trying to find the words to express himself. 'I think it is the only place where they would find the strength and the comfort to carry on. Remember what they have been through. They would need… they would need something permanent to draw on to give them the will to keep going.'

'Something permanent?' Mai asked.

'The stones, Mai. The stone circle,' Carder replied. 'I can't explain it. They're strange. They've been there for thousands of years and seen people come and go. They seem to almost give out something. I felt it.'

'Carder! I can't believe you're talking like this!' Tennison exclaimed. 'It would have been impossible for you to come out with something like that back on the moonbase.'

Mai smiled as she drove along. She knew that Tennison was in great pain from his wounds but this trip would do him good, she thought.

Carder looked across at Tennison. Poor Tennison, his grisly empty eye sockets hidden by the white bandage wrapped round his head. Brave Tennison. This special day would not have been possible without his courage and refusal to speak despite the butchery of Tariq's knife. Carder was glad to have Tennison with him to share this special day.

'Slow down, Mai,' Carder said looking out of his window. 'Stop here.'

'Just here?' Mai asked.

'Yes, just for a few minutes.'

'What's he up to now?' Tennison asked as Carder got out of the car and started to walk across the nearby field.

'I've no idea, Joe,' Mai replied, 'but I'm learning something new about him every day.'

Carder came back to the car and got in.

'Mai, in about a mile you'll see a narrow road to the left. Can you take it and drive along for about a mile. I want to show you something.'

Mai followed the instructions and Carder asked her to stop the car again.

They were parked next to a burnt-out farmhouse.

'Come with me,' Carder said.

They followed. Mai carefully leading Tennison across the old farmyard.

She could see Carder stooping down and looking at something on the ground.

As she got closer, she could see a mound of earth and a pile of stones.

Carder set about tidying up the area which was overgrown with grass and weeds. He spotted some fresh daffodils which had just burst into life following the long cold winter. He carefully uprooted them and brought them over to the mound of earth where he then re-planted them.

'You remember I told you about the boy, Charlie?' Carder asked.

'I do,' Mai said. 'I'm looking forward to meeting him.'

'This is his mother's grave,' Carder said, still looking down at the mound of earth before continuing.

'She and Charlie's father did a fine job on their boy. We should all be grateful for that. One of the things we must teach ourselves is... to remember the good.' He paused for a moment. Mai and Tennison remained silent.

'There have been a lot of bad things happen and a lot of bad people. But there have also been plenty of good things and good people. Brave people. We must remember them.'

Mai nodded. 'You're right. All that we have been doing for years is planning for tomorrow. Nothing else has really mattered. But you're right. This does matter.'

And the three of them stood there by the grave. People from another place. Outsiders. They stood there in a silent tribute to one of the many good lives that had been lost.

CHAPTER 78

'It's over the next hill,' Carder said anxiously.

He was eagerly anticipating seeing Sarah again but it was only now, as the car drew closer, that he suddenly began to have doubts that they would have all come back to the site of the old Village. They may after all have fled north. He would never find them then.

The doubts clouded over his mind as the car climbed the hill.

The sun was high in the sky as eventually the car nosed over the crest and Carder could gaze down at the scene below.

'There... the stones.' He pointed as he saw them first, 'and...' his heart leapt with joy as he saw a small cluster of buildings down in the valley, with little wisps of smoke coming from fires. And he saw the distant shapes of people and animals. He was right. They had returned.

In that instant, he remembered the same scene that had greeted him and Charlie as they rode their bicycles over the same hill more than a year ago.

'They're here,' Carder let out a huge sigh of relief.

'It looks like it,' Mai said. 'You have found them again. We will park the car here and walk down. I don't want anyone to be alarmed.'

They were a strange sight as they climbed out of the car and started walking down the hill, Tennison in the middle, arms linked with Mai and Carder on each side.

Carder and Tennison towered above the tiny figure of Mai as Carder glanced over at her.

The breeze was blowing her short, jet-black hair backwards but her determined chin was pushed forward.

Some lady, Carder thought. Maldini could not have done this in the same way. But his pupil Mai was ready. She had waited a lifetime for this moment.

At first, no-one from the Village saw the three figures walking down the hill, but then a face looked up from near the gate and pointed. Other faces then turned towards them.

'Connor. I see Connor!' Carder shouted with glee as the familiar shape of the giant lumbered up to the front gate and leant on the post, peering up at the three figures making their way towards them.

'Mister Carder! It's Mister Carder!' he heard a voice he recognised shouting his name.

Charlie had burst through the gathering crowd. He was about to run up to greet Carder but a voice called him back.

Carder's eyes searched in vain for Sarah. She was nowhere to be seen. He then had a dark thought. Surely, surely she was okay? Please let her be alive.

The crowd at the gate was about thirty strong as the three of them approached.

'They sound excited,' Tennison said.

Carder was desperately searching the faces for Sarah. The crowd seemed to part to form a pathway between the two groups. The pathway led to the Village gate and Carder looked straight down it.

Sarah was walking slowly towards him. Her long, dark hair was blowing across her face but Carder could see that she was radiant. Her eyes sparkled and she had a mischievous smile.

And Carder smiled back.

Sarah walked through the people on both sides and as she came closer to him, Carder gasped.

He saw her hugely swollen belly.

Sarah saw the astonishment on Carder's face and stopped walking. She stood there smiling warmly at him.

'Well, it seems like you have been busy!' Mai chuckled as Carder rushed forward to greet Sarah, gently hugging her and kissing her tenderly on the lips.

'Oh, Sarah, you are so beautiful. You... Sarah.' Carder looked again into her green eyes and softly said, 'I love you, Sarah Hanson.'

'I love you too, David Carder,' came the reply.

And they gently embraced again to the sound of wild cheering on either side.

CHAPTER 79

'Let's get these people something to eat,' Connor called out and the crowd gradually began to disperse.

Mai had introduced herself to some of the Villagers and was walking along to the dining hall deep in conversation with Connor, who was practically bent double as he stooped to listen to her.

Carder chuckled as he saw Mai and thought again how she wasted so little time in getting to know people.

'I knew you'd return.' Charlie had sidled up to Carder, and looked a little embarrassed to be interrupting Carder and Sarah's intimate talk.

Carder turned to the boy and noticed that he had grown a lot since he had last seen him. 'I'm glad to be back, Charlie. You've done a great job looking after Sarah. Thank you.'

'Charlie has been a great source of strength to me, David, and he never stopped telling me that that you'd come back.' Sarah looked affectionately at Charlie before adding, 'and I think Connor will have a lot to say about Charlie too. He has been a great help getting us all back on our feet here. In fact, it was Charlie's suggestion that we all came back here.'

'Well done, Charlie,' Carder said, 'your suggestion was right. This is where these people belong.'

Carder and Sarah spent some time together before joining the others for some food.

Carder was on unfamiliar ground and struggled to find the words.

'When did you…?' he started.

'I realised soon after you left,' Sarah interrupted. 'There were a few signs.'

'How have you been? Have you been well?' Carder asked.

'Mostly okay,' Sarah replied. 'The worst was the cold this winter. Why has it suddenly turned so much colder? Charlie says the whole weather is changing.'

'What do you mean?'

'You'll have to ask Charlie. Something his parents told him. He talks about something called the gulf stream but I don't really understand.'

Something rang a bell in the back of Carder's mind. It had only been a brief conversation a long time ago. Something Maldini had told him. He had talked about the ice cap melting at the northern tip of the planet, and how the higher sea levels would affect the weather patterns. He had mentioned the gulf stream. He had said there could be change. Maybe a very short-term change. Maybe much longer.

'I'll talk to Charlie when I get a chance,' Carder said.

'You look worried,' Sarah said.

'No… no, it's okay,' Carder realised that now was not the time to raise new concerns. 'I'll talk to him. But for now, let's go and get something to eat.'

'Yes,' Sarah agreed, 'and afterwards, we can go up to the stones and think about names. What we are going to call our child.'

CHAPTER 80

Connor had invited half a dozen Villagers to join Mai, Tennison and Carder for the meal.

Asif, the calm, mild-mannered doctor was there having cleaned Tennison's wounds and given him a fresh bandage.

'So then, Carder, are you going to tell us what you have been up to over the last six months?' Connor asked as he tore into his chicken leg.

And so Carder told his tale. Every now and then, Mai would add something and give them a perspective from the newly-arrived moonbasers.

The Villagers asked some questions, but mostly they listened fascinated and horrified at the same time.

Eleanor shook her head sadly and looking directly at Mai, spoke in her frail voice.

'So all this time you people were up there. Safe from the virus. Out of harm's way. Then when it looks to be safe, you choose to come here and... your people set about destroying everything and... killing and stealing. How... how can we ever trust you?'

Carder stood up to protest but Mai touched his arm lightly and he sat down.

Mai stood up and looked slowly around at everyone seated around the table.

Connor, Sarah, Asif, Mary, Charlie and Eleanor had all paused in their eating and all their eyes were fixed on Mai.

Tennison sat there listening, feeling the tension in the air.

Mai took a deep breath.

'In every community, there is always going to be good and bad. You have heard David mention a man called Maldini. He was our leader at the moonbase and he had growing fears about the bad in our community.'

She paused for a long moment before continuing.

'As it turned out, he found out too late who the bad ones were.'

Mai walked slowly round the table.

Carder knew that her mind was working furiously to make sure that she chose the right words, but she appeared calm and composed as she carried on.

'Maldini had vision and he had principles. He would have been very interested in what you have achieved at the Village because, despite all the hardships, you have put into practice all of the things that he would have wanted us to try to achieve when we arrived here. You have done things the right way.'

Carder could see that she had everyone's rapt attention and even Eleanor's expression had softened.

'I would like us to learn from you,' Mai continued.

'You have met David already. And now, Joe. There are others though, like them and like me, who want to be a part of a peaceful re-building of lives here. I don't know yet where or how we can help, but I would like the chance to find out. You may choose not to want us to stay or feel that you have no need of us. Or...' Mai looked at Eleanor, 'you may choose to let us be your friends. It will be your choice. Not ours.'

'That seems fair to me,' Asif muttered.

'I would very much like to spend a week here with you, if I can. For you to get to know me and for me to get to know you,' Mai continued. 'It could be the start of a long, trusting partnership or you may wish to be left in peace. That choice will be yours but please give yourselves a week to decide.'

Mai looked at everyone once more and then sat down.

There was a silence before Connor spoke.

'Mai, we will talk amongst ourselves and let you know later today.'

Mai nodded. 'Thank you, Connor,' and then went back to her meal.

'And can I just say,' Tennison spoke, 'this food is the best I have tasted in a long while!'

Everyone laughed and the mood lightened for the rest of the meal.

Sarah and Carder helped to clear up and then Sarah took Carder's hand, leading him out of the dining hall and into the afternoon's sunshine.

'Come on, David. We shall go and choose a name. Two names. For a boy and for a girl.'

Carder felt a deep pride and joy surging through his body as he walked hand-in-hand with Sarah through the Village. He also felt a dread and a guilt though about what he must shortly tell her.

CHAPTER 81

'What's that they're doing?' Carder asked as he looked over at some children playing by the Village boundary.

'It's called cricket,' Sarah laughed. 'In a few years maybe our child will be an expert at it.'

Carder looked puzzled as he watched the children. 'Well, I must get Charlie to teach me how to play it sometime soon.'

They laughed and chatted as they walked slowly away from the Village and up the track to the stones.

They had to stop a couple of times for Sarah to recover her breath. Carder was concerned. 'Sarah, we must go back,' he said. 'This is not good for you.'

'I'm alright, David. A little exercise is what I need,' Sarah replied. She gave him an indignant look but inside she was so happy that he was back with her.

Eventually they reached the stones and Sarah carefully sat down on the blanket Carder had brought with him, and they looked round at the surrounding countryside.

'It never fails to move me, this view,' Sarah said.

'I know,' Carder nodded, looking at the endless soft green fields and rolling gentle hills which fanned out in all directions. 'It feels like you're at the centre of everything here. It's very calm. Very peaceful.'

Their thoughts turned towards the baby then, and they discussed and argued in good nature for a long time before they finally reached agreement.

'Okay,' Sarah said, smiling, 'it's Jack for a boy and Louisa for a girl.'

'Agreed,' Carder laughed. Maldini had told him that Jack was his father's name.

Louisa was the name of Sarah's mother and grandmother.

They sat there in silence for a few minutes just holding hands, and Carder realised with reluctance that the time had come to tell Sarah.

He took a deep breath.

'Sarah, there is a problem that I still have to deal with.'

Sarah looked across at him and fixed him with those green eyes.

'There was a man called Straker,' he continued. 'I mentioned him back in the dining hall. He got away. Escaped. And… and I have to go with a man called Lenton to get him.'

'Can't someone else go?' Sarah asked. 'Can't it wait?'

Carder shook his head. 'I have to go, Sarah. It can't wait. But I shall be away for no more than a week. Then it will be done. We will all be able to put the horrors of the past behind us.'

'A week?' Sarah asked. 'Well, I suppose I've waited this long. I can put up with one more week. But why do you have to go?'

'Because…' Carder paused, 'because they need someone who can pilot a ship and someone who knows their way very well around the moonbase. And it has to be someone Mai can completely trust.'

'What?' Sarah cried out. 'Moonbase! What? Are you going back?'

She looked horrified. 'But there are no ships. You told us all of them had been destroyed.'

'All but one,' Carder replied. 'Mai knows where Pirrin kept his ship. In a hangar, somewhere to the north of London.'

He looked into Sarah's eyes which betrayed how frightened she was.

'Yes, it is the moon. I have to go back there Sarah… to get Straker.'

'Why? Why is it so important?' Sarah was shaking her head now.

'Mai thinks that he's gone back there and that he can get hold of… get access to the virus. And bring it back here.'

Sarah looked at Carder and he saw the anger cloud over in her eyes.

'The virus?' she said slowly. 'You have stocks of the virus up there?'

'Yes… for the research. Maldini was trying to develop a cure,' he replied.

'And now this madman can get hold of it?' Sarah asked incredulously.

'Yes,' Carder nodded. 'And I have to go tomorrow to stop him doing just that.'

Slowly, Sarah stood up and walked carefully over to the centre of the stone circle.

She said nothing for a few minutes and Carder walked over to join her.

'Look,' Sarah said quietly, pointing.

Carder followed her gaze and could see the sun low in the western sky, just above a gap between two stones. As it continued to drop in the sky, Carder could see that it would slide down that gap until it finally disappeared below the horizon. It was a curious sight.

'Now, look over there.' Sarah had turned right around and Carder looked at where she was pointing. It was due east.

He could see the moon, pale in the late daytime sky but very nearly full as it sat there low in the sky.

Carder could see that it was almost, but not quite, in line with another gap between two stones which themselves were directly at the opposite side of the circle to the ones they had just been looking at.

He whistled softly.

'Amazing,' he said quietly. Nearly perfect symmetry. 'It's as if the stones...' he trailed off.

'Every now and then it happens like this,' Sarah said. 'I have seen it before but it still amazes me. Everything falls into place. For thousands of years in the past, and thousands more still to come, there have been and will be moments or days when everything is aligned and falls into place.'

'Whoever built these stones must have known this,' Carder said quietly.

She looked round at Carder.

'David, I want us to be together always. Always aligned. Everything falling into place. Always. If you must go... then come back soon. You are needed here now.'

Carder hugged her gently.

'Sarah, I will come back. One week and I will be back.'

CHAPTER 82

They walked back down the track to the Village.

'Do you think Mai should stay for the week?' Carder asked.

'Yes, of course,' Sarah replied. 'Eleanor will take some convincing, but I think Mai is right. We will have a lot to learn from each other.'

The light-hearted chatter had gone. Carder felt terrible about hurting Sarah again. She had said that she understood why he had to go but Carder knew that she was hurting inside.

At the evening meal, Connor told Mai that she was welcome to stay for the week.

When Carder told them that he had to go away for a week, he had to explain why in the same way that he done for Sarah.

They were all horrified that Straker might get hold of the virus and agreed that Carder had to go without delay.

After the meal though, Connor came up to Carder.

'You're brave, Carder, but you've also been lucky so far.' He glanced over at Sarah before continuing. 'Be lucky again. Sarah is hurting now. Be lucky for her, Carder.'

Carder nodded.

'I'll be back, Connor, and when I do it will be to stay,' Carder smiled grimly before adding, 'that is if you let me and if you finally accept me as one of your own.'

Connor laughed. 'You can stay Carder! You can stay. Sarah needs you. But to me, you will always be an outsider.'

Then to Carder's surprise, Connor stretched out his huge arm towards Carder and after an awkward moment, Carder responded and the two men shook hands and embraced.

'One day Connor,' Carder said. 'One day, there will be no more talks of outsiders.'

Carder and Sarah talked for most of the night. They lay there in the dark talking about what their child might be like, whether he or she would look like them.

It was a magical night for them both. Full of excitement but also laced with a sadness, and a worry that Carder had to leave in the morning and place himself at risk once more.

They eventually drifted off to sleep, Sarah's head on Carder's chest.

It was still there when Carder woke first and listened to the cockerel crowing.

He knew there and then that he had found his home and his whole reason for living.

He said his farewells to everyone again and once more, he asked Charlie to look after Sarah.

'I will look after her, Mister Carder, and I know you'll be back. You once told me to make the right choices. Will you make them mister?'

Carder smiled at the boy who was fast becoming a man. 'I will, Charlie. Don't worry, I will.'

Mai would be the driver. She would take Carder back to Heathrow and pick up Lenton, and then drive them both to Pirrin's hangar before returning to the Village.

Tennison had asked to stay in the Village and everyone had agreed. Charlie was bombarding him with questions about his life on the moonbase, and Tennison was clearly enjoying the attention.

Before climbing into the car, Carder hugged Sarah and kissed her gently.

'Be strong, Sarah. I will see you in a week,' he said to her softly.

Sarah nodded and her moist eyes stared into Carder's. 'Come home, David. Come home to me.'

And Carder turned and got into the car.

CHAPTER 83

Lenton was ready for them at Heathrow and before long, Mai was navigating the car away from the Heathrow base and out towards the great orbital road. They sped along the empty motorway with the City lying silently to the south and east of them.

After half an hour, they drew nearer. Mai turned onto a slip road and they were soon driving along country lanes with high, overgrown hedges on either side.

Suddenly Lenton jumped in his seat. 'What is that?' he cried out pointing directly ahead.

In the middle of the road and in front of the car, a magnificent large animal had walked out of the hedge and had paused to look at them.

'It has bones coming out of its head,' Carder said. 'Charlie would be able to tell us what it is. A bit like a cow and a bit like a horse.'

'Look at its eyes,' Mai said. 'They are so calm, so beautiful. That animal looks like a king. It seems to be judging us.'

They sat there for a long moment staring at the beast, before it eventually moved off slowly through a gap in the hedge and disappeared.

'You know, it's not just the human population that have stories of hardship and survival.' Mai spoke softly. 'All the animals on the planet have also been through it.' She drove on in a thoughtful silence.

'This place just never stops surprising me,' Lenton said.

The car slowed down and stopped at some gates, and Carder could see an airfield beyond.

'Remote but secure,' Mai said. 'Perfect for Pirrin.'

They got out of the car and walked over to the gate. Lenton fired at the large bolt and it shattered into many pieces.

The shot rang out loud in the quiet countryside but there was no-one around to hear it.

'Over there,' Mai said, pointing to a large hangar on the other side of an old airstrip which had become overgrown with weeds.

They walked over to the hangar. Carder and Lenton carried their spacesuits. Mai was a tiny figure next to them.

Lenton had to fire his gun again to break the door on the hangar door.

Carder pushed the door open and some birds fluttered out, their peace disturbed.

As the light flooded in Pirrin's ship was illuminated, sitting there silently in the middle of the hangar.

Lenton leapt up onto the ship's platform and tried the door. It slid open smoothly and he stepped inside.

'The key is here,' he yelled from inside the cockpit.

He pressed a few buttons and after a minute shouted again. 'Fuelled up and ready to go!'

'Give me a couple of minutes,' Carder yelled back at him.

He turned to Mai.

'Enjoy your week in the Village,' he said smiling 'and don't go upsetting them. And… keep an eye on Sarah for me.'

'I will, David. You and Lenton… make the right decisions up there. You will have some to make,' she replied with some concern in her eyes.

'Don't worry, Mai, we will,' Carder replied and turned to climb into the ship. He suddenly remembered something though and turned back to Mai.

'Mai, one question that's been on my mind for a long time. Seville. Why was the Seville trip pulled? Maldini never really explained that one to me.'

Mai looked at him for a long moment and frowned.

'I puzzled over that one too. Maldini told me most things but he never told me much about that one. He was holding something back, I think… I can't be sure… why do you ask?'

'Just puzzled. It never made sense to me then and it still doesn't now,' he paused before adding, 'one more thing, Mai.'

She looked up at him enquiringly.

'Maldini would be proud of you.'

And with that Carder turned and climbed into the ship.

Mai walked out of the hangar and into the fresh air.

After a few minutes, Lenton started up the ship and slowly nosed it out of the hangar.

From his window Carder could see the tiny figure of Mai waving up at him from the ground.

Carder waved back and then the ship slowly began to rise.

Mai became a dot in the vast green of the airfield as the ship continued to rise, and then Lenton turned the ship around and they sped off upwards.

Mai watched them until they had disappeared completely and then she slowly walked back to the car.

CHAPTER 84

Carder looked out of his window at the planet below. He could make out coastlines, snow-capped mountain ranges and weather systems but he was struck most of all by something else. There was almost no ice at the North Pole.

He wondered why he hadn't noticed it when he had arrived. His mind turned back to what Maldini had said to him. He had warned that this might happen. He had said that it may re-appear quickly or it may not. Either way, Carder could see that a noticeable change had happened.

Lenton had put the ship into its second orbit before the slingshot across to the moon, and Carder was gazing down now with increasing anticipation as they passed over the plains of eastern Europe.

Soon he would be able to see the strange shaped island he now called home. Just off the main continent and just before the vast blue of the Atlantic.

'Beautiful sight, Carder,' Lenton called out from the pilot's seat.

'It's home now, Lenton. Home.' Carder replied and as he did so, the British Isles came into view and Carder peered down at the spot where he imagined that the

Village was. Where Sarah was. Where his child would grow up.

They only had an hour or so more daylight down there, he thought. Sarah would be having her evening meal. Carder longed to be with her.

Too soon the islands sped by and the ship was over the Atlantic.

'How much damage will Straker have done by now?' Lenton asked.

'Hopefully none,' Carder replied. 'The trouble is that the moonbase crew will welcome him and trust him. They will be totally unsuspecting and off-guard.'

'He'll be moving fast then whilst he has their trust. Although he won't know that we're coming after him.'

Over the next two days they both took turns at piloting the ship and alternately grabbed some sleep as the ship sped towards the moon.

Looking back, Carder saw the Earth diminishing in size and was once again struck by how delicate and fragile it was. A beautiful blue and white sphere just hanging there in the black void.

There may be other worlds that support life out there he thought, but none could be so beautiful.

After Carder had put the ship into moon orbit, he woke Lenton.

'Nearly time for action,' he said.

They went round the far side of the moon, into the bleak darkness and Carder felt uneasy. Cut off from his home. It was with some relief when they came back round and could see the Earth again.

As the ship slowly descended, the barren and craggy surface of the moon came up to meet them. It was a hard and soulless place contrasting sharply with the world they had left behind.

They hovered at a thousand feet above the moonbase.

'No lights,' Lenton said, 'none at all. That's odd.'

'Not good,' Carder said. 'Let's take her down a bit... towards the landing area.'

As they slowly descended both men peered out of the window at the base below. The layout of the buildings was so familiar to them, as were the network of connecting corridors. They could see the accommodation quarters. Everything was intact but there were no signs of any activity.

'No welcoming party then,' Carder said.

'Look, there's the ship.' Lenton pointed and Carder could see Mai's ship parked a few hundred yards from the main reception area.

'He made no attempt to hide it then,' Carder muttered. 'Where is he though, and where are the others?'

'Let's bring her down,' Lenton said and Carder gently brought the ship down onto the lunar surface, close to where Straker had landed.

He closed off the engines and switched off the power. The silence was deafening.

'Still nothing' Lenton said looking towards the reception area. 'No-one around.'

They climbed out of the ship and stepped onto the surface. It felt familiar and strange at the same time to Carder.

He had forgotten the feeling of walking without the heavy gravitational pull.

They made their way to the reception area and arrived at the sliding doors. Lenton hit the button to open them but nothing happened.

Lenton had a laser gun which he used to carefully break the seal, and eventually they prised the doors apart and squeezed in.

'No power' Carder spoke into his headset microphone. 'And also no oxygen.'

They both had to keep their helmets on as they looked around the large room.

'Which way?' Lenton asked.

Carder thought for a moment.

'The laboratories. We'll make our way there.'

Something was badly wrong and Carder knew that they had no time to waste.

They headed down a long connecting walkway, Lenton using his laser gun to open the doors.

When they came to the end of the walkway they turned right. They were heading for the laboratories but they would be passing the central control room on the way.

They reached this and Lenton fired open the door. They stepped inside the room from which all of the moonbase's power and resources were controlled.

And that was when they saw the first body.

CHAPTER 85

'I would like to go up there one day,' Charlie said, gazing up at the huge moon. 'It seems so close tonight.'

'There's not much to see up there,' Tennison chuckled, 'but it has, of course, got the most beautiful sight in the universe.'

'What's that?' Charlie asked.

'Here. You can look across at this place' Tennison said. 'The Earthrise is the most amazing thing. It always got to me. Every time.'

They sat in silence for a while. They were on a bench in front of the schoolhouse. The moon was casting a strong light and Charlie glanced across at the bandaged face of Tennison and felt sorry for his new friend. He had been describing the beauty of something he had once enjoyed looking at, but would now never be able to see again.

'Do you know Mister Carder well?' he asked.

'Yes, I do know him well, Charlie. He's a good man. A very brave man I'd say... he's changed though.'

'How do you mean?' Charlie asked.

'Up on the moonbase, Carder was always very single-minded. He was driven. He took risks that other people would not take. He upset some people though. They thought he was cold and hard. Well, perhaps he was a bit but... now, since he came here, he's changed a little. He's more aware.'

'More aware?' Charlie asked, not understanding.

'Meeting you and Sarah were the best things that have ever happened to him. You have both, in your own different ways opened his mind a bit. You have both touched his heart and unlocked something. And it will make him more careful now. Which is a good thing.'

'What is he afraid of?' Charlie said.

'He will be afraid of not protecting you, Sarah and the Village well enough. That's why he went. He couldn't trust anyone else to do the job. It was too important to let someone else do it.'

Charlie was thoughtful for a moment and then spoke again.

'Connor calls him an outsider still but I don't agree. We are all the same really. There are no outsiders.'

Tennison smiled. 'You'll go far, Charlie. You've already seen a lot of things and had to cope with a lot in your life, and I'm sure that you'll be having to cope with a lot more. But keep that level head of yours. Others will lose theirs but they will turn to you more and more.'

'Are you going to stay here?' Charlie asked Tennison, turning back to gaze up at the moon.

'That depends,' Tennison said. 'It depends on what everyone at the Village thinks by the end of the week. On what Mai thinks. On what Connor thinks. But I do want to stay, Charlie.'

'I'd like you to stay,' Charlie said quietly, still looking up at the moon.

'Do you two ever stop talking?' Mai had walked up to them unnoticed.

'There's so much to talk about Mai,' Tennison laughed. 'I think we could talk forever!'

Mai looked at Charlie and followed his gaze.

'It's been four days now,' she said. 'They will be at the moonbase and taking care of Straker.'

Charlie looked round at her and said, 'They should be back soon then. Three more days. I can just imagine Mister Carder running round there sorting things out. He won't waste any time. That man Straker won't stand a chance.'

Mai smiled 'I'll see you both in the morning,' and she turned to walk back to the schoolhouse.

Sarah had asked her to stay there and she was glad. She could tell that it would not be long before there was a new arrival at the Village, and Mai was pleased to be asked to be close by to help when that moment came.

CHAPTER 86

Carder stooped down to look at the body lying on the floor.

'It's N'Gomo,' he said bitterly. 'His throat has been cut.'

Carder could imagine that N'Gomo had been taken by surprise. He still had a screwdriver in his hand. As ever, he would have been working on something. N'Gomo never went anywhere around the moonbase without his toolbox. He was the person who made sure everything worked. He had been a great friend to Carder.

Straker had given him no chance.

'I think Straker would have come in here first to switch off the power. N'Gomo got in his way,' Lenton said. 'Straker is going to pay for this.'

'And for all the others,' Carder agreed.

He looked around the control room. He remembered this place as a hive of activity. There was always a buzz in here with Maldini usually in the middle of it all, checking on all the monitors, speaking to the technicians and issuing instructions.

Maldini would also spend hours looking through the huge glass windows which stretched from floor to ceiling.

He would gaze out at the lunar surface and watch the vehicles that would often be working out there. And he would spend hours looking at the Earth whenever it appeared majestically above the horizon.

But the room now was empty and silent. There were no lights or monitors on.

'Straker would have turned the power off and then gone to hunt out the others. Mai told me that there were five others that had stayed behind with N'Gomo,' Carder said as he paced around the room.

'Let's get the power back on,' Lenton said. 'My guess is that Straker will know he has company now.'

'Yes, switch it back on. We'll head for the laboratories.'

Lenton was trying a few buttons but getting no response. The computers were not responding.

'Over there,' Carder pointed. 'I think there's a master switch on that panel somewhere.' He remembered Maldini talking about the emergency procedures once, a long time ago.

Never in all his worst nightmares though would Maldini have imagined this scenario. One of his own people destroying his dream.

Lenton saw a red switch and with his gloved finger, he flicked it up.

Immediately the control room was flooded with light and burst into life.

The computer screens blinked and beeped at them, as if protesting at being cut off mid-programme.

Carder knew though that there would be some faults and malfunctions because of the crude way that everything had been shut down. His main need though was for the air system to be working. He needed the oxygen flow to be restored so that they could move around unhindered by the space suits.

He walked over to the air monitor panel on the wall and let out a sigh of relief.

It had fired into life and the oxygen levels were already increasing.

'Okay, let's go.' Carder beckoned to Lenton. 'Let's get to the laboratories. It's a long walk. By the time we get there the oxygen levels should be fully restored.'

'Yes. No time to lose,' Lenton replied 'It may already be too late.'

Carder had thought the same thing. They were too far behind Straker. He would have had time by now to deal with all the others and get hold of the virus. He had been here a few days already. Maybe he took his time before making his move. Carder's hope was that Straker would have been so confident that he would not have been followed that he would have taken longer than he needed. N'Gomo did not look as though he'd been dead too long. Maybe there was still a chance.

They headed back out into the corridor and then turned left, before coming to one of the long connecting walkways.

As they walked along the long glass tube, Carder glanced out. He could see two of the lunar vehicles parked neatly nearby, but behind them was a third one which looked as though it had been parked in a hurry, at an odd angle.

Carder stared at it and then he saw the arm dangling out from behind the driver's door.

Whoever had been driving the vehicle was now dead. Probably, they had rushed back to the base when they saw the lights and power go off and had been met by Straker with his gun.

'One more accounted for,' Carder said into his headset and Lenton looked to where Carder was pointing.

'Hell... that'll be Sonia... she drove that digger... hell...' Lenton stared out for a long moment before he grimly marched on, and Carder remembered that Lenton and Sonia had been in a brief relationship a few years ago. Sonia had been young and very pretty, and a great worker too. Maldini had handpicked the team to remain on the moonbase. It was an elite group.

'I'm sorry, Lenton...' Carder muttered. 'We'll get him.'

They reached the end of the glass walkway and entered the next building. This one housed the dining room, fitness suite and gymnasium, and also the medical centre.

Carder checked the air monitor panel and nodded at Lenton.

They both took off their helmets and discarded their spacesuits.

Now they could move more quickly.

They hurried past the gymnasium and were just about to set off down the next glass walkway, when Lenton shouted and called Carder back.

'Back here, Carder. There's someone in the gym.'

They both walked through the door with their guns raised and then rushed over to the stricken body crawling in agony across the polished laminated wood floor. A trail of blood stretched back to the rowing machine in the far corner.

It was Paulin, the French medical officer, and he had been shot in the stomach.

He looked up at Carder and Lenton with wide disbelieving eyes and opened his mouth to speak. All he could manage was a whisper and Carder and Lenton bent down to help him.

He was beyond help though. Carder could see that they could not do anything for him. Paulin himself would have realised that he was near the end.

He was holding his stomach and blood was oozing through his fingers.

'Straker,' he whispered. 'Stop him... he's...' His words trailed off and he slumped to the floor as his last breath left him.

Lenton and Carder stared at him in a horrified silence for a moment, before they both sprang up and started running.

They ran out of the gymnasium and then into the next glass walkway.

The walkway snaked over a quarter of a mile of the lunar surface, before disappearing underground and then continuing for another hundred yards, before terminating at the research centre. At Maldini's laboratories.

CHAPTER 87

Connor was pacing around outside the schoolhouse wearing a worried frown on his face.

'Don't worry, Connor. It is all quite normal,' Doctor Asif chuckled. 'Sarah is doing just fine. She has got two good helpers in Mai and Mary and everything is going okay.'

Connor looked unconvinced. He had heard the yells from inside and they didn't sound normal to him.

Doctor Asif disappeared inside again and left Connor to continue his pacing around. This was something outside of his control. He was helpless and he didn't like that. Also, he was worried because his Mary also had a baby growing inside her and he feared for her when her time came.

The morning was warm and he could see the Village waking up all around and people starting to go about their daily business. He started to feel better. This was a good place for a child to grow up, he thought. A safe place. Safe that is, providing that Carder was successful.

Carder, what was he up to now? Probably on his way home. He would be too late though to be with Sarah for the birth. His child was not going to wait for him.

And as if on cue, his thoughts were interrupted by a different type of cry from inside the schoolhouse. A baby's cry. A newborn's cry.

Connor had never heard the sound before but he knew without any doubt what it must be. He roared with delight and rushed in through the schoolhouse door.

'Slow down, Connor,' Doctor Asif said. 'We need some calm round here. Not you stampeding around and making such a noise. And wash your hands first if you must come in!'

Mai looked over and smiled at Connor. He looked so ungainly and uncomfortable but she could tell that he was as excited as the rest of them.

'Come through now,' she said after he had washed his hands, and she held the curtain open for him.

Connor walked through and gave Mary a little hug.

'Look Connor, look,' Mary said, her eyes shining in a way Connor had never seen before.

The giant stared down at Sarah sitting up in her bed, clutching close to her a little bundle wrapped in a white blanket.

Sarah looked up at Connor with an expression of sheer joy on her face. 'It's a boy, Connor. A son. Connor, this is Jack.'

Connor just stood there with his mouth open.

He didn't know what to say or do.

Mai and Mary laughed. Sarah just looked up at him and then she too started laughing.

'Perhaps, Connor,' Doctor Asif said, 'perhaps you could let the Village know that we have a new arrival, and that Sarah and her baby are fine. Everyone will be wanting to know.'

Connor looked at Asif and nodded.

He then looked back at Mary. She smiled at him and he just shrugged, and then turned round and left. He hadn't spoken a word.

The women all chuckled again.

'I'll tell you what, Sarah,' Mary said, 'your baby Jack is the first person that I have ever known to make Connor speechless!'

Sarah looked at Mary and Mai and smiled. 'Thank you. Thank you both for helping me. I couldn't have done it without you.'

Doctor Asif left the women alone and walked out into the fresh air. A new baby was so rare these days. A new life beginning. He had become so used to dealing with the sick and the dying. He would always treasure this moment. This made everything worthwhile.

Maybe, he thought, this will be the start of something better.

CHAPTER 88

Carder and Lenton arrived at the research centre out of breath. They had run all the way despite the oxygen levels not yet being fully restored.

Their heads were swimming but they knew that had very little time. With guns raised, they slowly walked up to the sliding doors at the entrance to the centre.

Straker was near. They could sense it.

Carder hit the entry button and the doors slid silently open. They stepped into the reception area.

A sofa and chairs were set out in front of a glass-topped desk.

The computer screen on the desk was on but the screen was locked, awaiting a password to be keyed in. It blinked silently at Carder and Lenton.

Leading off from the reception area were four corridors.

'Do you know the layout?' Lenton asked.

'I've been down those two corridors before,' Carder replied pointing to the two on his left. I don't know what's down the other two. And you?'

'No.' Lenton shook his head. 'I've not been in here before.'

Carder thought for a few seconds. 'We will have to split up. All four corridors might have to be checked. Shout if you think he's near you. Let's do these two first.' He pointed to the two on the left.

Carder chose his corridor and started to walk down slowly. It was dimly lit with rooms on either side.

He pushed open the first door.

The laboratory was empty. There were just a couple of benches in the middle of the room but nothing else.

Carder moved on to the second room. Same as the first. They had cleared out all the equipment long ago.

As he approached the third room Carder heard the shots. Rapid firing. It sounded like Lenton's gun but he couldn't be sure. Why hadn't Lenton shouted for him though?

Carder ran back down the corridor and into the reception area.

The firing had stopped and there was silence. The computer screen still blinked at him as he moved towards the corridor that Lenton had gone down.

'Lenton?' he called. 'Are you there?'

There was no reply, The only sound Carder could hear was his own breathing.

He saw a smear of blood on the floor. And then another one. There was a trail leading across the reception area. It looked like someone had been dragged right across it and down one of the other corridors.

Straker held all the aces now. Carder knew the odds had tipped and that he was in trouble. Lenton had been shot. It was just him and Straker left now.

'Straker!' He yelled. 'Straker, its Carder! Come out here and give yourself up!'

There was no reply and Carder looked down the corridor that the blood trail led to.

The lights were off.

He reached for the light switch but a shot rang out and he reeled backwards as the bullet nicked his right shoulder.

The bullet had not lodged but he was in great pain, and he had dropped his gun which had clattered across the floor out of reach.

There were more shots and Carder's gun bounced up and down on the floor as the bullets rained into it.

Eventually the firing stopped and Carder looked across at his wrecked gun. The odds had tipped further.

He picked himself up slowly from the floor and started to move towards the other corridor and seek cover, but he wasn't quick enough.

He heard the loud and chilling click of the gun behind him.

Slowly he raised his left arm, his right one hanging uselessly at his side.

'Yes, get your arms up and turn around slowly,' came the voice behind him. Cold, smooth. A voice that had total command.

He turned round slowly and looked into the familiar face. Blond hair, steely blue eyes. He saw the familiar smile. He saw the face of evil. He had found Straker.

CHAPTER 89

Mai was experiencing emotions that she had never had before.

Looking at Sarah clutching her newborn baby had made her thoughtful. Firstly because she had never seen a newborn before. It was one of the odd mysteries of the moonbase that not one child had been conceived there. She knew that it was also one of Maldini's biggest worries. He had not talked about it much, but she knew that he had been precoccupied with trying to solve the mystery. He would have been overjoyed to have been here for this moment.

The other emotion was very new to her. Motherhood. Mai could see that Sarah's joy at becoming a mother was obvious. She now had another dimension to her life. Another reason for her to go on.

Mai wondered if she would ever feel that other dimension in her life. She had been involved in relationships but only fleeting ones. That they had never lasted long had never bothered her. But now it seemed as though new thoughts and new feelings were beginning to creep into her mind.

Sarah had let her hold Jack for a few minutes and she marvelled at his tiny but perfectly formed features. What an achievement, she realized, to make another human being. Surely it must be the greatest achievement of all?

Her thoughts turned to Carder as she handed Jack back to Sarah. He must return to see this. His son. The happiness of Sarah. He must see this.

Mai had seen some subtle changes in Carder already but she knew that this would change him forever. He would finally find an inner peace.

Doctor Asif had come back in and suggested that they left Sarah alone to rest.

As Mai walked out of the schoolhouse, she was greeted by Charlie who ran up to her.

'Miss Sarah has a boy then?' he asked excitedly.

'Yes, Charlie. A fine little boy,' Mai replied, 'and they are both doing really well.'

'This baby is very special, isn't he?' Charlie asked and Mai looked at him and nodded.

Charlie carried on. 'He's the link. Between the moonbase people and the people here. Now there is just one group of people. Not two.'

Mai looked at the boy in surprise.

'Yes, you are right, Charlie. You are absolutely right. This baby is indeed very special.'

And she walked on through the Village with a new happiness in her heart.

It is a start, she thought. Just a start. But it is perhaps the best thing that has happened in a very long time.

CHAPTER 90

In his right hand Straker held the gun which was pointed at Carder's chest. In his left hand he held two sealed glass tubes, both half filled with a reddish brown liquid. Carder knew what it was.

'Why?' he asked Straker. 'Why the virus?'

'It is the key for me, Carder. The key that will unlock the control and the power.'

His startling blue eyes didn't appear to blink. His cropped blond hair seemed to accentuate them. His clipped but smooth tone oozed confidence.

'I should have finished you off long ago, Carder. You were an irritant. Maybe even a threat. But not now.'

Carder stared steadily at him 'I can't let you go Straker. I can't let you leave here. Not with that.'

Straker smiled. 'Always the hero, Carder. Always the man with the solutions. Maldini used to say, Carder will find a way. Carder will solve it. Well not this time.' He paused before continuing. 'You have no choice but to let me leave. You have run out of choices. Out of options. You cannot stop me now.'

'Where is Lenton?' Carder asked.

'He interrupted me,' Straker replied. 'That wasn't very wise.'

'The others?' Carder asked. 'There were six people left on this moonbase. Three men and three women. They were brave people. Good people. I've seen three of them. Butchered by you. Where are the others, Straker?'

Straker's eyes hardened. 'They all had to be dealt with. But I was doing them a favour. They were going nowhere. There was never going to be a trip to Earth for them.'

Straker smiled before continuing. 'Carla was good for me you know. Very good. You meant nothing to her, did you know that?'

'She found me, Straker. She gave her life to save us. I saw her,' Carder replied.

'What?'

'How do you think we got out of there? Carla warned us. She warned us about you.'

Straker was thrown for a moment and looked astonished. Then he regained his composure and just shrugged.

'It was good while it lasted with Carla. But she was another one who just got in the way.'

Carder was silent. His hatred of Straker was consuming his mind but he had to keep calm and find a way. It couldn't end like this.

'So what next, Straker?' he asked. 'You could have killed me by now. Why am I still alive?'

Straker's smile returned. 'I want you to see something first. Then you can die.'

He beckoned with his gun. 'Move. This way.'

Straker was leading Carder towards the corridor that Lenton had disappeared down.

'I was setting something up for you to see when Lenton came in and interrupted me. I heard your ship land and watched the two of you getting out. I don't know where you got that ship from but as soon as it I saw it, I knew it would be you. You shouldn't have brought Lenton with you though. He would still be alive now.'

Straker was talking as he pushed Carder along the corridor, with the gun pressed into his back.

Carder's shoulder was throbbing. But his head was clearing.

He had to wait for his opportunity. He had to wait for the slimmest of chances. He had to find a way to stop Straker.

'In here,' Straker said as he pushed Carder into the last room at the end of the corridor.

There was just one chair in the room and a television set on a table in front of it.

Carder had been in the room once before with Maldini. It had been for a training session. Maldini had showed video footage and maps and diagrams of London so that Carder would be familiar with the layout and geography. Maldini had bombarded him with facts and figures about the City. They were all irrelevant now, Carder thought bitterly. Pirrin and Straker had seen to that.

'Sit down. Sit there and watch the screen,' Straker said as he watched Carder carefully, keeping his gun trained on him.

He put the two glass tubes carefully into an inside pocket and in his left hand he now held a remote control pad.

He pressed a button and the television screen sprang into life.

Carder stared at the screen.

A man's face had appeared. A young man, Carder placed him in his early twenties.

He looked vaguely familiar but Carder couldn't remember where he had seen the face before.

The man was seated in front of a table with a white wall behind him. It looked like he was in some sort of a medical room.

A voice said, 'Okay, speak now,' and the man on the screen coughed to clear his throat.

As he did so, in the top right hand corner of the screen some words and numbers appeared. At first, they didn't register with Carder, but then he found himself staring in disbelief at what they were saying.

The block-capitals were clear and spelt out a name and a date:

JACK CARDER - 26.06.2077

Carder read and re-read them.

The man was speaking. He was looking directly into the camera and was reading from a script. Carder listened, breathing deeply.

'My name is Jack Carder. I am twenty one years of age. I confirm that I have come to the Sheffield Collection Centre of my own free will, and that I have willingly provided a sperm sample to the officials here.'

Straker hit the pause button.

'Very watchable isn't it, Carder? Now, do you want to die? No, you want to see some more first.'

Carder said nothing. He just stared at the frozen face on the television screen. The face. Of course it was familiar. It was almost like looking in the mirror. A younger version, yes. But the features were his. This man was… must be… his father.

Straker hit the play button and the man on the screen started talking again.

'The year is two thousand and seventy seven. I am from Bamford, a village fifteen miles from here. I confirm that I have no living relatives.'

There was a pause whilst Jack Carder breathed in deeply. He had the same mannerisms, Carder thought as he stared at the screen. When the voice continued there was an edge in it that hadn't been there before. He was no longer reading from the script.

'I hope that somehow my line will live on... and my descendants will live... will live in a better time than I have.'

Jack Carder looked directly and defiantly at the camera.

'If you are listening to this sometime in the future, remember that the name Carder is a good one. Remember that and have a good life.'

And then Jack Carder stood up and walked away from the table, and out of the room.

Seconds afterwards, another young man walked in and took Jack Carder's place on the seat behind the table, and looked up at the camera.

Straker hit a button on the remote and the screen went blank.

CHAPTER 91

Carder sat staring at the empty screen in silence and in disbelief.

Straker broke the silence.

'Now, think about it, Carder. Think about the year. Two thousand and seventy seven. Nearly fifty years ago.' He paused as he put the remote down. 'And yet... and yet here you are. You don't look fifty to me.'

Carder looked up at Straker. 'It is not possible. You have doctored it.'

'I didn't think it was possible either at first,' Straker replied 'until I saw Maldini's files.'

'What do you mean?'

'Take a look for yourself. That folder on the table.'

Carder hadn't noticed before but there was a slim brown folder next to the television set on the table. He stood up and walked over to pick it up.

'Slowly, don't try anything,' Straker warned.

Carder walked over to the table, grimacing in pain.

He picked up the folder and looked at the cover page. The title read, 'MALDINI - SECURE.'

Carder opened it up.

At first, he didn't understand what he was looking at but as he flicked through the pages, it gradually dawned on him.

Maldini's file was a series of notes and charts and diagrams. The subject matter was egg development and fertilisation. The first section described the stages and procedures for creating a human egg. The second section started with a brief description of an artificial fertilisation process, and then moved on to show a list of names and dates.

He scanned down the list which was in date order.

The list was long. There were a few hundred names on it, many of which he recognised.

Finally he saw it. The entry read simply:

'01.05.2090 – JACK CARDER – SUCCESSFUL.'

Carder stared at this, trying to piece together the full scale of what he was looking at.

'Maldini... did this?' Carder asked.

'Yes. Pirrin didn't know all the details but he did know that Maldini was hiding something major. He knew that he was holding back on something that affected everyone. He told me that Maldini had some confidential files that would be worth a read one day. He wasn't wrong. The only two obvious names that do not appear in the lists are Maldini and Pirrin.'

Carder's mind was racing. 'Maldini stored... stored the sperm samples. He froze them and then brought them out to carry out the fertilisation?'

Straker nodded. 'Him and Doctor Lubierski, yes.'

'Where is the doctor, where is she now?' Carder asked but as he did so, he realised that he could guess where she was.

Straker just smiled.

'Don't you see though, Carder. It's even worse than you think. You've skipped over something. Something very important. Maldini made the eggs himself. He created them. Look at his notes. Look at the dates.' He paused for a moment. 'There is no natural mother.'

Carder felt the blood drain from him. He suddenly realised the enormity of what Maldini had done. He had created his own community.

'In a sense,' Straker chuckled, 'Maldini is our mother. He provided the eggs.' He laughed again. 'Carder, we must be brothers!'

Carder's anger tipped over the edge.

'No!' he shouted and threw the folder at Straker, catching him by surprise.

Seeing that Straker was caught off balance for a moment Carder launched himself at him.

The shot rang out and Carder fell to the ground.

This time the bullet had lodged. In his leg. Even in his pain Carder realised that Straker had not shot to kill. He had shot him just below the knee. Straker had not wanted Carder to die just yet.

Carder clutched his leg in agony. The blood was seeping through his fingers and he could feel the mess of his leg underneath.

'Why Straker?' he shouted. 'Why not finish it?'

Straker smiled down at Carder.

'That would be far too simple, Carder. Now that you know who or rather what you are that would be far too simple,' he chuckled. 'No, you can dwell on this in your agony and you can choose your own moment to end it all. Call it a farewell present from me if you like.' He walked around Carder, carefully watching him before continuing.

'I will return to Earth now. With this precious cargo' he patted his inside pocket where the two glass tubes were.

'When I am there I will choose where and how much of the virus to release. I will have total control. I think though I will start with that interfering Mai. She has caused me too much trouble. Yes, I will find Mai and whoever she is with and start there.'

He looked down at the stricken Carder. 'You will stay here. Every time you see the Earth rise you can think of me, Carder. Think of me releasing the virus. Think of me and all the power I will have.'

'You are insane, Straker! If you don't kill me now I will hunt you down and find you.'

Straker laughed. 'No, Carder. You are staying here. And the last decision you will need to make is for the time when you can bear it no longer, when you are being driven mad with the agony and the loneliness. It is then, Carder, that you can choose to end it all.'

And with that Straker left the room and Carder heard him walk down the corridor, into the reception area and then out into the glass walkway.

He fell back onto the ground clutching his leg in fresh agony.

He had been beaten. Straker had left him to die a lonely death. He had left with the virus in those glass tubes. Straker had won.

CHAPTER 92

Something deep inside Carder made him keep on fighting. Something made him slowly raise himself up onto all fours and start to crawl out of the door and along the corridor, and then into the reception area. Something inside him gave him the strength to stand up through the agony and put all his weight on his good leg and start to shuffle along. One leg and one arm were useless but he managed to move along and get to the glass walkway. Something was keeping him going. And that something was Sarah Hanson and the child inside her.

He had a reason to live. A reason to keep fighting and survive. He wanted to see Sarah again. He wanted to hold his child.

Slowly, he shuffled along the glass walkway.

His head was thumping and his vision was blurring but he managed to keep going.

He made it to the medical rooms and after rummaging through some desk draws, he found what he was looking for.

He sat on the floor and injected the morphine into his leg. He found a bandage and with great difficulty, did what he could for his wounds.

The morphine would take some time to work and he should have rested there. He knew that he had no time to waste though and he hauled himself forward again.

He made it to the next glass walkway. His leg and arm were now numb and it was only the thought of Sarah and his child that was driving him on. His progress was slow and he stumbled over twice, but eventually he reached the end of the walkway.

He knew that Straker would head for his ship now with the virus safely in his pocket. He knew that he had no chance of reaching him and stopping him from taking off in the ship.

But Carder had remembered something.

Something that Maldini had shown him once.

He arrived at the control room. The lights blazed and the computer screens were blinking out at him from all sides. N'Gomo's body lay on the floor.

As he walked in though, he glanced at the huge glass window and looked out on the sight he had been dreading.

Straker was in the pilot's seat of the ship. Except that it was the ship Carder and Lenton had arrived in. The one from Pirrin's secret hangar.

Carder wondered for a few seconds why Straker had swapped ships but then, with an icy dread, he realised.

Straker had fired up the ship and it was slowly rising up from the lunar surface.

Carder walked over to the central control panel and hit the intercom button.

Immediately Straker's face came up on the computer screen in front of him. Even inside his helmet, Carder could see that Straker was smiling.

Carder turned his attention to the glass window and looked out as Straker manoeuvred the ship sideways over to and above Mai's ship.

Carder realised what was about to happen and cried out. 'No, Straker! Wait! There must be another way.'

On the computer screen Carder saw Straker turn to the camera and his voice came over and echoed around the empty control room.

'It's time to say goodbye, Carder. You know now what we are. You know that you don't belong anyway. You must stay here.'

'No, Straker. I belong on Earth now, not here,' Carder replied.

Straker laughed.

'Read Maldini's files. You can take as long as you like to read them. Look at his film clips. Study his records. All his statistics. And then look over at the Earth. And think of me.'

Carder picked up the screen and threw it on the floor.

'I will come to get you, Straker. I will hunt you down. You should have finished me.'

'No, Carder, you will not. Your words and threats are empty. You will stay here on this barren rock for the rest of your miserable days.' Straker laughed as he hit the vaporiser button.

'No!' Carder shouted, shielding his eyes but he knew that it was too late.

The light flooded in and the blast rocked the control room windows.

When Carder removed his hand from his eyes he could only see one ship. Mai's ship had disappeared.

Straker was still laughing as he brought his ship round to face directly down at Carder in the control room.

'We've been here before, Carder. In this position before.' Straker's smooth voice came over the intercom again.

'Last time I would have killed you if I could have. This time I could kill you easily. But I will let you live. Because you cannot follow me. Not now or ever. Wait to see the Earth rise. That is as close as you will ever get. Think of me choosing who lives and who dies Carder. Now that is what I call real power.'

'You are a madman, Straker.' Carder's voice was calm. 'Maldini created both good and bad. With you, he just got the mix wrong. He should have just poured you away.'

'Well, thank you, Carder. And goodbye. Have a good life.' Straker laughed again and turned the ship around.

Carder watched as the ship started to rise slowly and he remembered again what Maldini had once showed him. He shuffled wearily over to a panel on the wall.

CHAPTER 93

Night had fallen on the Village.

It was not a warm night but there was a solitary figure sitting out on the boundary fence.

Charlie had been sitting there for some time now and he was looking up at the moon. He was looking at the features that Carder had pointed out to him. The ridges and higher ground. The lighter and darker shades. The huge craters. And he could see the area known as the Sea of Tranquillity. Where man had first set foot on the moon. And where the moonbase now lay.

An owl hooted in the night but that didn't disturb the boy's thoughts.

'He'll be back soon,' a quiet voice spoke from behind Charlie.

It was Mai. She hadn't been able to sleep after all the excitement of the day.

'Sorry if I surprised you,' she said.

'Why did they put the base up there?' Charlie asked.

Mai gazed up at the moon. 'Why do you ask?'

'Well... couldn't Mister Maldini have found somewhere remote on the Earth. Somewhere safe from the virus.'

'It wasn't Maldini,' Mai replied. 'It was the people before him that chose the location.' Mai spoke softly. 'Maldini just carried on what other people had started. 'And there was nowhere safe on Earth.'

Charlie looked across at Mai.

'But there were places where no humans lived. Why didn't they go there and build the base?' Charlie persisted.

Mai was silent for a moment before replying.

'There are a lot of unanswered questions. One day, we may find the answers. Or maybe we never will and it won't matter. We have a new world to think about now.'

'I hope he's alright,' Charlie said, looking back up at the moon.

'He will be, Charlie,' Mai replied and put her arm round the boy's shoulders. 'David Carder is a survivor. He will be back.'

Mai walked back towards the schoolhouse leaving Charlie alone again. As she opened the door she turned to look back. He was still there. She could see his hunched figure just sitting there on the fence looking at the moon.

Something the boy had said was ringing a bell in her mind. A distant memory had been triggered. Maybe something Maldini had said once. She struggled to remember it but gave up after a while. It had been an exhausting day. She let out a long sigh.

Beyond Charlie, she could see the great stones on the hill. They glowed a strange colour in the moonlight and Mai stood for a few minutes looking at them before eventually turning and walking back into the schoolhouse.

CHAPTER 94

Maldini had always liked to allocate his secrets. He parcelled out different pieces of confidential information to different people. He had shared most with Mai, but Carder had remembered one of the things Maldini had once shown him.

The moonbase had a vaporiser missile which could be fired from the central control room.

When Maldini had told Carder, he said that only N'Gomo, Carder and himself would know about it. He said that it could be used to deflect or destroy incoming asteroids, but Carder wondered if perhaps he also had a sixth sense that there might be another important use it could be put to. Maldini could always see the big picture.

Carder tapped in the security code which he had no difficulty in remembering: 01-01-63, which Maldini had said was the day he had arrived at the moonbase.

Carder had no time to dwell on it but the date on the television screen behind Jack Carder had been fourteen years later. He would have to try and puzzle that one out at another time.

The security code was accepted.

Carder's vision was blurring again and now his co-ordination was beginning to fail him.

With great difficulty, he moved his finger over the button. Pressing the button would start the one minute countdown. Time was short because Straker would be speeding away fast and would soon be out of range.

He pressed the button and the countdown started. After sixty seconds, the missile would launch from its pad about half a mile away and scream up from the lunar surface until it reached the orbit level. At that point it would settle into an orbit and would start hunting the heat source. It would lock onto the heat and then nothing could stop it.

The heat emitted from Straker's ship would draw it in faster and faster.

Carder shuffled over to the window. He tripped on a cable and fell. He bumped his head on something and his vision started to swim. Yet again, he managed to draw on his dwindling energy levels and picked himself up. He heard a noise from a computer screen behind him. The countdown had completed.

In the same instant, the ground vibrated and the glass window rattled again as the missile shot out of its pod.

Carder looked out of the window and in the distance saw a thin silver tube streaking up from the ground. He stayed watching and the silver tube turned into two and then four as he lost his focus.

He forced himself to watch the missile until it disappeared out of sight and then in exhaustion and pain, he slumped back onto the floor.

As he lay there on his side, he could see out of the glass window. He could see the barren ground with the odd shaped rocks lying around. He could see the sharp rim of a crater in the distance.

The pain was taking him over again. He looked along the rim, his vision clearing and then blurring repeatedly.

Then his eyes stopped moving along the rim and fixed on an object. They fixed on the blue and white crescent that was hanging just above the horizon. For a minute the crescent was clear and then it blurred.

Carder cried out. 'Sarah… Sarah!' as his vision finally deserted him and he could see nothing but a grey featureless void.

And his mind slipped into a vivid and colourful scene as he descended into unconsciousness.

He was in a field with Sarah. And a young boy. They were all playing a game with a bat and a ball. Charlie was there too. Connor also. They were all playing the strange game. Carder was helping the little boy hold the bat and hit the ball. Everyone was laughing.

The boy was called Jack. It was his boy… his Jack.

And there was Maldini's face. Large and distorted, etched into a great stone looking down on them all playing their game. There were some other stones near the one with Maldini's face. There was a circle of stones. Maldini was talking. Constantly talking about statistics. About the oceans. About the population count. About landings. Maldini's mouth was moving all the time and talking, but no-one was taking any notice. Carder and Sarah were hugging and holding hands with the little boy. He could hear his little boy's voice and laughter. He could hear Sarah. There were blues and greens and reds. Such vivid colours. They seemed to get brighter with each minute. He could hear some birds singing and Charlie saying something. There was a hawk in the sky and it swooped down. They all pointed and laughed in excitement.

All the time Maldini was talking. He could hear him saying 'Just five million left. Population decreasing.'

And then the sounds started to fade. The colours were still there and Maldini's mouth was still moving, but no words could be heard.

Carder was running round to each of them. To Sarah. To Jack. He couldn't hear them. They were all talking and smiling but he couldn't hear them.

There were more people now. More people had come. There was a crowd. He could see Mai.

His boy ran out of the crowd and jumped up to hug him. Sarah smiled at him. Carder called out to her but he couldn't hear his own voice.

Jack's face was right in front of his. He was happy. Smiling and saying something.

And then the colours faded. The grey returned. Then there was nothing.

And Carder fell face down on the floor.

CHAPTER 95

Straker had settled into an orbit of the moon. He was feeling good. Everything had turned out easier than he had expected. And he had the added pleasure of having made sure that Carder could never bother him again.

He would make a circuit of the moon and then catapault across to the Earth.

He looked back at the barren pitted land below him and was glad to be leaving. For too long he had bided his time. Following orders. Not now though. Not ever again.

He glanced down at the two glass tubes holding their lethal liquid and smiled.

He had done it. He had known that he would. He would now return to Earth and people would listen to him. He would control them. He would control everything. This was how it was meant to be.

A screen flashed up a message in front of him.

At first, Straker didn't understand. A red block-capital message flashed at him repeatedly. It said simply, 'APPROACHING.'

'Impossible,' Straker muttered aloud. He wasn't approaching anything. He was in orbit at a steady height above the surface. And he was alone. He had destroyed the other ship.

Below him he could see just the barren craters of the moon. In his right hand window he could see the Earth. It looked tantalizingly close. He turned back to the screen. Something must be malfunctioning. Something...

His thoughts died in his head and he frowned as he realised what the message was actually telling him. For a split second, the chill spread over his body. He twisted in his seat to look behind him but he ran out of time.

The impact came first.

Out of the corners of his panicked eyes, Straker saw the two glass tubes explode and the liquid fly out.

Then he felt the heat as the fire consumed him.

He screamed once and then stopped. Then he screamed again until the sound died in his throat.

CHAPTER 96

The party had been in full swing for a couple of hours when Mai led an embarrassed Sarah out into the centre of the boisterous crowd.

Mai was dwarfed by all the people around her but she was smiling as she brought Sarah with her. Sarah was holding Jack who was managing to sleep through all the noise.

'Quiet, please!' Mai cried out and raised her arms to the air.

It was a struggle but eventually the noise died down.

'Give us a song, Mai!' shouted Connor, who had drunk more than his share of the homemade wine. Everyone laughed.

'Please, quiet everyone,' Mai repeated. 'A song, Connor? Well... tonight I have to say that there is a song in my heart. A song in all our hearts. And here is the reason why.' She pointed at Sarah and Jack and wild cheering broke out.

After it had gone quiet again, Mai continued.

'Jack's birth is a very special event. For us all,' she paused and looked round at everyone.

'You have all been through so much. You have suffered such hardships and seen some terrible things. I have wondered how you kept going. Where did you find the strength to keep going? I know now that you did this because you believed. You believed that a new start was possible. You believed in a future and that good would prevail.'

It had gone quiet around her now as Mai continued. Jack had not stirred in Sarah's arms.

'We are here, me and Joe as outsiders. I said we wanted to learn from you. Well, now we are learning. You are showing us why the human spirit is special. Why it is so strong.'

She turned to Sarah and spoke softly.

'You have shown us the greatest of all achievements, Sarah. Nothing surpasses the creation and birth of a new life. You have shown us this and I thank you. We all thank you.'

Everyone clapped and cheered and Sarah looked sheepishly round and smiled. 'Thank you, Mai, and, thank all of you. If… If Benjamin could see this tonight he would be very happy. My baby Jack has been very fortunate to be born into this community. Thank you all for giving me the strength to keep going.'

Connor joined Mai and Sarah in the centre and raised his arms to quieten everyone again.

'Mai. You and Tennison have been here for a week now. We have talked and if… if you want to stay on then please do. You are welcome here.'

Again everyone cheered and Mai smiled.

'Thank you, Connor. Thank you, everyone. We will stay. We have so much to learn. Anytime now we are expecting another reason to celebrate. David Carder should be back with us very soon. And when he arrives here,' she paused and looked at Sarah and Jack, 'he will have the best possible homecoming present!'

Sarah smiled at Mai. Mai walked over and hugged her gently. 'Not long now, Sarah. Not long.'

Connor went back to leading the celebrations and the noise level rose again. Someone had a flute and another person had a guitar. The dancing was not in step with the music but no-one cared.

Charlie had been watching the celebrations at the side with Tennison. They had both cheered as loudly as everyone else, but now Charlie turned to his blind friend.

'Joe. Something is not right. I don't know what but I feel it. Something has gone wrong.'

And he glanced up at the night sky.

CHAPTER 97

Three weeks later.

Sarah asked Mai to walk up to the stones with her. She carried Jack in a sling that Charlie had made for her. Mai knew what was coming.

The sun was getting stronger each day as the early summer approached. The harsh cold of the long winter seemed a long way away as the two women made their way up the track towards the stones. The scent and colours of the flowers were everywhere around them. The birds were in full song, but both women walked up the track with heavy hearts.

They reached the stones and Mai put a blanket on the ground for them to sit on.

Jack was sleeping soundly and Sarah laid him down gently on the blanket.

Sarah turned her green eyes onto Mai and Mai saw the hurt and the pain swimming in them.

'He's not coming back is he?' she asked quietly.

Mai didn't reply for a moment. Then she slowly shook her head.

'No, Sarah. I'm sorry but I don't think he is.'

Sarah was silent, staring down at the Village.

Mai continued. 'There are a number of... possibilities. We may never be sure, but... but I think he must have stopped Straker. I think that if Straker had got away and come back to Earth, then we would have known about it by now.'

'But... if he stopped Straker... why hasn't he returned?' Sarah asked.

'I don't know,' Mai replied. 'Something must have gone wrong. Maybe with the ship. Maybe...'

'Maybe... David died stopping Straker.' Sarah finished the sentence for Mai.

'Yes, maybe,' Mai said, 'although... it is possible... but not likely, that he survived but... but he's stranded up there. He and Lenton may be alive but are not be able to get back.'

Sarah stared at Mai. 'Stranded? They could be alive. But... how long could they survive?'

'A long time,' Mai replied. 'Many years. Maldini told me that the food and water reserves were getting low. But he was thinking in terms of five hundred people. If there are just a few of them up there, then they could survive for a long time.'

'If they want to survive,' Sarah said, 'it would drive them mad. Knowing that they could never get off the moon.'

Mai didn't answer. She wanted to say that Carder would want to live to see Sarah and his child, but she didn't want to give Sarah false hope. If Carder had survived, he would be agonisingly lonely. It would surely break him.

'Do you think he is alive, Mai?' Sarah asked.

Mai looked at Sarah. She was ashen-faced and looked so vulnerable as she sat there on the blanket next to her baby boy.

'Sarah... it is what you believe that is important. I believe that David has saved us all and given us the chance to re-build our lives in peace. You must make your own mind up about what you believe.'

Sarah nodded and slowly stood up.

She picked Jack up and slowly walked around the stones, touching them from time to time, brushing them with her fingertips.

Then with great care, she raised Jack in her arms and lifted him up to the skies.

Mai could see the tears sliding down her cheeks as she cried out. 'David. David Carder. I believe that you are still alive. We will wait for you. We will wait for you forever.'

And Sarah sank to her knees, hugging Jack close and closed her eyes.

Mai watched her new friend suffering in her grief and for the first time that she could ever remember, the tears came for her also.

The day gave way to night and when Jack was sleeping soundly with Mai watching over him, Sarah slipped out of the schoolhouse and walked over to where she knew that she would find Charlie.

He had been carrying out his lonely vigil for three weeks now. Always there on the fence. Sometimes alone, sometimes with Tennison.

Tonight he was alone. Above him the clouds were quite numerous, but every now and then they parted to allow the moon to reveal itself. It somehow seemed further away than usual that night.

As Charlie gazed upwards, he realised that there would be more challenges ahead. More journeys and more people to meet. Somehow he knew, deep down, that he would play a big part in the fight for survival. Somehow he knew that Carder would want him to lead the fight and to make his own decisions when the time came.

Sarah looked up at the moon with Charlie, and then spoke softly.

'We need to be strong, Charlie. He is up there and he is watching over us. He wants us to be strong. He wants us to get on with our lives.'

Charlie looked across at Sarah. His strong chin jutted out. He was summoning his own defiance and determination.

'Do you really think he can see us, Miss Sarah?' he asked.

'Yes, Charlie, I do believe that he can.'